MARRIED MEN

MARRIED MEN

by

Georgie Carter

Dales Large Print Books
Long Preston, North Yorkshire,
BD23 4ND, England.

British Library Cataloguing in Publication Data.

Carter, Georgie
Married men.

A catalogue record of this book is
available from the British Library

ISBN 978-1-84262-836-2 pbk

Published in Large Print 2011 by arrangement with
Working Partners Two

Dales Large Print is an imprint of Library Magna Books Ltd.

Printed and bound in Great Britain by
T.J. (International) Ltd., Cornwall, PL28 8RW

MARRIED MEN

If you are a wedding planner by trade then it's best not to have affairs with married men. This is a view that Robyn Hood (yes, her parents really did do this to her) would subscribe to, but when she meets Jonathan sticking to principles suddenly seems pointless... After a delicious dalliance the pressures organising the high profile wedding of a rock star's daughter, Robyn comes to see that there are some interesting single Best Men about...

Chapter One

October

I have *always* loved weddings. As a kid I used to spend ages wrapping my Barbie up in loo roll and then conducting long intricate ceremonies at which my teddy officiated and poor Barbie was joined in holy matrimony to the cross-eyed Action Man I'd picked up at a jumble sale. Barbie always looked distinctly unimpressed with her groom, whom, I seem to recall, didn't have a willy. No wonder Barbie was fed up. These days, in my book, this physical abnormality makes Action Man a strong contender for the title of Ideal Boyfriend. My ex-fiancé, Patrick, would have been a lot less trouble without that particular part of his anatomy. Not that I want to waste another second of my life thinking about *him*, despite the fact that he is one of the ushers today at Adam and Samantha's wedding.

It's because of him that I'm in hiding! OK. Not *hiding* exactly, actively avoiding someone describes it better, but the end result is hopefully the same.

Maybe behind a potted bay tree at the reception isn't the best hiding place? I breathe in and turn sideways. Mmm. I'm not convinced this helps. The plant is a gigantic specimen but my fuchsia pink dress doesn't blend in. I couldn't stick out more if I jumped out naked and started to dance the can-can.

Drat!

Why didn't I wear my emerald dress? At least I'd have been camouflaged. There's so much greenery in this room that I could take my pick of plants and avoid Patrick all evening. I could even stroll out onto the terrace and blend into the shrubbery if I really had the urge.

Why didn't I wear the green?

Looking around, the answer is obvious. As wedding planner, I'm officially responsible for the pinkest wedding reception in the history of the colour pink. From the balloons to the flowers to the bridesmaids' dresses, everything is pink. I've even included myself in the colour scheme, great for matching the table decorations but not quite so great for going unnoticed. I hasten to add that this would not be my choice of colour scheme, but one learns to rise *above* the occasion in this business.

I *will* talk to Patrick later, I tell myself, ducking my head when he turns around. I'll paste on a smile and talk about trivia. But it won't be easy; the man has seen my wobbly bits for Heaven's sake! I'm not sure if I'm up to discussing the weather with him yet.

Not that Pat will want to discuss the weather. He probably can't wait to gloat about, I mean introduce me to, the slim redhead who is the 'plus one' on his invitation. I'm really not in the mood for his games. Not when I've got a missing DJ and a confetti-eating flower girl to contend with. Besides, I don't know if I'm ready to meet the latest member of the Patrick McNicholas fan club even though I cancelled *my* subscription long ago. A girl has her pride, doesn't she?

Pat's a stand up comedian, which I used to find romantic, especially when he proposed to me on stage. His combination of intelligent near geekiness and lilting Irish accent was seriously appealing and I found myself accepting, much to the delight of the audience. I suspect Patrick was thrilled as much by the laughter and applause. Cutting a sorry story short I lost my sense of humour when a week before our wedding Patrick confessed to a fling with another woman. Actually, confessed is pushing the truth a little. Pulling Patrick's intestines out with a cocktail stick would have been easier than getting him to admit that he'd been having a fling with some girl called Jo, one of the comedy groupies. One cancelled wedding and one broken heart later I think I'm just about over the horror of it all. I saw Pat at a party several months ago and managed to resist ripping off his gonads and stuffing them down his throat.

This is progress.

It's a constant relief to me that despite having my own special day wrecked in spectacular fashion I still adore weddings. Becoming a cynic would have been professional suicide. But right now I'm not here to discuss my personal life. I'm here to work and I want everything kept on a professional footing. Hence my taking cover behind a bay tree.

I peek through the foliage and feel a glow of pride at the perfect scene. I've pulled it off. Even if I do say so myself, this wedding reception is looking pretty damn professional. Well done me.

The elegant drawing room of Taply Manor is festooned with pink and white fairy lights, which twinkle gently against the gathering dusk of the evening. The tables are draped with crisp white cloths, freckled with pink confetti and set off with deep pink damask napkins. The centrepiece of each table is a vase crammed with waxy white lilies, fat pink roses and bright pink teddy bears with *Adam and Samantha* embroidered across their tummies. The bride insisted upon this particular detail even though I wasn't convinced. But, as my best friend Faye pointed out, it is *their* wedding, and Sam was right, the bears actually suit the whole fluffy pink theme. Phew!

From behind my plant I observe the

guests enjoying the wedding breakfast. The salmon has been demolished and the scraping of cutlery against china suggests that every mouthful has been savoured. Patrick is busy entertaining his companions, which means the coast is clear for me to give the caterers the go ahead to serve the dessert.

I whiz around for a good ten minutes giving instructions to the waitresses. Then I check that the wedding cake is ready to be wheeled out and that the champagne is chilled for the toast. One of the bridesmaids has a headache so I fetch some headache tablets from my emergency wedding kit (you name it and I bet I have it, from spare tights and safety pins, to plain wedding rings because yes, it has been known!) and when the DJ calls in a panic, because he's lost, I become a human SatNav system and guide him to the reception venue. Once all this is done and everyone's tucking into their puddings I treat myself to a glass of rosé and retreat back behind the trusty bay tree for a few minutes. Deciding to take advantage of the peace I flip open my mobile and call my friend Simon. Si's been my best friend for so long that dinosaurs were roaming Ladbroke Grove when we first met. OK, that's a *slight* exaggeration but you get the gist! We actually met at Uni as terrified Freshers while we were settling into our rooms in a truly gruesome 1960s tower block

‘This is shit!’ Si had groaned, as with arms full of the obligatory pot plants, biscuit tins and posters, we squeezed into the creaky lift, ‘Still, at least, if the course is dire, suicide will be easy!’ and he’d thrown back his head and laughed. Two packets of biscuits, a bucket of coffee and discussion of our A-Level grades later and we were well on our way to being firm friends.

West Granite House was indeed shit. Built in the early sixties it dominated the skyline like the proverbial sore thumb, only this thumb wasn’t so much sore as gangrenous and in desperate need of amputation. The lifts conked out on a regular basis, the previous intake of Freshers had bankrupted the bar, the rooms were little more than glorified cupboards and as for the toilets … well, I’d rather forget about those. Si and I were on the eleventh floor and our view was either spectacular or nauseating, depending on how you feel about heights. The windows opened wide and it was trick at many a late night party to slide across on the ledge from one bedroom to another, a trick which Si was more than capable of performing.

Lots of people assumed Si and I were a couple but this couldn’t have been further from the truth. I love Si, but I don’t fancy him. At all. He’s just my big rugby-playing, beer-swilling comfort blanket of a mate. I don’t care about all the *When Harry Met*

Sally hype, men and women *can* be just friends. Si and I have helped each other through broken romances, horrendous hangovers and once I even stayed up all night to write an essay for him, but we have never, ever blurred the boundaries of our friendship. When Si met Faye, the stunning blonde he later married, I couldn't have been happier for him. And although Faye was a little cool at first it didn't take long before she realized I really wasn't a threat of any kind.

It's strange but in many ways I'm probably closer to Faye now than I am to Si. We're girls after all, and there are some things that you just can't discuss with a man, no matter how good a mate he is. Si also has a really high-powered job as a barrister and works all the hours that God sends plus a few more. Lately he's more elusive than the Scarlet Pimpernel which means I've seen far more of Faye. But no matter how hard Simon works, it's tradition that I call him from my weddings with an update. It's payback for all the rugby matches I've had to watch over the years!

I've been running *Perfect Day Weddings* for just over eight months now and this is my sixth wedding (not bad for someone who's only twenty-nine!) – and sixth running commentary.

OK. So the six weddings aren't technically mine but when I think back to my own *almost* wedding I'm pretty sure that I prefer arranging my clients' special days. Other people's weddings are a lot less heartache.

'Robyn!' Si answers promptly, 'One minute!' I hear the hiss of a ring pull followed by the silencing of the rugby, 'How's it going? Did Samantha dye her poor sod of a fiancé pink as well?'

'Not yet,' I giggle, 'It's going well. The reception's pretty much perfect.'

At the top table laughter floats up and pops like the Möet bubbles fizzing in the champagne flutes. The bride and groom are feeding each other great spoonfuls of raspberry crème brulée and I find that I'm holding my breath in case a big splat of garish pink syrup lands on the delicate silk wedding dress. I'll want to strangle myself with the streamers if anything happens to that dress. The bride and I trawled practially every wedding emporium and design studio in London for it, howling in desperation when each dress was just slightly wrong. Some dresses were too white, some were not quite white enough, some were too plain and some were too fussy. It was the wedding dress equivalent of Goldilocks' porridge-tasting. I'd almost lost the will to live when Samantha finally declared that the final dress was just right.

I will *not* let her wreck that dress before their first dance.

I'm just on the brink of snapping shut my mobile and snatching the dangerous dessert away when the groom leans forward and gently wipes a smudge of brulée from the corner of his new wife's mouth. The tenderness and pride in his eyes when he smiles at her stop me in my tracks. I feel my eyes begin to moisten.

'What?' demands Si when I go quiet.

'It's so romantic,' I gulp. 'Adam's feeding Samantha.'

Simon makes vomiting sounds. 'Is this the same Samantha you said was so self-absorbed that if she was cut in half the word *me* would run through her like seaside rock?'

Did I say that? It must have been after the marathon wedding dress hunt. Looking at Samantha now, all smiles and Swarovski crystals, I know every stressful minute has been worthwhile.

'She looks beautiful,' I whisper, watching the happy couple share a lingering kiss. 'I love weddings, Si, I really do.'

'You're a hopeless romantic,' Simon says indulgently, 'Totally and utterly hopeless. Two in three marriages end in divorce, remember?'

'Says you, the most happily married man I know.'

Simon's end of the line goes quiet. He's probably got distracted by the rugby in the background, but then he adds soberly, 'It's not all moonlight and roses, Robs. Marriage is bloody hard work. It's about who's bought the milk and who's picking up the dirty socks. But, yes, I am lucky.'

'Faye deserves a medal for picking up your socks,' I shudder, 'I still have nightmares about those ones that grew mould.'

'OK,' grumbles Si, 'Dig up the past why don't you?'

'I had to dig up your socks from the carpet!'

'You exaggerated about that,' Simon laughs, 'But the point is that marriage is about mundane stuff most of the time.'

'I'm sure you're right,' I agree, 'I should know how hard marriage really is. My parents have hardly set the best example.'

My parents' marriage survived for about six years and I can't remember the last time they had a civil word to say to each other. I try not to focus on this, concentrating instead on creating perfect wedding days for other people. At least I can get that right. The happily ever after bit I leave to my clients.

My eyes are all misty from watching the bride and groom so I blink furiously and focus instead on my remaining tasks. I can't believe that I still well up like this at the idea of true love because I've experienced all kinds of emotions since Pat and I split up, seesawing wildly from total disillusionment to a fervent optimism that true love can still overcome all.

So long as there are no comedy circuit groupies around, obviously.

Blast. Sometimes disillusionment wins.

'Introspection over,' I inform Si, who expresses his relief. 'My pragmatic head is now firmly back in place and ... oh God,' I add, my heart sinking when I see who is coming my way. 'Not a minute too soon either. I'll call you back, Si.'

So much for my cunning hiding place.

It's Patrick. And he's making a beeline for me.

Here we go.

Chapter Two

My ex-fiancé is looking ridiculously handsome in his morning suit. The thick chestnut curls, which I used to love threading my fingers through, are longer than I remember, but the lopsided smile and twinkling eyes haven't changed one bit. He broke my heart and totally humiliated me. I will *not* still find him attractive.

Even so, butterflies flutter in my stomach. The scars remain pretty tender. I take a deep breath and prepare myself for a game of social chess.

Maybe this is what's known as an occupational hazard?

Snapping the phone shut I paste a bright

'I'm fine' smile onto my face. And I am fine; it's just that no girl wants her ex to see her teary-eyed at a wedding. Patrick would be bound to think I'm blubbing over him and, let's be honest, he's certainly given me enough cause to cry in the past.

'Hello, Robyn,' smiles Patrick, his peat-brown eyes twinkling, 'You're looking lovely, so you are. How's it going?'

Patrick is a born flirt. He probably drew his first breath and then started chatting up the midwife. With his dark good looks, razor-sharp wit and that Irish blarney, he's pretty irresistible. Or so he thinks. Believe me, I'm resisting these days.

'Fine, thanks.' My smile is so forced it feels as though my skin is going to rip. I don't love Patrick any more but I'm a long way off from forgiving him.

Faye thinks that I have issues to resolve. Simon says Pat's a tosser.

No prizes for guessing that I'm with Si on this one.

'I haven't seen you for ages,' he continues, loosening his tie and raising an eyebrow Roger Moore style. The suave effect of the gesture is ruined rather because I know he practises it in the mirror, 'Have you been away?'

Patrick may not have seen me for several months but unfortunately I've been seeing an awful lot of him and so has the rest of

Dewsbury Library

Tel: (01484) 414 868
Email: Dewsbury.lic@kirklees.gov.uk

Customer ID: *****4017

Items that you have borrowed

Title: Married men
ID: 800194591
Due: 04 December 2025

Title: Marrying for money
ID: 351727306
Due: 04 December 2025

Title: The edge
ID: 800893570
Due: 04 December 2025

Total items: 3
Checked out: 3
Overdue: 0
Hold requests: 0
13/11/2025 15:39

Thank you for using the bibliotheca SelfCheck System.
We hope to see you soon.

www.kirklees.gov.uk/community/libraries

Britain. I haven't encountered him in the flesh but there's no escaping Patrick on the telly. Judging by the expensive cut of his suit and the silk tie, Patrick McNicholas has come a long way from the impoverished standup comedian/book shop assistant that I used to know. His agent must have made a pact with Satan or something because now Pat has a lead part in the cult BBC 3 sitcom *Nosh!* and regularly appears to make smart-alec comments on shows like *Have I Got News for You*. He's also started to feature in the tabloids for his exploits out and about with other celebrities while kids the length and breadth of Britain are driving their parents insane with his catch phrase *'Jaysus!'*

It's a catch phrase I feel like uttering right now as I face my cheating scumbag, wedding-wrecking ex-fiancé and try to prevent myself from punching him on the nose.

Maybe Faye has a point about issues?

'I'm fine thanks, Pat,' I say, and am delighted that my voice is calm and low, 'I've been really busy with the wedding planning business. It's doing OK. More than OK, actually.'

If the mention of weddings embarrasses Pat then he does a good job of hiding it. Instead he nods approvingly and helps himself to a flute of champagne from a passing waiter.

'Adam said that this was one of your dos.'

Pat glances around the room before turning the charm back onto me, his eyes lazily sweeping my body in that old familiar way. 'It looks amazing, Robs, and so do you. I love that dress. Very, very sexy.'

'Thanks, Pat.' I say.

Is there anything more awkward that trying to make small talk with a man who once had you in positions that Yoga teachers baulk at? Fortunately I've been anticipating this encounter ever since I noticed that Patrick was on the guest list, and I've had weeks to psych myself up for it. I'm determined to look gorgeous and be every bit the successful business woman rather than the tragic weeping figure he might expect.

I love to be well prepared for any eventuality and I can't understand why so many of my friends and family think that it's a contradiction that I can be both a hopeless romantic and a pragmatist. How do they think I'd manage to co-ordinate all these weddings if I didn't have a practical streak?

I am woman. I can multi task!

Anyway, much as I don't want Patrick back there's no harm in showing him exactly what he's missing, is there? And I know that I'm looking good today. My vintage 1950s prom style dress nips my waist in to a hand's span and flares out over my hips, the black netting underneath holding the skirt out ballerina style and drawing attention to my legs, which are actually looking slender as they taper into delicate strappy sandals. The bodice of the dress is strapless and boned and pushes up my boobs in a frankly amazing manner. Wow! I must patent these optical illusions!

'Is there a Merry Man with you, Miss Hood?' asks Patrick. He always did love to play on the fact that my name is Robyn Hood. Yes, that's right, as in green tights, Sherwood Forest and the Sheriff of Nottingham. School was a right barrel of laughs, saddled with this moniker. Thanks a lot, Mum and Dad.

'I'm working, Pat.' I point out coolly, 'I'm not here to socialise.'

'Jo's with me,' continues Pat, gesturing towards the redhead who is hovering by the stack of pink iced fairy cakes.

'Jo?' I parrot, 'That's *the* Jo?'

Pat nods, 'You must remember, Jo, Robs?'

Duh. Of course I do. Only Pat could be this tactless. Thank God I don't have an open wound; he'd be shovelling salt into it by now. 'She was worried about introducing herself; worried about your reaction,' he continues, 'I told her not to be a sissy, that everything between us is fine now, but she still isn't sure. Come and say hello?'

Patrick has all the sensitivity of a bull rampaging through the china department of Liberty's. Since Jo is the Comedy Store groupie that he was shagging behind my back, presumably from the moment that the ink was dry on our wedding invitations, it wouldn't take Einstein to suss out that we are not destined to be best friends. I refrain from throttling him since the whole point of this exercise is to prove to Patrick that I'm fine about things now. I no longer love him but part of me wishes that he was on his knees pleading for a second chance just so that I could have the pleasure of turning him down.

Hmmm. In my dreams. If Pat had groupies *before* he was famous then I dread to imagine what it's like now. He hardly needs to beg girls to be with him. I stare at Jo, who looks so pale and worried, and feel nothing but relief that I'm not in her Jimmy Choos.

'Sure,' I say airily. 'Why not?'

Patrick drains his champagne and, placing his warm hand in the small of my back, guides me towards Jo. Her pale skin blanches as we approach, and I wonder quite what Pat has told her about me.

'Hi, Jo,' I hold out my hand. 'Good to meet you finally.'

'Robyn, hi.' Jo's green eyes can hardly bear to meet mine and instead she seems to find her scarlet toenails fascinating. 'Er, you too.'

'Thanks for taking Patrick off my hands,' I add. 'I owe you.'

Patrick puts his arm around Jo and pulls her close, dropping a kiss onto the top of her head. 'See!' he laughs, 'I told you that Robyn was fine about us. She knows what a lucky escape she's had. You did her a favour, darlin'!'

'You certainly did,' I agree, suddenly realising that I mean it. Something about the way that Jo is gazing up at Patrick reminds me of the way my neighbour Gideon's dog looks at him. Patrick laps up adoration. One of his biggest complaints when we were together was that I spent far too much time working rather than traipsing round the comedy circuit supporting him. Comedians are hideously insecure. At the time I wasn't self-employed and gave so much energy to my demanding boss, Hester Dunnaway, that there was nothing left for shoring up Pat's ego. Jo looks like a girl whose sole aim in life is to please her man, exactly what Pat needs.

I love my work. Adore it even. Did I love it more that Patrick? Did I neglect him? Do all men secretly want a little wife at home rather than a career woman? Why can't we have it all? And what is 'it all' anyway?

'So, Robyn Hood,' grins Pat, 'Why were you skulking behind a pot plant? Was it the nearest thing to Sherwood Forest you could find?

'I wasn't skulking,' I say.

Up goes the famous eyebrow, 'Not planning to shoot me with your bow and arrows then?'

'No,' I say, 'Bows and arrows are far too good for you. I thought I'd just rip your head off and hit you with the soggy end.'

Actually I don't say this but I'd like to. What I actually say is, 'No. I was er ... distance wedding planning.'

'Distance wedding planning?'

'Yes,' I warm to my theme, 'It's wedding planning but-'

'From a distance?' Pat finishes for me.

'Exactly.'

'And always behind a plant?'

'Plants are optional,' I tell him, 'But very useful.'

'I'll remember that, so I will,' Pat nods, 'Next time I'm up to something I shouldn't be I'll just tuck myself behind a plant,' He grins. 'Jaysus! I'd better buy up Kew Gardens!'

When Pat laughs at himself I remember why I liked him so much as a friend long before we became romantically involved. Should I be glad that Jo has turned out to be a significant relationship? Would it have been worse to have gone through all that heartbreak over a meaningless fumble in the dressing room?

'Here, give me one of your business cards, Robs,' says Pat, 'You never know, somebody might want to marry me one day.'

He winks at Jo who flushes the colour of strawberry milkshake.

I'm under no illusions here. Patrick commit to someone? As if. Against my better judgement I pluck a card from my bag. It's destined for the bin but I suppose it's the thought that counts.

Time to make my excuses and tend to Samantha's guests. Several of them are looking rather puce in the face and it may be a nice idea to throw open the French doors.

'Isn't it hot?' I fan my face with my hand. 'I think that I'd better let some air in before somebody passes out. Good to see you again, Pat. Nice to meet you, Jo.' And I hurry away. I might be over Pat but I've never claimed to be a saint.

I also don't like to be reminded that while Pat is all cosied up with Jo I'm well and truly up on the shelf and gathering dust.

Where are all the eligible men anyway? All the half-decent ones are already married and as for the rest... Well, let's not go there.

What a depressing thought. The nearest I'll probably ever get to sex now will be walking past Ann Summers.

With a sigh I throw open the French windows. The cool evening air soothes my hot cheeks and lifts the table cloths. But it isn't just the breeze that drifts into the room but also the unmistakable undertones of a row on the terrace.

'I've had enough!' hisses a woman's voice.

Arguing at a wedding? Honestly, some

people have no manners.

'This marriage is nothing but a farce!' she continues, 'I should have left you years ago!'

Why is Fate trying to convince me that all relationships end in tears?

Tutting to myself, I'm about to fasten back the doors when I feel a horrible prickling nausea of the variety known only to wedding planners who have just made an enormous error of judgement.

I think I know that voice.

Chapter Three

'I've had enough, Geoffrey!'

I do know that voice! I know it because it's been berating/thanking/bossing me around for the past six months. These not so dulcet tones belong to none other than Susan Ellis, mother of the bride.

This is so not good.

I peep around the French windows and sure enough there she is, hands on hips and mouth wide open, out of sight of the top table but now louder and, unfortunately, within earshot.

'Do you hear me? Enough!' Susan yells at her husband, drowning out his muttered response. 'Our marriage is over!'

The guests nearest the windows hear every word. Those seated further away notice the unease of the faces of the bride and groom and fall silent. Even the musicians in the string quartet sense the atmosphere, their instruments scraping to a discordant halt. The absence of the beautiful music highlights the ugly words, which slice through the stillness.

I'm mortified. What's the etiquette in such a situation? Do I go outside and tell them to keep it down, or do I shut the French windows quickly and hope that we are all English enough to pretend that this isn't happening? Deciding on the latter I start to wrestle with the doors. I think I'll get away with it.

And I would have done too if the doors didn't stick and if Susan Ellis didn't yell with more volume than a 747 taking off.

'I've kept quiet because I didn't want to ruin our Samantha's big day,' she hollers. 'But she's married now so I don't have to lie any longer. I know you're sleeping with Marion from next door, and do you know what? She's welcome to you!'

A large woman dressed in violent magenta linen blushes the same colour as her frock.

Oh God. It's my worst dream come true. My lovely wedding, Sam and Adam's perfect day, has turned into *The Jerry Springer Show*.

'I'm not wasting another minute with you!' shouts Susan and then, just in case Geoffrey misses the point, 'I want a divorce!'

A gasp of shock/outrage/callous enjoyment ripples through the guests. Samantha squeals in horror and for one awful moment I think she's going to faint. I have smelling salts in my emergency wedding kit and start to rummage for them.

'Sam!' Susan steps into the room, realising too late that every ugly word has been overheard. 'Oh, darling!'

'Sweetheart,' Geoffrey Ellis is right behind her, 'I'm so sorry.'

'Not half as sorry as me, Daddy,' Sam sobs. 'How could you? It's my wedding day!'

'Darling...' Susan reaches out to Sam who recoils furiously.

'Don't touch me! I hate you, both of you! You've ruined my wedding! I'll never forgive you!'

Leaping up from her seat, Sam flees from the room, sobbing wretchedly, while her groom and the guests look on in stunned horror. The chief bridesmaid bunches her skirts up into her fists and follows.

Susan glares at her husband. 'This is your fault, Geoffrey.'

'My fault?' he echoes, 'Why is everything always my fault?'

'Because it is, that's why! I'm sick of this marriage!'

'That makes two of us,' he retorts, 'Thirty years of being struck with you. People get less for murder!'

No! Stop! This isn't the way that it is supposed to go. Weddings are supposed to mean happy ever after. This is a disaster!

Scooping up my emergency wedding bag I follow the bride, whose sobbing can still be heard. I'll do my best to sort this somehow, but I think it might take more than headache tablets and a sewing kit.

Sam has locked herself in the Honeymoon suite's bathroom where she is weeping wretchedly.

'Sam,' I tap on the door, 'It's Robyn. Let me in, please.'

'It's no good,' the bridesmaid shakes her head, 'She won't listen.'

But I am wedding planner extraordinaire. As well as knowing where to find the best antique lace or freshest flowers I also have peace-keeping skills that would land me a job at the UN.

Luckily.

'Sam, this is your special day,' I say, 'Yours and Adam's. You are the bride. Everyone is looking at *you*, not your parents.'

There's another sob from behind the door.

'The guests are taking their cue from you,' I continue, 'If you dry your eyes and come back down they'll think it's all blown over, I promise. Honey, only you can decide how this turns out. You can stay here and I'll send the guests away, or you can dry your eyes and join poor Adam. He's your husband now and he really needs you down there.'

'Really?' she says. Or at least I think she does. It's hard to tell because her voice is so clotted with tears.

'Really,' I say firmly, 'It's your call, Sam.'

I cross my fingers and hold my breath. Then there's the sound of a key turning and the door swings open. Sam, bottom lip wobbling and with makeup smeared all over her face, is perched on the edge of the bath.

'I'm a mess,' she hiccups, 'My face is ruined.'

'Nothing we can't fix,' I take her chin between my thumb and forefinger and gently wipe the tears away with a tissue from my magic box of wedding saving tricks. Once her face is clean I pull out my emergency makeup bag, 'I'll have you looking as good as new, I promise.'

Sam takes a shaky breath, 'Thanks, Robyn. Whatever would I have done without you today?'

'All part of the service, hon.' I say.

I squeeze tinted moisturiser onto a sponge and set to work. Thanks to Pat and his antics I'm an expert at restoring tear-stained cheeks to peachy glory.

After ten minutes Sam feels brave enough to venture back to the reception. Luckily everything seems to have calmed down. The DJ has arrived and is playing a selection of upbeat tunes. Fortunately the Ellis Seniors are nowhere to be seen. Sam, every inch the dignified bride again, rejoins Adam, while the caterers whiz around filling champagne flutes for the toast. Helping myself to one I gulp it gratefully, relief and alcohol hitting my blood stream in equal measure.

Next time I need an adrenalin rush I'll take up something more sedate than wedding planning, like bungee jumping or white-water rafting.

From across the room Patrick catches my eye, grins at me and raises that trademark eyebrow.

'Jaysus!' he mouths.

And I must admit that I couldn't have put it better myself.

Chapter Four

November

'Welcome to Swing Heaven!
The place to be if you're passionate about swing dancing!'

At last, I think, scrolling down the advertisement. My internet quest to locate a Swing dancing course has certainly opened my eyes. I've not exactly led a sheltered life but some of the websites that popped up on my computer practically turned the monitor blue.

Maybe I was asking for trouble typing 'Swing' into the search engine? 'I want to Lindy Hop,' I mutter, 'not bed hop.'

Maybe you want to lose some weight?

Do I? I prod my stomach thoughtfully. I've been doing a lot of desk work in the months since I started Perfect Day and my stomach isn't as toned as I'd like it to be, although I'm hardly a dead ringer for the Pillsbury Dough Boy. Still, it wouldn't hurt to get a bit more exercise. Running up and down the stairs to my tree level flat probably isn't enough.

Swing Heaven is a great way to keep fit. Come along and begin a love affair with the 1950s dance craze.

I scan the details, noting that the class takes place in an Adult Education Centre only a few streets away from my favourite bespoke lace shop. Making a note to sign up the next time I'm in the area, I exit the advert and surf for a bit; anything to distract me from the fact that I'm a freelance wedding planner, with no weddings in sight. It's scary just how addictive the internet is. I must have been surfing for at least an hour. I stop at a couple of my favourite 1950s message boards and visit eBay to drool over the vintage clothes.

EBay is such a nightmare for a 1950s addict like me. My flat is full of my treasures and bargains, from the original Roberts radio in the kitchen to the big kidney shaped dressing table that takes pride of place in my bedroom. My wardrobe is bursting with vintage fifties clothes and the TV cabinet groans with DVDs of all the greats from Doris Day to Marilyn Monroe.

I click the mouse and drool over all the bargains. There's the sweetest 1956 prom dress in damson organza that I'm tempted to bid on, as well as a gorgeous beaded clutch bag and the most amazing satin slippers

With mammoth self-control I log out. Once I land some really big clients I'll bid away to my heart's content. When *Perfect Day* is right up there with major players, like Hester Dunnaway's *Catch the Bouquet*, I'll treat myself to something really special, but until that day comes I guess I'd better stick to cheaper options.

I shut the computer down and spin around in my wheelie chair, chewing thoughtfully on my pencil. Hester hasn't taken particularly well to my leaving her employment to set up my own wedding agency. Defecting Russian spies probably get a warmer reaction from the KGB than I do from Hester these days. Luckily she operates out of her plush office in Fulham while I'm working from my kitchen in Ladbroke Grove so our paths haven't crossed much, but she's let it be known to mutual contacts that I'm no threat to someone with her experience and connections.

Unfortunately she seems to be right because so far only friends of friends and family have employed Perfect Day to arrange their weddings. The A-list celebrities have yet to call.

'What I really need,' I say aloud, 'Is a really high-profile wedding to put *Perfect Day* on the map.'

Of course there's nobody to reply apart from Poppy, Gideon's dog, and she is fast asleep under my desk. I'm not sure how it's happened but since I began to work from home I've become an unofficial dog-sitter. Gideon and James work long hours so it's become a daily routine to drop Poppy off with me when they set off for work in their purple convertible Beetle. So as well as being Wedding Planner extraordinaire I'm also Doggy Day Care! But I don't really mind. Gideon, the finance director of high-class home ware company *Impressions*, has been brilliant helping me set up the business. I've picked his brains for months and he's spent hours helping me with my business plan and accounts, so dog-sitting is the least I can do.

I haul myself out of my chair and fill the kettle. While it boils I lean on the window sill and watch the world outside. I love my flat in Ladbroke Square. Gideon and James have the garden flat and I have the top one but the hike up the four flights of stairs is more than compensated by the roof terrace and views over the tree tops towards Portobello Road and Notting Hill. Though I've yet to bump into Hugh Grant a girl can live in hope, can't she?

I sip my coffee and check the clock. Faye has invited me over for lunch so I'd better get moving if I'm going to give Poppy a run first. I love going to Faye's. Not only is she an amazing cook but she's the best company in the world. An afternoon drinking tea at her kitchen table and putting the world to rights is just what I need.

'Come on,' I say to Poppy, 'Wake up. If you're lucky you might even get a walk on the Heath.'

At the word 'walk' Poppy comes to life. She thumps her tail, knocking a vase onto the floor.

'Why didn't Gideon get a Chihuahua?' I groan, wrinkling my nose at the stench of the water. 'Or a Paris Hilton handbag dog?'

But Gideon and James like Staffordshire bull terriers. Sighing I mop up the water, wrestle Poppy into her harness and prepare for battle.

It's a beautiful morning. The birds are singing away and a fried egg sun sparkles on the frost crunching under my boots. I ram my cute cloche hat onto my head, snuggle into my suede driving coat and clamber into the car. Then Poppy and I stomp round Hampstead Heath for an hour.

By the time we turn into Faye's road I feel glowing and healthy from the exercise. OK, my shoulder may be dislocated thanks to Poppy's enthusiasm, but being away from my desk has done wonders for my creativity. In my bag are assorted leaves, glossy conkers and greenery that I've collected for colour matches on an autumnal mood board. As I ring Faye's doorbell I think about designing an autumn wedding. Lots of crimson and terracotta and a wedding dress as gossamer light as the iced spiders' webs stretching between the trees.

Poppy pogos in excitement when Faye answers the door. Like me, she loves coming to visit her. There are the spaniels to play with and Faye always has something tasty for her to eat. Food is Faye's passion as well as her livelihood. She creates amazing novelty cakes and is the writer of the best-selling children's cookery book, *Kidz Kan Kook!* As well as professional success, a beautiful Victorian house just off the Heath and the kind of figure that supermodels envy.

Just as well I love her so much.

'Robyn!' The door swings open and Faye throws her arms around me. 'It's so good to see you!'

'Poppy's really muddy,' I warn.

'Don't worry about mud,' laughs Faye, as though expensive carpets don't matter a jot, 'I'll put Poppy with my dogs.'

Amazingly Poppy transforms from the lunatic hound that hauled me through the undergrowth into a meek and obedient dog. I follow Faye into the boot room, listening to her chatting about her latest cake idea.

'Honestly!' she exclaims 'I've even started dreaming about this cake.'

I have every sympathy. I've started to have dreams lately about *Perfect Day*, although since they involve my bank manager and a gloating Hester these could be more accurately classed as nightmares.

'Sit Gordon! Sit Nigella! Sit Poppy!' Faye takes three chews from a cupboard and gives them to the delighted dogs, 'You enjoy those. We're going to have a nice glass of wine.'

'We are?'

'Don't look at me like that,' says Faye, tucking her arm through mine and leading the way down the stairs to the basement kitchen. 'If you'd spent the best part of four hours trying to make a lump of chocolate sponge look like Balamory you'd need a drink too.'

In Faye's kitchen, which I always think looks like something out of *Country Living* magazine, the most amazing cake takes up at least half of the table. I've worked from home long enough to recognise the set of Balamory, which is arranged in various chunks of pastel butter-iced cottages around a fondant icing harbour. It's incredible.

'Please, please make wedding cakes,' I beg, imagining the fantastic creations that Faye could dream up, 'And work exclusively for me!'

Faye shudders. 'No thanks. Adults are far too critical. I'll stick to children. They're a much more appreciative audience.' She darts to the Aga and stirs a pan before opening the fridge and fishing out a bottle of Chablis.

'This must have taken for ever.'

'It did,' Faye agrees, while pouring the wine, 'But it should lead to greater things, with any luck. It's a major client with brilliant connections which is why I asked you to lunch.'

'Really?' Intrigued I take a seat at the table, peering closely at the fabulous cake. It could probably win the Turner Prize. 'Who's that?'

'Saffron Scott, the editor of *Scorching!*' cries Faye, and her eyes sparkle with excitement. 'She's ordered the cake for her goddaughter's birthday.'

I'm impressed. *Scorching!* is the only celebrity gossip magazine worth reading. Celebs practically queue up to give it interviews, probably due to the fact that Saffron Scott is herself no stranger to the world of fame. The only daughter of sixties rock star Davie Scott, Saffron has lived most of her life in the public eye. She spent the late years of the nineties being photographed in various drunken states, taking a cocktail of drugs and having a spectacular nervous breakdown. After a spell in the Priory Saffron reinvented herself as a showbiz correspondent on *This Morning* before eventually landing the job of editing *Scorching!* In her late twenties now she's still frequently papped lunching with celebrities.

'Wow,' I say.

'Davie Scott's a client of Simon's,' explains Faye. 'He put her in touch with me.'

I take a sip of Chablis and the biscuity flavour bursts across my tongue. Simon's taste in wine has certainly improved since we used to swill Liebfraumilch out of mugs at college.

'That's great, hon,' I'm pleased for Faye; she works so hard and is so talented. 'She'll be able to get you millions of commissions.'

'Probably,' Faye agrees. 'But that isn't really the point, Robyn. I've got quite enough on my plate right now.'

We both look at the cake and then laugh.

'Literally!' smiles Faye. 'But I did have contacts in mind, only not for me but for you...'

'Me? I can't cook.'

'I know that.' Faye rolls her eyes. 'You may burn water but you can plan the most fantastic weddings.' She looks dreamy. 'Ours was perfect. Davie Scott was admiring the wedding photo on Si's desk. Si told Davie what a fantastic wedding planner you are.'

'Good,' I say.

'It's better than good!' cries Faye. 'I've been dying to tell you! Davie was really impressed with what you'd done, Robs, and borrowed our wedding album. Apparently Saffron and Fergus are about to announce their engagement and are looking for a wedding planner so Davie showed her our photos. She loved what you did for us and wants you to pitch for the job of planning her wedding!'

It's just as well I'm sitting down because my legs have gone wobbly. This could be it! A chance to break into the big time and plan the kinds of weddings that I only dream of!

'Saffron Scott wants *Perfect Day* to pitch for her wedding?'

'She certainly does,' Faye rummages in her huge shoulder bag and plucks out a card which she hands to me. 'She wants you to call her. Remember me when you're hired to arrange Prince William's wedding.'

Oh. My. God. I can't believe it! This could be it, the life changing opportunity that I've been waiting for! My dreams are so close to coming true that I can almost taste them!

I gaze at the card but I don't see it because I'm visualising the fabulous wedding that I could organise for Saffron. My stomach seesaws in excitement. This is my golden opportunity to show the world exactly what I can do.

'I'll call her as soon as I get home,' I

promise, wondering how I'll manage to contain myself until then. 'Thanks, Faye. I owe you one.'

'You certainly do.' Faye looks serious. 'I'm fully intending to call in this favour.'

'Anything.' I promise, and then wonder what I'm letting myself in for. The last favour I did for Faye was attending one of her dinner parties where I spent a dismal few hours feeling like Bridget Jones and swigging wine. I'd rather be locked in a broom cupboard with Patrick and Jo than go through that again.

'Don't look so scared.' Faye opens in a cupboard and pulls out a slab of sponge. 'It's not another dinner party.'

Don't you hate it when your friends can read your mind?

'It was a great dinner party,' I say, crossing my toes, fingers and anything else crossable.

'You always were a useless liar,' Faye says. 'Here, take these.'

She hands me a tub full of green goo and a palette knife.

'What's this?' I sniff it.

'It's your payment for my networking,' says Faye. 'Once we've had lunch you are icing the Balamory hillside.'

'For getting the chance to pitch for Saffron Scott's wedding I'll ice twenty hillsides,' I declare.

'Excellent,' grins my friend, flinging open

another cupboard to reveal an Everest of containers. 'By a strange coincidence I seem to have at least twenty more.'

Chapter Five

The next morning I wake up late and it feels as though someone is break-dancing inside my skull. Even though my eyes are tightly shut I can sense the daylight burning through the windows ready to blast me into dust. The churning in my stomach would make even Ellen MacArthur spew.

This is all Gideon's fault. When he popped in to collect Poppy I was so wound up with excitement, after having spoken with Saffron Scott and tendering for her wedding, that I was practically nailing myself into the floor. My notebook was brimming with sketches and notes, scraps of fabric for mood boards had drifted onto the carpet like pastel autumn leaves and I'd drunk so much coffee that I could have moonlighted as a Pro Plus tablet.

'Christ!' Gideon exclaimed when I opened the door. 'What's happened to you?'

Glimpsing in the mirror I saw a pink-cheeked woman with glittering eyes and a mass of curly dark hair pinned up with a biro.

I looked manic.

'Something really exciting,' I'd said, inviting Gideon in. His eyes were like saucers when I mentioned Saffron Scott – he adores *Scorching!* – and he was almost as excited as I was by the thought that I could be planning a wedding where the likes of Posh and Becks would be guests.

'We have got to celebrate,' Gideon declared, pulling me into his arms and waltzing around the kitchen. 'This is it, Robs!'

'I haven't got the job yet,' I pointed out, but to Gideon this was a minor detail. Pushing aside my protests that I had to work/watch EastEnders/clean the flat, he dragged me down the stairs to his place where I ended up sampling James's whiskey collection until the small hours.

I may have sampled his wine and spirit collection too...

I will never drink again.

Honestly!

I open my poor eyes but needles of light stab my retinas and my brain swivels inside my skull. I stagger to the bathroom, slosh cold water onto my face and wince when I glance in the mirror. Not only is the sunlight glinting evilly off the glass but my eyes have practically disappeared into my face. My skin looks grey and on my chin a lovely spot has decided to make an appearance. Why am I the only 29-year-old I know who still gets spots? Surely now I have to worry about fine lines and tax returns it wouldn't be too much to ask not to have to worry about spots any more? I look terrible.

I hate getting older. I resent the fact that I'm nearly thirty and can't stay up all night any more and look radiant – or at least my version of it – the next morning. I remember the days when Simon and I would go out on the beer, smoke until daylight and still manage to go to lectures. We even managed to pull.

Those days are gone for ever.

I drag myself into the shower and blast my body with hot water, rinsing the hangover away. I do a face pack, deep condition my hair and use an entire tube of invigorating lemon shower gel. Several coffees and paracetamol later I'm almost human again. The mirror reveals that apart from being a bit pale I won't scare small children if I venture outside.

I'm feeling really inspired by the whole Saffron Scott thing. I look through the notes I made and then put them aside. A pale winter sun pokes through the blinds and decide to go out and get some fresh air, or what passes for it in London. I'll visit the lace shop to pick up some samples and on my way I'll sign up for that Swing Dancing class.

Shrugging on my suede coat and hitching

my Chloe bag onto my shoulder I prepare to face the world. To give myself a boost I decide against wearing my knee boots and plump instead for a really cute pair of low-heeled character shoes in a vibrant crimson.

It's just past noon when I leave the flat. The sunshine is starting to turn a sickly hue and the sky is bruised with lemony clouds. Wind whisks up the remaining autumn leaves and spots of rain patter on the bin bags. Experience tells me there'll soon be a downpour of the type only found in London where the rain leaves the skin gritty, the cars hiss through puddles and people scuttle by with their heads bowed. I turn up my collar and hurry towards the station, glad to hide underground for a few stops.

When I surface the rain is falling in earnest, big dollops that splat onto the soft suede of my coat and pool into large puddles. I'm furious with myself for forgetting to bring an umbrella. Soon my lovely shoes bleed red dye everywhere and my feet look as though a vertically challenged vampire has popped in for lunch. By the time I arrive at the Adult Education Centre my hair, so carefully straightened after my shower, springs back into ringlets and my makeup is sliding down my cheeks.

Maybe I should have stayed in bed?

When I try to push open the door of the centre and discover that it's locked I know I should have definitely stayed under the duvet.

'Closed for lunch,' I read, while the rain plasters my hair to my head and turns my coat into soggy chamois leather. 'Fan-flipping-tastic.'

I back into a shop doorway in a feeble attempt to get some shelter, pointless really because I'm so wet now that you could wring me out, and decide to wait until the centre reopens. I really want to try this Swing class. I'm already looking forward to rummaging around in some of my favourite thrift shops to find some authentic dancing outfits and – look ruefully down at my stained feet – some new dancing shoes.

I'm standing outside a small shop that sells the most amazing lingerie, all pink satins, peach ribbons and frothing cream lace, exactly the sort of underwear that I used to hope Patrick would buy me one day. Not that it would have occurred to my ex to buy me underwear. For the last birthday that we were together he'd proudly presented me with a state-of-the-art food processor which he'd ended up wearing on his head. A food processor? What a sexless present. Was that really how little my fiancé knew me? In the kitchen I'm not so much Raymond Blanc as totally blank. I stare at the pretty bras and French knickers like a Dickensian pauper staring at buns, and feel rather sorry for myself.

I'm trying to mop up the water dripping down my neck when a man appears beside me and attempts to enter the building. It would be hard not to notice him because not only is he tall and ridiculously handsome with glossy dark hair and sapphire eyes, but he is hammering on the door so hard that the glass panes rattle.

'It's closed,' I tell him, rather unhelpfully since he's probably figured this out. 'It's lunchtime.'

'What sort of place closes at lunchtime?' growls the man, giving the door another bash.

It's on the tip of my tongue to reply the sort of place where the employees want to eat something, but the grim set of his mouth and the muscle ticking in his check tell me that he probably won't care. From the expensive cut of his suit and the Rolex on his wrist he's probably one of those city types who think lunch is for wimps.

I must be a wimp because my tummy is growling. To cover the unladylike noises I say brightly, 'I'm here to sign up for a course!'

The man looks at me as though I'm insane. 'It's an Adult Education Centre,' he points out.

'I know that,' I say. 'I'm signing up for the Swing Dancing Course. I'm going to learn to Jive, or I am if I ever get in to put my name down, I can't wait to start. I love all that 1950s dancing. Apparently its brilliant exercise and really good for keeping fit and…'

Normally I'm such an energetic talker that you could wire me to the National Grid and use me to power Britain, but the man is looking at me really strangely, his amazing blue eyes trained on my face in a powerful gaze, and my words peter away. I feel quite giddy at being the subject of that intense scrutiny. Staring back at him, I'm shocked to find myself thinking how plump and kissable his lips are. He looks rather familiar too. Maybe we've met before? Is that why he's staring at me?

Stop it, Robyn! It isn't you he's looking at. That horrible spot has probably escaped from its twenty layers of *Touche Éclat*. Either that, or he can't believe how bedraggled and tatty you're looking.

Why is real life so unfair? In romantic novels heroines always look amazing in the rain, all pink cheeked and with their muslin gowns clinging tantalisingly to their curves. Just my luck that I meet the most attractive man in months when I look as though I've swum here from Ladbroke Grove. In a novel he would be captivated by my soggy beauty and offer to shelter me under his raincoat rather than continuing to stare.

Tearing my gaze from his, I sneak a glimpse of myself in the shop window. Yuk!

Not pretty. No wonder he's staring. I think I'll give this up as a bad job and come back another and hopefully drier day. Maybe I could shelter in the lingerie shop? Bruise my plastic and indulge my inner romantic heroine?

Just as I turn to push open the shop door his hand reaches out and brushes my elbow.

'Excuse me, but I'm sure I know you. You're Robyn, aren't you? Robyn Hood?'

I nod, wracking my brains to place him. I thought he looked familiar.

'We've met before,' he continues, and now that he's forgotten to be angry about the adult education centre he's smiling, a cute dimple playing hide and seek in his check, 'At the Harveys' dinner party?'

Good old Faye and her dinner parties.

'And you remembered my name, right?' I sigh. It's annoying when a random decision by your parents becomes your defining feature. Not for the first time I consider changing my name. I read somewhere that you can legally call yourself whatever you want, even Minnie Mouse if you feel like it.

On second thoughts maybe I'll stick with Robyn Hood.

'I remembered *you*,' says the man, his eyes warmer now and the lashes starry from the rain. 'You're the wedding planner who had to dash off to a comedy gig. I'm Jonathan Broadhead.'

The memory is hazy but it's coming back to me slowly. I met Jonathan at one of Faye's dinner parties ages ago and we'd been thrown together because our partners were absent. We'd chatted for a while and I'd told him about the wedding Hester and I were planning for a glamour model. Gazing up at him I realize how much I must have loved Patrick not to have been struck dumb by how incredibly handsome Jonathan is. He has the sort of face that makes you want to take a second look and then a third and maybe even a fourth. I can't help but look now. You could slice granite with those amazing cheekbones.

'You're a lawyer,' I recall, 'You work with Simon.'

He laughs, 'That makes me sound really dull. I wish I'd dropped out of school and joined the circus.'

'Oh I don't know,' I say, 'Ally McBeal always seemed to have a lot of fun.'

'My law firm isn't fun. Besides I look ridiculous in short skirts,' he says.

'Knee length is more you,' I reply and then the ice is broken and we're laughing.

'Look,' says Jonathan finally, 'I don't know about you but I think it might he a good idea to go inside until this rain stops. Pleasant as the view is,' he inclines his head in the direction of the lingerie shop, 'I don't think that I can really follow you in there.'

'Do you buy your fishnet stockings else

where then?' I tease, liking the way that his eyes crinkle when he laughs.

'I'm more M&S than S&M,' Jonathan says, 'I don't know where you get your preconceptions about we legal types, unless there's something about Simon Harvey I don't know. Come on, let's get in the warm somewhere, grab a coffee and dry out.'

Although I am trembling like a whippet because I'm soaked right through to my knickers I'm not in the habit of going for coffee with strangers, especially ones this attractive. And anyway I hardly know Jonathan Broadhead. It makes more sense to go home for a hot shower and try to sign up for swing dancing another day.

But sometimes fate likes to pull a moonie at me and today is no exception. Just as I'm telling Jonathan that I'm going back to Ladbroke Grove a lorry thunders past and showers us both with cold, dirty water. I splutter and the icy rivulets trickle down my cheeks like tears. I certainly feel like sobbing because my lovely suede coat is wrecked. Beaten, I sway wearily on the pavement.

'Right, that's it,' says Jonathan firmly, his hand steadying me, 'You're soaked and freezing. I'm taking you to Starbucks and thawing you out. Simon will never forgive me if I let his best friend get hypothermia. Here, come under my coat and get out of the rain.'

He's offering to shelter me under his

raincoat! I'm so bowled over by the sheer romance of this that I forget to protest and seconds later he's pulling me close against his side and gently draping the fabric across me. His hand grazes my cheek and then I'm snuggled beneath his arm, with the rain pitter pattering on the coat and breathing in the delicious tang of his skin. I must still be tucked up in my bed and dreaming.

Please don't let me wake up just yet!

'OK?' asks Jonathan.

Even though my goose bumps have got goose bumps and my favourite coat is ruined I haven't felt this OK for a very, very long time. Laughing, we venture into the street, dodging puddles and cannoning off one another as we try to walk in a straight line. Somehow we make it into Starbucks without stumbling from the kerb and falling under a bus. I'm almost sorry to enter the warm fug of the coffee shop because it's such fun trying to walk whilst huddled under his raincoat.

Nothing to do with the fact that it's nice to be held by an attractive man, of course!

'We made it,' Jonathan releases me and shrugs off his coat. His dark hair is beaded with raindrops but he doesn't seem to care. The cross expression of earlier has been replaced by a smile of incredible sweetness and that cute dimple is back too.

Not that I'm looking, of course.

'What would you like?' he asks, 'Coffee? Cake?'

Now there's the one million dollar question. I peer up at the menu board and then into the cabinet of yummy pastries. What I'd *like* is a big wedge of carrot cake washed down with syrupy white mocha latte, extra cream and about a zillion calories. What I ask for will, of course, be another matter entirely.

'Skinny latte, please,' I say, 'Nothing to eat, thanks.'

Jonathan rolls his eyes, 'You girls! Why are you always dieting? My wife, Anita, is exactly the same. You all look lovely as you are.'

His Wife? Ten bums in row! Typical of my Swiss cheese memory to forget that little snippet.

'I can't speak for your wife,' I smile, 'But maybe we look lovely *because* we're careful what we eat?'

'It's a shame,' Jonathan shakes his head, 'Take a seat, Robyn. I'll bring these over.'

What a gentleman! See, it's always the good ones who are taken.

I find a couple of battered chic armchairs and bag them for us. While I peel off my soggy coat and rearrange my hair by peering in the back of a teaspoon I try to dredge up anything that I might have once known about Jonathan Broadhead. He has a wife but she wasn't at Faye and Simon's dinner party. I seem to remember that she was held up at work and does something really high powered. Merchant banker? Neurosurgeon? Astronaut?

Oh dear, I really can't remember. Will that look rude? In my defence we last met at around the time things were going pear-shaped (or should I say Jo-shaped) with Pat. My mind wasn't exactly focused on making small talk.

Maybe I can wing it?

'Here we go,' Jonathan places the coffees and a large piece of carrot cake onto the table, 'Get warmed up.'

Carrot cake. The man has excellent taste!

'Thanks,' I wrap my hands around the mug and instantly the warmth starts to thaw my frozen fingers.

'What a shame about your coat,' Jonathan remarks, 'It's really lovely. Will it dry out?'

'I hope so,' I look sadly at my poor coat as it drips onto the floor, 'It's a 1950s Dior; quite my favourite thing. Collecting vintage clothes is one of my passions.'

'What are the others?' he asks, smiling at me.

I think about this, 'Weddings, obviously! I love all things fifties too. And,' I smile back at him, 'Carrot cake!'

Jonathan pushes the cake into the centre of the table, 'I suspected as much,' he says with mock seriousness, 'Which is why I brought two forks back.'

I laugh, 'Wow. A mind reader. What talent.'

'Not really,' Jonathan helps himself to a forkful, 'I saw you looking. But hey, I totally get the fifties thing. I love the music. Frank Sinatra. Dean Martin. Elvis. Actually, I've just spent an embarrassingly large amount of money on a genuine 1950s juke box which is now my pride and joy.'

'Worth every penny though,' I say, 'I feel the same about my vintage shoes.'

We chat happily for a while about all things 1950s and it's great to meet a kindred spirit. Most people look at me as though I'm mad when I talk about my fifties obsession. Gideon can't bear the 'clutter' in my flat, being more a chrome and black marble minimalist, and Faye tries hard not to wince at the very thought of second-hand shoes. Jonathan totally gets it though and we talk for so long that I fetch more coffees because we're hogging the table.

'So,' Jonathan tips sugar into his second latte, 'How's it going with that comedian chap? He's doing well, isn't he? I was reading in the paper that he's been given his own all male discussion show.'

I read that too. Apparently it's called *Talking Bollocks*. Need I say more?

'We're not together,' I say, stabbing at the carrot cake with my fork, 'It didn't work out.'

Stab. Stab. Stab.

'Hey,' Jonathan places his hand over mine,

halting the destruction, 'I'm sorry Robyn. I didn't mean to be nosey.'

'It's OK,' I say, 'It was a long while ago. I'm fine about it.'

Jonathan doesn't move his hand. It remains covering mine, warm strong and oddly comforting. It's a friendly gesture.

'It's not easy though, is it?' he sighs.

I slide my hand out from under his.

'How is Anita? Is she still a ... um...'

'A biochemist?' He pulls a face, 'Yeah. 'Fraid so.'

I'm not sure quite what a biochemist does exactly but I'm sure it's really important and I tell him so.

'It is important,' he agrees, and now it's his turn to attack the cake by mashing it with his fork.

I say nothing.

'And I try to be understanding, really.' I can tell he's wrestling with something. 'Like, last night, we had plans to catch a movie. I was making 'Nita supper when she called to cancel with some excuse to do with single-handedly revolutionising stem cell research. What could I say to that? "Well, you try re-suscitating the carbohydrates in a dried-out lasagne!" Of course I didn't say that. Instead, I said, *Of course, honey, I understand,* and then moped around all night feeling sorry for myself. God, sorry!' Jonathan laughs, awkwardly.

'We all do that,' I say, 'I'm the world's expert. Sit back and listen to some of the things that I've done.' And I start to tell him some stories about the occasions when Patrick did something outrageous to me and I tolerated it.

It's scary actually how many stories there are to choose from!

By the time that I've finished telling the story about the time Pat popped out for tea bags and ended up in Paris with a super-model ('Nothing happened Robs, so it didn't, I swear on my mammy's life!') Jonathan is laughing so hard that other shoppers are casting disapproving looks our way. I'm laughing too because looking back these stories are really funny and I'll probably dine out on them for years. Telling them no longer hurts, so hurrah! I really am over Patrick!

'Christ!' Jonathan exclaims, looking at his watch, 'It's nearly three! I'd better be going. My secretary's probably sent a search party out for me. At least the rain's stopped.'

'So it has,' I say, surprised, 'When did that happen?'

'No idea,' Jonathan shrugs, 'I was having far too much fun to notice. Thanks Robyn, I can't remember the last time I laughed this much.'

My sides are hurting from giggling, 'Neither can I,' I tell him, 'Thanks for rescuing me from the rain.'

'My pleasure,' he smiles, and I notice that his teeth are absolutely perfect. Does this man have any flaws? 'You've snapped me out of my bad mood so I owe you one! How about I come back tomorrow and sign us both up for our classes – me for business French and you for swing dancing? If you give me your mobile number I'll text you to let you know it's done.'

If he wasn't so clearly potty about his wife I would have hesitated, but Jonathan is so upfront and so genuine that I reel it off straight away.

'Great,' Jonathan saves my number and pockets his phone, then he leans forward and kisses me on the cheek, a kiss as soft and as delicious as a buttery croissant. 'It's been wonderful catching up with you. I feel like I've made a new friend.'

I can still feel the brush of his lips and I have to sit on my hands to stop myself touching my cheek.

'Me too,' I nod, 'Me too.'

'I'll text you,' promises Jonathan, his blue eyes crinkling at the corners, and then he's gone, a tall broad-shouldered figure striding through the crowd.

My hand slowly traces the place where his lips rested only seconds before.

Why, oh why, are the good ones always spoken for?

Chapter Six

OK, Robyn, count to ten.

You are *not* going to let her wind you up.

You're twenty-nine, with your own flat, your own business and your own overdraft. You do not answer to your mother!

Remember that yoga course you did with Faye? Exhale stress out and inhale tranquillity in. And repeat slowly, 'I will not let my mother get to me'.

I'm a natural!

Or at least I am for all of twenty seconds before my mother pushes her designer glasses up her nose and gives an exaggerated sigh. When she shuffles the papers and shakes her head for the fiftieth time my yogic calm is shattered.

Maybe I should have gone to more than two classes?

'What's wrong, mum?'

My mother looks up from perusing my accounts, 'Oh nothing, darling. Just ignore me.'

It would be easier to ignore a herd of wildebeest rampaging through my flat.

'It's obviously not *nothing*. You've been groaning for the last hour. What's up?'

'Your overdraft limit, I should think, my

girl! *Perfect Day*'s hardly making any profit. I wish you'd told me things were so bad.'

'Mum! *Perfect Day*'s breaking even after only eight months, which is excellent. All my clients have been more than happy.'

'Darling, there's nothing coming in this month and your VAT is due. I don't see how you can even draw a wage.'

I've had a few sleepless nights on this score actually but there's no way I'm telling my mother that. She's likely to drag me kicking and screaming back to Hester Dunnaway. And things aren't that bad.

Yet.

'There are weddings in the pipe line,' I say firmly, 'And guess what? Saffron Scott's asked me to pitch for her wedding.'

'Robyn! That's wonderful!'

'So stop worrying,' I say firmly, 'Things will be fine.'

My mother checks her Cartier watch, 'I'll never get through this before lunch. I promised Hester we'd try the new place off Henrietta Street.'

'Leave the accounts, mum.'

'Leave them?' Her eyebrows shoot into her hairline, 'That's what caused the problems! Why don't you have an accountant?'

'Because I can't afford one yet,' I lean over and shut the books. 'Anyway, Gideon's more than happy to help.'

And he's less critical than you, I add under

my breath. Mum can't help interfering with *Perfect Day*. I know she means well but I could really do without it.

'I know when I'm not wanted,' she huffs, 'I thought you'd jump at the opportunity of having some one with my business experience cast an eye over the figures. But if you don't think I'm good enough...'

'Of course I don't think that!' I say impatiently. My mother runs an incredibly successful soft furnishings shop which she built up from practically nothing, 'I've asked you for lots of advice since I started *Perfect Day*.'

'You didn't ask me what I thought about your leaving *Catch the Bouquet*. But you did ask your father.'

'That's not fair! Hester's your best friend. It would have put you in an impossible position.'

'Hester was terribly upset.'

I think the chances of Hester being genuinely sorry to see me leave are slimmer than Victoria Beckham. The charming letter that she had couriered over the next day, complete with threats of legal action if I dare use any of her contacts, hardly smacked of regret. Still, there's no point explaining this to my mother. She and Hester go back years.

'That's all in the past,' I say, 'Leave the accounts and have a coffee.'

'I can take a hint, I know when I'm not wanted...'

I grit my teeth so hard my fillings rattle.

'You are wanted, Mum.'

'You never were a very good liar,' she pauses, 'Unlike your father.'

Here we go. According to my mother Dad could knock Satan into cotton socks for pure evil. While I tend to the Gaggia machine that Si got me for my birthday I pretend to listen to mum complaining about my father. The way she goes on you'd think Dad had left yesterday.

'Did I tell you he's bought *her* a brand new Range Rover?' says my mother, 'And all those years he let us struggle with a clapped out old banger.'

By *her* mum means Hannah, Dad's new wife. Actually, hardly new since they've been married for eleven years and have ten year old twins. But as far as mum's concerned Hannah is a par venue interloper.

'Dad did his best,' I say, rummaging in the fridge for milk, 'At least he gave us a car. He wasn't well off back then.'

'That's right,' my mother snaps, 'Stick up for him as usual. I don't know why you bother, all the times he's let you down over the years, all those Saturdays when you waited for him. It used to break my heart. You'd press your little nose to the window and nothing I'd say could persuade you he'd let you down again.'

There's a lump in my throat. For a

moment I'm transported back to those long gone days, dressed up in my best frock and giddy with excitement as I waited for my Daddy to come.

'Then he'd phone with some pathetic excuse or another and you'd be distraught.'

'He had to work!'

'He worked in the bookies, Robyn, where he spent most of your maintenance, by the way. He wasn't splitting the atom.'

I close my eyes. So Dad liked a little flutter? He went on to buy the book makers and now runs a very successful chain, *Sure Bet*, which could probably finance a fleet of Range Rovers. When he did turn up to see me his pockets were always crammed with notes and he used to laugh and rustle them, promising me that I could have whatever I wanted if I smiled and was his happy little Robyn. Ballerina Barbies, trips to the zoo and more sweets than were probably good for me always followed. I loved it when he told me I was his special girl. It more than compensated for all the tears and disappointments.

'That's men for you,' Mum says bitterly, 'I've never yet met one who wasn't a total disappointment. But your father has to be the worst of the lot.'

'Do you want a biscuit?' I interrupt, sick of hearing my father's faults for the umpteenth time. I open the Marilyn Monroe barrel that I found on eBay and help myself to a couple. Hopefully munching digestives will keep her quiet for a few minutes.

Mum shakes her head, 'I'm doing no carbs!' she pats her stomach, 'Hester swears by it.'

Hester is a professional food Nazi so this is no surprise. And wherever her food fads take her, from the grapefruit diet to the boiled egg plan (believe me it was not pleasant in the office during that phase) mum is sure to follow. I hate diets. And I love my curves.

Most of the time.

'Do you know how many calories are in those?' Mum snatches the biscuit barrel from me.

'I'm starving!'

'You are not,' Mum tips the contents into the bin. 'Children in Africa are starving. Have an apple.'

'Who eats apples rather than biscuits?'

'A girl who's single and thirty.'

'Mum! You've just been telling me how crap men are!'

'Well, yes,' she agrees, 'But I've seen the sweetest hat in Philip Treacey. It's perfect for mother of the bride.'

I slosh coffee into spotty Emma Bridgewater mugs, 'It's not even a year since Patrick and I broke up.'

Mum places a hand on her heart, 'I still have nightmares about having to return all those presents. Great Auntie Ethel was really upset.'

Sod Auntie Ethel! I was pretty upset myself.

'I'm not ready for a relationship.'

My mother tuts, 'When you fall off the horse what do you do, Robyn?'

'Give up riding?'

'Darling! Do try and make an effort! You get back in the saddle, of course! And refuse to sign a pre-nup. Just like I do.'

This is no exaggeration. My mother, currently Anna Dexter, has been married and divorced no less than three times. To my great relief she's taking a break from nuptials recently, preferring to go on luxury cruises where she's wooed by men called Luigi who have Tango tans and large wallets. She's the only person I know who finds David Dickenson attractive.

So I think I can be forgiven for *not* taking relationship advice from her.

For a moment I think about meeting Jonathan Broadhead yesterday. I see again those amazing hyacinth eyes framed by inky lashes all starry with rain and feel the hard contours of his body when he pulled me beneath his raincoat. He was definitely attractive and not a hint of fake tan.

He was also married and totally off limits.

More proof that all the good ones really are taken.

I'm saved from discussing my love life any

further by Hester Dunnaway attacking the intercom and demanding admittance. I buzz her in and my stomach seesaws. Hester and I have had very little to do with each other since I resigned and I'm quite happy to keep it like that.

Imagine Cruella de Ville's meaner older sister and you've got a pretty good picture of Hester Dunaway. Groomed and plucked and waxed and suctioned to within an inch of her life she looks like a desiccated skeleton, albeit one dressed in Prada and with Chanel tipped talons. It costs a lot of money to look this well preserved so it's just as well Hester is one of the most successful wedding planners in the country. And luckily she always has a keen junior to do the donkey work because keeping her aging body embalmed is a full time occupation.

I should know. I may have learned an awful lot from working with Hester but she certainly got her money's worth. You haven't known telephone Hell until you've spent six hours calling every zoo in Europe to secure the services of twenty pink flamingos. Even months on I have the strongest Pavlovian impulse to jump to my feet and start working when in her presence.

'Hello Robyn,' says Hester, once she and mum have admired each other's outfits, 'How are you?'

'Good thanks,' I smile, 'And you?'

'Never busier. My latest wedding's going to feature in *Hello!* It's very high profile and totally secret.'

There's a pause while she waits for me to ask whose it is. No way am I going to give her the satisfaction. I'd rather eat Poppy's dog food.

But my mother has no such restraint, 'Who?'

'I really can't divulge, darling, but suffice it to say that the budget's hundreds of thousands.'

A poisoned arrow of envy scores a bulls-eye in my heart. What I wouldn't give to have that kind of money to play with. What a fantastic wedding I could plan!

And not a flipping flamingo in sight either.

'Any big weddings coming up?' Hester asks me.

This is where I'd love to say that every WAG in England is beating a path to my door but she'll know I'm fibbing.

'Nothing huge,' I hedge, 'Yet.'

'Oh dear,' sighs Hester, 'I did warn you. You have some lovely ideas, Robyn, but you're hardly in the same league as *Catch the Bouquet*. Still, I'm sure there's some satisfaction in helping people with tight budgets.'

'Robyn's really modest.' pipes up my mother, 'Saffron Scott's asked her to pitch for the job of planning her wedding.'

Hester tears her attention away from

admiring her reflection in my Brabantia bin, 'Yes, which will be a fantastic wedding. I can hardly wait to discuss my plans with Saffron and Fergus.'

'You're pitching too?'

'Of course,' Hester is triumphant 'Didn't you know I dated Davie Scott back in the sixties?'

Since Hester collects men like I'm currently collecting bank charges I shouldn't be surprised.

'The pitch will be wonderful experience for you, Robyn,' she continues, 'But don't get your hopes up too much. It's just a formality. The Scotts can afford the very best.'

'Maybe I'm the best?'

Hester smiles, the smile of a crocodile before it gobbles you up.

'You're ideas are sweet, darling, but you're hardly competition for me. I'm not about to lose any sleep over *Perfect Day.*' The discussion over as far as she's concerned Hester turns to my mother, 'Ready, Anna? I've booked the table for twelve thirty.'

I stand seething by the window long after they zoom off in Hester's pink Mercedes. Suddenly all my ideas for Saffron's wedding seem trite and clumsy. The mood boards are clichéd, the themes are too obvious. How can I possibly compete with someone who flies in flamingos? She'll probably come up with some amazing Arabian Nights scenario complete with camels or stage the first ever wedding on the moon.

I wander miserably to the fridge. I can stare at blank paper all afternoon and drive myself insane or I can do something a little more positive. I pull out my emergency bar of Dairy Milk and carry it into the sitting room where I slot a Doris Day DVD into the machine and settle onto the sofa. Doris and chocolate are my two favourite things and normally guaranteed to lift my spirits.

And once I'm feeling more positive I'm bound to have some good ideas, right?

I break off a square of chocolate, press play and try to put Hester's mocking words out of my mind.

I'll think of something brilliant soon.

Won't I?

Chapter Seven

'Two glasses of dry white wine and a packet of pork scratchings!' Gideon deposits the spoils of his trip to the bar onto the table, 'So what's going on? You drag me to the *Feathers* on a week night, swig wine like there's about to be a world shortage and look like shit.'

'I thought gay men were supposed to be sensitive?'

'Only in *Sex and the City*. darling. But I am sensitive enough to see something's up. Care to share?'

'I'm totally stuck for ideas to pitch for Saffron's wedding,' I sigh, 'And worse than that, Hester's pitching too and she's bound to have something incredible up her sleeve.'

'Bollocks,' says Gideon.

'Bollocks indeed.'

Even after chomping through the entire bar of Dairy Milk and watching two Doris Day movies I remained uninspired. I stared at my blank sketch pad until I'd gone cross-eyed before giving up and going to find Gideon. I've got the wedding planner's version of writers' block and since it's a truth universally acknowledged that a girl who cannot be cheered up by chocolate must be in want of alcohol I've dragged him out and left a message inviting Faye to join us.

'When's the pitch?' asks Gideon.

'Friday. If Hester gets the job she'll be unbearable. I'll have to emigrate so I can't hear her gloating. Saffron's bound to choose her because I can't possibly compete with Hester's extravagant ideas.'

'Maybe that's the problem?' says Gideon thoughtfully, 'Competing I mean? You're not Hester Dunaway so do something totally different. Be understated and elegant, classy not tacky. You've got bags of style, darling. Not everyone wants thrones and flamingoes.'

'That makes sense,' I agree slowly, 'I left Hester in the first place because I wanted to plan weddings my way. I wanted to be totally different.'

Suddenly I have a moment of blinding clarity. This is where I've been going wrong! I've been trying too hard to think like Hester and come up with themes that would make Jordan's wedding look understated when I should have been exploring my own ideas. I need to start thinking like me.

'Gideon, you're brilliant.'

'It has been said.'

'Now you've sorted Hester, maybe you could give me some help with my mother? She's convinced that once I'm over thirty I'll be well and truly left on the shelf.'

'There you are!' Faye weaves her way through the tables and beams at us both, 'It was Hell on the tube!'

'Sorry,' I say as we hug, 'I should have met you somewhere more central.'

'Don't be daft,' Faye unwinds a beautiful Hermes scarf and slips out of her velvet coat, 'This makes a great change. There are only so many themed gastro pubs a girl can take.'

'Robyn likes the *Feathers* too,' Gideon grins, 'Especially the bar staff!'

'Gideon!' I slosh him on the arm.

'Oh!' Faye's eyes widen, 'Is this where that Aussie barman works?'

'Sure is,' nods Gideon, 'Mr. Surf God himself.'

'Is he here now?' Faye spins round to see the bar so quickly that she probably gives herself whiplash, 'That blonde guy serving? He's the one that Robyn-'

'Hello, guys? I am here you know!' I interrupt waving a hand in front of my friends. I'm so hot with embarrassment I'm amazed I don't spontaneously combust and leave nothing but a smoking pair of boots, 'He's called Bradley and he's just a friend.'

'A friend she shags!' says Gideon, so good at stirring he could double as a teaspoon.

Faye's bottom jaw is almost on the table, 'You never told me that!'

'Some things are private,' I say, fixing Gideon with a look that in a just world ought to lay him out on the floor, 'And some people spend too much time spying on their neighbours.'

'Sorry,' says Gideon, not looking anything of the sort, 'But how could I ignore something that gorgeous wandering down the stairs?'

Note to self: when *Perfect Day* is floated on the stock market buy a very secluded house, miles away from nosey neighbours.

'He's lush Robs,' says Faye, settling next to me on a stool, 'Good for you.' She looks again towards the bar where Bradley is pulling a pint, his tanned fore arms strong and corded with muscle, 'And how was it?'

'Mind your own business, Faye Harvey!'

'Sorry,' says Faye, 'I'm a sad old married woman who doesn't get out much. Si works such long hours these days that I have to get my excitement vicariously.' She sneaks a look over her shoulder and winks at me, 'And *that* is seriously exciting.'

'Divine isn't he?' sighs Gideon.

Bradley, sensing that he's being talked about, catches my eye, beams a big white toothed Aussie smile and waves. In spite of my embarrassment and Fay and Gideon's nosey delight that I'm attracted to a man, any man, who isn't Patrick, I wave back.

'He's really is just a friend,' I say, 'He's been away for a couple of months too. There isn't anything going on.'

'Well, you're mad not to pursue that!' says Faye, fanning herself with a bar mat, 'He's like something out of *Neighbours*, and I don't mean Harold!'

Maybe I should explain myself before you decide that I'm some old slapper who regularly pulls Aussie bar men and drags them home for wild sex. As if. I can probably count my sexual partners on one hand and still have spare finger, not cool these days I know but that's just the way I am. Before a man sees my wobbly bits I normally like to know more than his name.

Normally.

But the night I met Bradley was the exception to the rule. To be fair the circumstances were unusual. It was about five months after Pat and I broke up and although I was still desperately sad I was past the stage of weeping until I looked like a goblin.

Or so I'd thought.

I'd had a long day. Hester had been in a vile mood after a row with her latest toyboy, a designer dress had been lost in the post and my computer had crashed losing most of our files. As I'd dragged my self up the steps from the tube and wandered down the high street I'd wanted nothing more than to collapse onto my sofa with a big glass of wine and a trashy magazine. With this aim in mind I'd popped into the corner shop and picked up *Scorching*, flicking through to find the coverage of *Catch the Bouquet's* latest wedding. I'd been expecting to see nothing more than the vacuous smiles of the boy band member and his new glamour model wife when a headline leapt from the glossy page and walloped me right between the eyes.

Patrick McNicholas
Britain's Sexiest Single Comic invites us to his Thameside Home

Although I knew this was the psychological equivalent of picking a scab I couldn't help flicking through the magazine, gobbling up every purple paragraph and feasting on the glossy pictures of his new apartment. Pat looked so handsome and was obviously so happy, especially when he raved about the fun he'd had leading the single life since his engagement ended. 'This is the life, so it is,' he bragged. 'I totally recommend being free!' Thanks a million, Pat, I'd thought, shoving the magazine back onto the shelf. I was furious with Pat for being so shallow and even more furious with myself for still letting his carelessness hurt me. I might not love him anymore but to have two years of my life dismissed so easily sliced through me like a hot knife through butter. Blinking away tears of rage and hurt I fled the shop and stumbled into *The Feathers* where I'd ordered an enormous glass of wine and downed it in one.

'Jeez!' the barman had exclaimed, 'Looks like you needed that!' and he'd fetched me another which I'd drunk in a similar fashion. To cut a long story short I'd ended up pouring out my tale of woe to my new best friend AKA Bradley the Australian barman. Bradley listened sympathetically and told me about breaking up with his girlfriend and then we'd bonded in that peculiar way you do when bitching about an ex. Eventually the pub closed, Bradley had cleared up and then walked me home.

And the rest you can figure out for yourself!

Anyway, he's a nice guy and really easy to talk to. He's not my soul mate but he's fun and he's taken my mind off Patrick on several occasions. There's nothing more to it than that. Not that you'd ever convince Gideon though. As far as he's concerned it's only a matter of time before I book tickets with Qantas and rack off to chuck a few shrimps on the Barbie. There's no way I'm going to mention meeting Jonathan Broadhead yesterday. Gids will die of excitement and Faye will think...

Actually, I don't know what Faye will think. I'll tell her another time, not that there's really anything to tell.

'Let me get you a drink,' I say to Faye, 'White wine?'

She nods, 'The drier the better, please.'

'Any excuse to see Mr. Love God,' Gideon stage whispers as I thread my way through the evening drinkers.

I roll my eyes. Bradley and I haven't hooked up for ages. I've been rushed off my feet with *Perfect Day* and recently he went home for two months. Like I said there's nothing serious between us but it's nice to see him again. And maybe if he's not busy later he could pop round for a coffee?

A coffee, that's all!

I lean against the bar and try to catch the

eye of the bar staff. Bradley is nowhere to be seen so I wait patiently until a girl I haven't seen before, small, tanned with a mane of white blonde hair, serves me.

'Hi,' she says. 'Sorry to keep you. Where are the men when you need them?'

Another Aussie! What is it with this pub?

'That's a question I ask most days,' I smile, counting out my money, 'Where are all the good men?'

'Hanging out with Santa?' she passes the wine across the bar and takes my change, 'They must be somewhere. Gotta live in hope.'

'Or die in despair,' I sigh, and, balancing drinks and crisps in my hands, rejoin my friends. It's one thing to joke about the man famine if you're a twenty two year old gorgeous Aussie surfer babe and quite another if you're nearly thirty and pretty average on a good day, wearing control knickers and your best frock. If all the good ones really are taken then where does that leave me?

Alone, that's where, unlike Gideon and Faye, both of whom will be going home tonight to their partners.

Totally alone.

Chapter Eight

By half ten I've drunk my way through a bottle of Blossom Hill, the table is littered with crisp packets and Bradley's becoming more and more attractive by the minute. Even if George Clooney popped in and offered me a full time job licking *Nutella* from his body I'd have turned him down. Every time Bradley scoots round collecting glasses I admire the way his biceps swell beneath his white t-shirt and the lines of his six pack under the clingy fabric. OK, so he can't discuss Chekov and once said that his greatest fantasy was Jordan naked on a trampoline, but you can't have everything.

And anyway with a body like that who cares about conversation?

I knock back the last of my wine. I'm going to ask him to come home with me. This is what feminist burned their bras for! Germaine Greer would be proud.

I am strong! I am woman!

And maybe a teeny bit pissed?

'Darling,' Gideon says, shrugging on his coat, 'Are you sure you don't want to come with us? I'm going to walk Faye to the tube and then home for tea and toast.'

At the mention of toast my stomach rumbles, but I ignore it. Gideon and James will cosy up and I'll feel like a spare part. They see quite enough of me as it is. 'It's fine,' I say, 'I'll stay here and chat to Bradley.'

'Can't say I blame you,' sighs Gideon, 'I wouldn't kick him out of bed for ... well for anything!'

Faye gives me a hug, 'I'll call you tomorrow,' she promises, 'We can have a chat about some ideas for Saffron Scott. I'll ask Si if Davie has dropped any hints.'

'Thanks babes.'

'And Robyn,' she whispers, 'Give him one from me!'

Blushing to the ends of my hair I hoist myself onto a bar stool, wishing that I had the kind of endless legs I could cross elegantly rather than short ones that just dangle in mid air. Catching sight of my flushed face in the chrome beer pumps I decide to order Diet Coke from now on.

'Diet Coke?' echoes Bradley, when I place my order, 'With Bacardi?'

'No!' I laugh.

'Jeez, Robyn,' Bradley shakes his head as he pours the drink, 'Have you any idea what's in this stuff?'

Now call me stupid but actually I haven't a clue. So while Bradley explains the evils of Coke I arrange my features into a riveted expression and decide not to tell him that they can include anything they want as long as they *don't* include calories. Bradley's a health freak and won't appreciate this. His body is a temple.

Hope I get to worship soon!

As Bradley serves and chats I'm distracted by the enormous flat screen TV at the end of the bar. It's showing one of those late evening chat shows and Patrick has just loped across the studio and is shaking the host's hand. I'm over Patrick but I still get a little jolt whenever I see him. It's weird to be close to someone, to have shared their life in every way, and then be relegated to the position of stranger. I know Pat always cleans his toothbrush under the hot tap and likes the left side of the bed but none of the other viewers are privy to these details.

Although, knowing Pat, maybe I shouldn't bet on this.

Repositioning my bar stool so I'm spared watching Patrick charm the socks off the audience I turn my attention back to Bradley. Physically he's the opposite of Pat in every way. Bradley's tall with sun bleached hair and so gym honed that even his muscles have muscles whereas Pat's tall and rangy and hasn't been to the gym in his life. Running a double love life is enough to keep him fit. Both guys have green eyes but Bradley's are like rock pools, clear and honest, whereas Patrick's are the shadowy hue of his beloved Irish peat bogs.

I'm through with complicated men. Who wants to discuss Yeats in bed when they could be having amazing sex?

Time to see if Bradley's in the mood for a coffee...

'How was your trip home?' I ask.

Bradley runs a hand through his thick blonde mane, 'Awesome! I'd almost forgotten what it was like to feel warm. And the surfing was great.'

I flick my hair back from my face, 'So are you pleased to be back?'

'Sure. There's lots to keep me here.'

I raise an eyebrow Patrick style, 'Such as? The weather's hideous, your job looks exhausting and there's not a lot of surf on the Thames. What could possibly bring you back?'

I'm more pissed than I thought. What seemed like a flirty, witty line in my head sounds cheesier than the Cheddar Factory.

But Bradley just smiles his dazzlingly white smile.

'Jeez! It sounds really lame but I came back because of a Sheila. I was thinking about staying in Brisbane but she's here and I'm useless without her.'

My chardonnay saturated brain is a bit slow at translating from Australian to English but I think he's just told me that he's come back because he wants to be with someone. Someone who lives in England...

Oh. My. God.

I like Bradley, he's a fun guy and everything, but I don't fancy him in a 'let's play at naming our children' kind of a way. It's a bit of a responsibility if he's come back to Britain because of me.

I clutch the bar because I'm in serious danger of falling off my stall.

'You've come back to be with a girl?'

Bradley's cheeks are as pink as my Kath Kidston mobile, 'Yep. She's right here. In this pub.'

'She is?'

Bradley nods, 'She's over there. Her name's Julia,' and rather than peering deeply into my eyes and dropping a bombshell he points towards the blonde Australian bar maid who'd joked with me earlier.

For a moment I'm speechless. I know he's not the love of my life and I definitely didn't want him to declare undying love for me or anything but it's something of a surprise to discover that my no strings mate, has fallen in love with another woman. And one who's tall, blonde and young to boot.

'I've known Jules for years,' Bradley says, as he pulls a tray of glasses from the dish washer, 'She was dating a mate of mine so I never dreamed we could be anything else. But when I went home she was single and,' he looks bashful, 'we kind of got it together, you know?'

I've got it together with Bradley a few times myself so, yes, I know.

'But Jules was about to go travelling,' he continues, 'And I couldn't bear to lose her so she persuaded me to come back with her.'

Julia looks over and smiles at him, a smile of such joy that it lights up the room.

'Isn't she great?'

'She's beautiful,' I say honestly.

He reaches across the bar, 'You and me have been really good friends, Robyn, so I want you to be the first to know! Before we flew here I asked Jules to marry me. And guess what? She said yes!'

'Wow!' I say, 'Congratulations!'

'Thanks. I know it's sudden but it's true what they say. You really do know when you meet the right one. Everything just falls into place.'

'I'm really pleased for you,' I lean across the bar and kiss his cheek, a very different kiss from the last one we shared, 'You deserve to be really happy.'

Bradley brushes my cheek with the back of his hand, 'And so do you Robyn,' His jerks his head in the direction of the television where Patrick is flirting with a stunning actress, 'Especially after your narrow escape from that idiot.'

It's really late by the time I finally leave the pub after buying champagne and listening to Julia's excited plans. I've offered *Perfect Day*'s services for free as a wedding present and I'm over the moon for them, I really am. The tears that slide silently down my cheeks aren't because I want Bradley for myself or wish that I were in Julia's Uggs. No way. I'm just so sad at always being the one left behind. Everybody is moving on but I'm always left alone, standing on the shore and watching them sail over the horizon to new and exciting lands. I'm not jealous of Bradley and Julia but I am jealous of what they have.

I'm tired of always being on my own.

I'm just pushing open the gate to Gideon's garden, and peering carefully at the path just in case Poppy's been out for a late night loo visit, when my phone beeps from deep within my bag. I root around and fish it out, trying not to scatter sweet wrappers and fluffy Tampax onto the grass.

That's strange, I don't recognise the number.

I open the message and scan it. When the words sink into my wine sodden brain I'm taken aback because the text is from Jonathan Broadhead. He's signed me up for the Swing Dancing course just like he promised.

A thoughtful man who keeps his word too? No wonder he's married.

I unlock the front door and switch on the light. Suddenly my heart doesn't feel as though it's encased in concrete. It feels all floaty and happy. Jonathan's been thinking about me. He's been in my thoughts too, maybe a little more that he ought to be.

I re-read the message and in spite of myself I find that I'm smiling.

I may be an old spinster of the parish, gathering dust on her shelf but things are looking up.

Robyn Hood is going swing dancing!

Chapter Nine

I've always hated job interviews.

Before I went self employed I dreaded squeezing into my strait jacket interview suit, bullying my curls into a chignon and pasting a keen expression onto my face. Nerves always overwhelmed me and I'd end up either totally tongue tied or gabbling away at Formula One speed. I'm much happier in an informal setting than I am being interrogated in an office and I'd been delighted Saffron Scott wanted to discuss the pitch in the comfort of her Chelsea flat.

So when Saffron's PA called my mobile and changed the venue of my pitch to

Scorching's HQ in Covent Garden my heart sank. I'd almost reached Chelsea and had to retrace my journey, cutting it fine to say the least. No matter how many times I try to convince myself that this is a pitch *not* an interview it doesn't feel like it and the closer the tube gets to Covent Garden the more nervous I feel.

And being nervous is never good, especially when pitching against Hester Dunaway, a woman so cool that she makes cucumbers appear hot and bothered.

Sighing, I check my reflection in the carriage window. When I planned my outfit I'd plumped for a look with just the right amount of edge, hoping this would sum up the ethos of *Perfect Day*, saying I'm a creative individual and someone with whom Saffron can identify. I'd imagined sipping coffee while Saffron flicked through my portfolio in a relaxed and friendly fashion. I hadn't prepared for a serious grilling in her office and I hope I'm not breaking some unspoken dress code by not wearing a power suit and stilettos so sharp they could puncture the pavement. I'm not sure what magazine editors wear but I've seen *The Devil Wears Prada* and I'm beginning to worry that I may have got it wrong.

I'm wearing a black vintage flared skirt with a full net underskirt and with red roses appliquéd onto it, a black cross over sweater with a rose corsage and my favourite pillar box red swing coat and cute velvet scarf. It all looked great when I twirled in front of the mirror and just the thing for a frosty November morning. But now I'm just wondering why I decided to wear my Camden knee boots, biker style and with platform soles higher than Ben Nevis. They seemed like a really funky statement when I pulled them on but I probably look like Minnie Mouse in a skirt.

I *had* looked great but I hadn't legislated for the London Underground system which has decided to flick a v at me and pack up somewhere between Russell Square and Covent Garden. As we all sit in polite silence and slowly cook I know my face is the same hue as my coat.

I check out my hair and groan. I spent hours straightening it but after thirty minutes stuck on the Tube it looks like a pair of starlings have taken up residence. Reaching into my pocket I fish out a hair band and pull it back into what will hopefully pass for a trendy high pony tail. Ouch! Although the Vicky Pollard style face lift is quite flattering it feels like every hair is being plucked from my scalp and I can't help worrying that my watering eyes are turning me into a dead ringer for Alice Cooper. Much as I loved those student nights head banging to *Poison* with Si, I don't think I'd want Alice to plan my wedding. Squinting in the glass I rub at my mascara but only make things worse. I'll just have to sort it later.

If I make it to *Scorching!* that is. Won't Hester love it if I'm late?

Just as I'm contemplating prising the doors open and running along the top of the carriages Bruce Willis style the train jerks into life and crawls into Covent Garden station. As myself and several hundred other commuters spew onto the platform I elbow my way to the lifts, cursing my boots that make running difficult and racing up the hundred odd steps to the surface an impossibility. So I wait my turn, shoehorn myself inside and eventually the elevator jolts me to the surface where I slam my Oyster card onto the yellow pad and tear into the street, blinking like a mole in the sunlight and gulping the air.

My watch reads ten forty six, my appointment with Saffron is at eleven, so by some absolute miracle, I'm not late. Sending up a silent prayer of thanks to my guardian angel – who's on the ball for once – I dash across the Piazza, ignoring *Karen Millen* and the human robot man, and locate Floral Street, home to the hive of celebrity news and gossip that is *Scorching!* magazine.

'Robyn Hood,' I pant to the glamorous receptionist whose makeup's such a work of art that the Louvre is probably bidding for it, 'I have an appointment with Ms. Scott at eleven?'

'Welcome to *Scorching*,' she smiles, 'Ms. Scott's in a meeting at the moment but she is expecting you. Please take a seat.'

I perch on what appears to be an art installation but is actually a chair and take a deep breath. OK, Robyn, you've made it. Calm and relaxed, remember? You can do this.

As I sit and get my breath back I indulge in some people watching. The hallowed offices of *Scorching!* are peopled by women who all look like they've been genetically modified in order to meet some unwritten company policy. While I nervously clutch my portfolio and wince as the trendy couch bites into my backside, a mind boggling army of tall thin people mince past balancing like tightrope walkers on their Jimmy Choos and Manolo Blaniks.

It really is another world. How ever did I think I could compete with Hester and plan A list weddings? The closest I come to designer labels these days is drooling over them on eBay.

I glance down at my portfolio. In it are designs and plans for Saffron's wedding that I've been slaving over. Gideon's advice about following my own instincts breached the dam of my wedding planner's block and for the last three days I've been sketching and creating themes from dawn to dusk. I don't think I've ever been so inspired in all my life or that I've ever been so creative. I just hope Saffron likes some of my ideas because I really couldn't have worked harder if I'd tried.

I put the folder down, flexing fingers that tingle from holding it so tightly, and decide to check my makeup. I reach into my bag and fish around for my make up, easier said than done when the bag leaps from my lap to spew its contents all over the floor.

'Bugger!' I say, 'I mean, oops!'

I glance towards the enormous chrome and glass desk just in case the receptionist is looking in my direction but she's on the telephone, her narrow back to me, so I seize my chance and fall onto my knees, cramming the detritus back in and hoping that the reclaimed oak floor boards don't ladder my stockings. You can bet your life that the one thing I *won't* have in my bag was an emergency pair of tights.

'Robyn, you don't need to get on your knees in my presence!' drawls an amused voice.

Looking up from a pair of gorgeous Christian Louboutin boots – and let's be honest unless I pull some major clients out of the bag soon this is the closest I'll ever get to such beautiful shoes – my gaze travels up past a pair of slender ankles and classic black Chanel suit, via this season's must have Mulberry bag, to Hester's beady gooseberry green eyes.

'Hello, Hester,' I say.

Come on floor, open up and swallow me.

Now, if it isn't too much trouble?

'Darling,' Hester drawls, 'Why on earth are you sprawled on the floor?'

I cram the contents of my bag back inside as quickly as I can and scramble to my feet.

'Yoga,' I tell her, 'Just a quick salute to the sun to supple up my mind!'

'Yoga?' echoes my ex boss, 'How very last season, Robyn. Any one who is anyone is doing Pilates now. Sienna and Gwyneth both attend my class.'

What sort of world is it where even crawling around on the floor has to he done fashionably? If Hester's celebrity friends were blasting themselves into space and orbiting the sun for ten years in order to lose weight then she'd give it a try.

Actually…

'I'm pitching to Saffron at eleven,' I say, smoothing down my skirt and arranging my face into an expression of yogic serenity.

'Really?' Hester smiles, or at least I think she does because Botox can do strange things to a woman's facial expression, 'And you've dressed up especially. How sweet. You look like Little Red Riding Hood.'

Luckily for Hester I'm twenty-nine not nine which means that I don't smack her in the face.

'And you look very smart,' I say, because she does.

Hester inclines her blonde head graciously, the hair so bouffant today that she looks like a coneless Mr. Whippy, 'How one dresses reflects one's status and experience, Robyn.'

Hester has certainly taken power dressing to the max today. Think Joan Collins in her *Dynasty* years and then some. She must be wearing every status item in her wardrobe, from the diamonds in her ears and gold bracelets jangling on her wrists, to Gucci shades and her Louis Vuitton attaché case, everything about Hester is screaming success and money. Her nose is held so high that Air Traffic Control is probably tracking it.

'Tarquin!' Hester barks to her assistant, 'Pass me the folder.'

Her slave does as he's told and Hester flips through myriad glossy pictures until settling on one.

'You see, Robyn,' Hester says, 'In this game experience and contacts are everything. How else would I be able to give people the weddings of their dreams?'

'By listening to them and giving them what they want?'

But Hester isn't paying attention to insignificant little old me, 'How else,' she continues, 'would I have been able to devise a wedding such as this? A wedding of such grandeur and vision that Saffron was left speechless after my presentation?'

And she shoves the folder under my nose so that I have little choice but to look at the bright images.

I'm not surprised that Saffron was speechless.

I'm pretty lost for words myself.

The glossy scene before me is of a medieval style wedding. Everyone is in period costume, including the groom who is encased in shiny armour. The bride is seated on a grey horse and wearing an ice cream cone contraption on her head, from which yards and yards of fabric sweep to the floor. Jesters turn frozen somersaults, five hogs are roasted on spits and in the background a joust is taking place.

Hester has out flamingoed herself, that's for sure.

'Goodness,' I say weakly, thinking that if Saffron loves this I may as well just go home now, 'That's really something else, Hester.'

'Isn't it?' Hester agrees, snapping the folder shut, 'The armour alone is worth one hundred thousand pounds, and, between you and me, HRH is not averse to renting out Windsor Castle for the day. Stella McCartney is *desperate* to design the dress. Have you got anything planned that can compete with that?'

'I can safely say that I haven't.'

'Oh Robyn,' Hester shakes her head sorrowfully, 'Did you listen to anything I said when you worked for me? Didn't I always tell you to stick to the golden rule, always go for the most expensive wedding possible? Nobody wants to be stingy when it comes to their wedding.'

I think of the plans in my portfolio where I've opted for simplicity and elegance. If Saffron is crazy about Hester's medieval idea then I've blown it. Blown it but at least kept to my principles, which are that a wedding isn't about how much cash the planner can make but actually about a couple being in love and celebrating their union.

Call me old fashioned but there you are. Maybe this is why Hester shops in designer boutiques and I go to Primark?

'Anyway, darling,' Hester says, 'I can't stay chatting all day. I need to source some peacocks and quinces,' and, point made, she bids me a swift farewell and sails out of the office. The cloying scent of *Poison* lingers in her wake, making me feel sick.

At least I think it's the *Poison* making me feel sick...

'Robyn Hood,' the receptionist calls, smiling at me from her desk, 'Ms. Scott will see you now. Go on up. Top of the stairs and first left.'

'Thanks,' I croak and clutching my portfolio in my cold and clammy fingers I make my way up the stairs.

I don't think I've ever felt so worried in my life.

And since I was once engaged to Patrick McNicholas, that's really saying something.

Luckily the text alert from my mobile distracts me from my nerves and flipping it open I see that Jonathan has sent me a message.

Best of luck with the pitch! x

It's really sweet of him to remember I'm meeting Saffron today and this thoughtful message makes me smile in spite of my nerves. We've sent each other several messages since I texted back to thank him for booking the Swing Dancing class and I've come to look forward to his messages. I know he's married but that doesn't mean we can't be friends. After all, I'm friends with Si.

I switch off my mobile. Knowing Jonathan's sending me positive vibes has a wonderful effect on my state of mind and my legs no longer feel like over cooked spaghetti. By the time Saffron's PA escorts me into the office I'm actually looking forward to making my pitch and giving Hester a run for her money.

Bring it on!

'Hi Robyn!' Saffron crosses her office, a slender figure with a glorious mane of red hair and skin like double cream, 'Thanks so much for coming over. I'm so sorry about changing the arrangements at the last minute, but Hester insisted she'd never be able to make it to Chelsea for ten.'

I bet she did!

'That's no problem,' I shake her hand, noticing the simple but elegant French manicure, 'I'm just pleased to be here. There was signal trouble on the tube, I thought we were all going to boil alive.'

Saffron shudders, 'Poor you. Take a seat and I'll get my PA to fetch you a coffee. I take mine black, how about you?'

'Just milk, thanks,' I'm relieved she's indicated that I sit on a black leather sofa rather than perching in interview style in front of the desk. Saffron seems really friendly. I love the simple green trouser suit she's wearing; it compliments her fiery hair and clear blue eyes perfectly and the big platform boots that peek out from beneath the boot leg trousers make a perfect contrast.

While Saffron calls her PA I check out her office and in *Through the Keyhole* style try to decide 'who works in an office like this?' The walls are white, the floor the same reclaimed oak as the reception and at the furthest end of the room are two ceiling to floor length sash windows through which pours in watery winter sunlight. Saffron's desk faces these windows and its surface is empty apart from a black Mac and a large silver framed photo of Saffron and a handsome blonde guy. The whole effect's very restful and elegant. By the time my coffee arrives I'm feeling much more at ease. Saffron and I chat for a while, laughing over our love of platform boots, and I'm delighted when she admires my vintage 1920s bag.

'It's very F Scott Fitzgerald,' she says, '*The Great Gatsby* has to be one of my favourite books. In fact I've just come back from the Hamptons. Have you ever been?'

On my budget I'd be lucky to make it to Littlehampton, and even then I'd have to borrow the petrol money from Gideon.

'I've not made it there yet,' I admit, 'but it's definitely on my list of places to visit one day.'

Saffron tells me about all about her holiday in the Hamptons and how excited she was to bump into Mia Farrow while she was there.

'She's still beautiful,' says Saffron, 'She has the most amazing bone structure. If I had to name a style icon I'd have to say it was her, especially in the sixties. I love that simple chic look. I guess that's why I adore the twenties so much. It was such an elegant age.'

'I like the fifties myself' I say, 'I buy loads of vintage clothes on eBay. That's where I found this skirt, and the handbag.'

Saffron is holding my bag, raving about the teak handles and gold embroidery, when something clicks into place. Although my portfolio is brimming with all the elaborate sketches and themed details that I've always dreamed of being able to put together something tells me Saffron's wedding is not going to be the one where these become reality. I'm really disappointed that I can't indulge myself but what the client wants the client gets, in my book.

'So,' says Saffron finally, "What ideas have you got for my wedding?'

I take a deep breath, 'I'll be honest, Saffron, I've spent ages thinking up ideas, making mood boards and sketches but now I've actually met you I don't think any of my ideas are right.'

Saffron's mouth is open, she was probably waiting for more hog roasts and jesters.

'You're welcome to look at my portfolio,' I plough on, 'But I've had a better idea. Why don't we use your love of the Hamptons and *The Great Gatsby* as the spring board for a 1920s themed wedding? It could be fantastic! Lots of understated glamour and beautiful 1920s clothes. We could even take some old black and white films as our starting points.'

Saffron stares at me. Oh God, I've blown it. I should have stuck to flamingos. Then her mouth curves into a smile.

'It's brilliant! I adore that look! Do you think we could really pull it off?'

'Of course we can!' I'm nearly bursting with ideas for utilising all my experience of rummaging through vintage clothes boutiques and antique stores, 'We could have so much fun sourcing all the materials. In fact,' I add thinking of my favourite little shop in Camden, 'I know a great place to start. If you want to start, I mean. I don't want to presume anything. I know Hester had some amazing ideas.'

'Yes, she certainly did,' deadpans Saffron, 'Absolutely amazing.' Then she catches my eye, her lips twitch and she convulses with laughter, 'Sorry! Sorry!' she gasps, 'I shouldn't laugh but can you really imagine me wearing an ice cream cone on my head and an edible chastity belt?'

'Not really,' I admit.

'Or poor Fergus in a suit of armour? I'd need a can opener to get him out on the wedding night!'

I start to laugh, 'But what about the medieval banquet? You need to think carefully before you turn down a stuffed swan.'

Saffron shudders, 'Apparently we're going to be eating pottage. I haven't the foggiest what pottage is, have you?'

'No idea.'

'God,' she shakes her head, 'I don't think I've ever been so horrified in all my life. I'm really not that sort of girl. Her ostentatious ideas were such a turn off. Is that really how people see me?'

'Not if they know you,' I promise, 'Hester just likes to go to town.'

'That's one way of putting it. I wasn't impressed either when she suggested I delay the date of the wedding so we can really go all out. Fergus would have gone mental.'

'That's totally understandable. The whole point of the wedding is so that you can be together; it shouldn't be keeping you apart!'

'You're a romantic!' Saffron cries, clapping her hands, 'That's perfect! A wedding planner who actually believes in love *and* who has brilliant ideas! That does it! Robyn, I'd love you to plan my wedding, if you'd like to?'

'If I'd like to?' I parrot, only needing a cage and some seed to complete the look, 'Of course I'd like to if you're sure you want me?'

'Oh I'm sure,' says Saffron, '*Perfect Day is* exactly what Fergus and I have been looking for. I can hardly wait to get started.'

'Nor can I,' I say, as we shake hands, 'Nor can I!'

Chapter Ten

December

'You know what you should do with this car,' the AA Patrolman says from beneath the bonnet, 'scrap it and get something new. My missus has got a lovely Fiesta.'

'Right,' I say, fighting the impulse to ram his head into the engine, 'I'll bear it in mind.'

'Besides, we've been called out for this car too many times and we're within our rights to refuse to give you any more assistance.'

'Maybe I should join the RAC instead?'

'They'll only tell you the same. Get rid of this monstrosity and find yourself a practical car.'

'I love my car!' I protest, 'She's a design classic!'

He snorts, 'If you say so. But you'd be better off with a Fiesta and a nice big boot for all your shopping.'

So much for very nice men and you've got AA friend. Thanks a lot, advertising executives. Here I am, broken down on a drizzly December evening, a woman on her own at the side of the A4 and my knight of the road turns out to he the same grumpy git who's attended Dolly the Mercedes' previous two hissy fits. And I literally mean hissy fits. I haven't seen this much steam since I last went to the Sanctuary Spa.

While the Patrol Man delves under the bonnet I turn up the collar on my poor suede coat and wish I was the sort of girl who always has an umbrella in the boot. I need to add my inability to ever have a brolly to the list of things I really hate about my life right now.

At this particular point in time my list of

pet hates is topped by know it all AA patrolmen, this particularly British mizzling rain that *may* look like nothing but gets you soaked to your knickers in less time than Casanova could get them off, and, of course, my car breaking down.

My ancient Mercedes can be a little temperamental but Dolly's over twenty years old and probably feels she's earned the right to flip a v at the world. I'd have sympathy except I wish she'd chosen a better time. A dark, wet December night should be spent watching rubbish telly and drinking wine not shivering at the road side while being lectured about my car. One minute I was cruising down the A4 singing along to Capital Radio, the next Dolly was doing an impression of a kettle as her temperature gauge soared to critical levels. Somehow I managed to reach the side of the road, dodging thundering juggernauts and speeding cars, and dial the AA.

Why do things like this always happen to me? Am I some kind of bad luck magnet? This morning I had a phone call telling me the beautiful Art Deco hotel Saffron's had her heart set on for the wedding venue is double booked, a stern letter arrived from the Inland Revenue and then Faye cancelled lunch. Add to this feeling bloated and tearful thanks to an unfortunate combination of PMT and realising that it's a year since Pat and I split and there you have it a totally crap day.

Actually, make that a totally crap festive season. Make no mistake about it, Christmas isn't for kids, it's for couples. Every shop is full of them. Couples holding hands as they peer into jewellers' window or coyly eying the mistletoe sprigs in the florists. Or they wheel their Bugaboo prams and fatly wrapped babies into the Department stores to coo over the toys and tinsel. Even the supermarkets are in on it with their jumbo sized turkeys, multi packs of mince pies and family sized Christmas puddings. Where are all the Christmas dinners for one?

I kick the verge with the toe of my Ugg Boot. I'm so fed up with Christmas that I could give Scrooge a run for his money. Gideon and James are off skiing, my mother's taking yet another cruise so it looks like I'll be watching the Queen's speech with Poppy and tucking into a Lean Cuisine. I'm not going to impose myself on Dad nor am I going to take Faye up on her offer of spending Christmas with her and Simon like I did last year. Their entire family descended last year and it was Hell in Boden. What with four married sisters between them and a cavalcade of nephews and nieces, the talk the whole festivities revolved around when Faye and Simon were going to start having children too. In between working my way through the alcohol and trying to pretend that my heart wasn't in Patrick sized pieces I'd had to listen to endless baby talk and tactless comments about biological clocks. Simon quipped that unless conjugal visits were brought into being in his office, the chance of procreating would be a fine one. Faye had laughed but the taut skin across her cheekbones suggested that she wasn't particularly amused. By the end of it all Faye and Si were bickering and frazzled and adamant they weren't thinking of a family. I couldn't help being relieved. I love kids but I don't want to lose my best friends to nappies and sleepless nights just yet.

So Christmas alone it is then, unless something mega happens in the next two weeks.

Maybe in a parallel universe the patrolman attending this breakdown is some Brad Pitt look-a-like, all rippling muscles and six pack under his yellow overalls? And as he climbs from the cab we take one look at each other before he scoops me into his arms, carries me into his low loader. Then he'll turn out be the love of my life and we'll live happily ever after...

Hmm, just my luck I live in the *crappy* parallel universe where AA men are bald and grumpy and I'm so cold I'm starting to lose feeling in my fingers and toes. I couldn't be wetter if I'd swum the Channel. If I don't get home soon I'll get hypothermia.

Maybe I should look on the bright side? After all there is one sunbeam on an otherwise gloomy horizon and a pretty impressive sunbeam it is too. I can still hardly believe that I'm going to he planning Saffron's wedding! I'm still pinching myself because I can't believe I've been given the green light to source fabulous designers and genuine 1920s accessories. I haven't seen Hester since Saffron made her decision but I know she won't forgive me for winning this pitch in a hurry and I'd better have my wits about me if I'm to prevent her from deliberately sabotaging the wedding. Hester could knock Machiavelli into cotton stocks when it comes to underhanded tricks and plotting.

I turn my attention back to the car. I wouldn't put it past Hester to have sabotaged that either.

'Can you fix it?' I ask the AA man.

'It looks like the radiator. I'll do my best to patch it up so you can get home but you'll probably need to replace it.'

'Is that expensive?'

'About two hundred quid.'

Great. My bank manager will need Valium if I go any more overdrawn this month.

'Don't look so worried,' the AA man says, wiping his hands on a rag before delving into the back of his truck, 'Worse things happen at sea.'

'I'm not at sea. I'm on the A4,' I wail.

What a way to spend a Saturday night! I look at the cosy lit windows of the houses that haven't succumbed to compulsory purchase and imagine the people curled up inside. Just to add insult to injury the golden arches of MacDonald's shimmer through the drizzle, calling me to come in and cram grease into my mouth. I'd be there quicker than you can say 'Quarter Pounder' if it wasn't for the six lanes of furious traffic that some sadistic bastard has placed in the way.

I perch on the crash barrier, which defeats the object but is a better option than sitting on the grass verge. The rain speckles my coat and trickles down my neck. Surely things can't get worse?

When my phone buzzes and Patrick's number flashes up on the screen I could kick myself for tempting fate. What do I have to do to get rid of this man? I've erased his number but the digits remain ingrained in my memory. Which, seeing as I struggle to remember my pin number, is very annoying.

I flip my phone open.

'What?'

'And hello to you too,' says Patrick cheerfully, 'Sure, isn't that a lovely way to greet your friends?'

'What makes you think you're my friend?'

Pat laughs, 'I love your dry sense of humour, so I do.'

He might not find me such a hoot if he

knew I wasn't joking.

'This really isn't a good time for a social call. Dolly's broken down.'

'Jaysus! Not again? How many times is it now? Eight?'

'No!' I retort hotly, 'Only six actually.'

'Only six?' although I can't see him I know that Pat's eyes will be crinkly with mirth, 'Oh, that's OK then, so it is! Honestly, Robs, it's time you gave up with that old car and got yourself a newer model.'

'Like you did?' I nearly say, and only just stop myself in time. Instead I say, 'You never did like Dolly, did you?'

'Robyn, what sort of man wants to be seen in a Barbie car?'

'Ken?'

Pat laughs, 'A man with no dick! I rest my case. Anyways, Robs, I haven't called just to talk dirty, fun though that is.'

'I can't imagine we have anything to talk about, Patrick. We said it all the last time we met at the wedding.'

'About that,' he says, 'I really appreciated you being so nice to Jo. It could've been awkward.'

I sigh, 'It's all in the past, Pat. We're adults, after all.'

'Absolutely, that's what I told Jo! Rob's a good old girl, I said, she's not one to hold a grudge. Sure, things weren't exactly going well between us, were they?'

I think of my lovely wedding dress still hanging in the closet, my mum's distress at having to send back the presents and all the nights I cried so hard that I looked like a frog, and say nothing. I'm a good old girl, after all.

Patrick, the guilt equivalent of a non stick saucepan, carries blithely on, 'So I was wondering if you fancied coming out for lunch sometime? Maybe Wednesday?'

I've always known he's tactless but this doesn't so much take the biscuit as the entire McVities factory. Our first wedding anniversary would have been next week. What's going on? I hope he's not about to suggest we have sex for old time's sake or something equally ridiculous. I wouldn't put anything past Patrick. I never trusted him when we were together – rightly as it turned out – and I certainly don't trust him now.

'I'm really busy next week. I've lots of winter weddings.'

Weddings. Hint. Hint.

'Ah, feck it,' Pat sighs, 'I really wanted to see you. There's something I need to tell you.'

'Everything's OK, isn't it?'

Pat is silent.

'Pat? You're not ill or anything, are you?

'Sure, we're fine!' he says swiftly, 'Especially Jo. She's really well. In fact, you could say she's blooming.'

Now it's my turn to be lost for words.

'That's why I'm calling,' he murmurs, 'I wanted to tell you personally, Robs, before it becomes common knowledge. I know we've been apart for ages but I just thought it was right that you heard it first from us.'

I feel as though my legs have turned into over cooked noodles. Thank goodness I'm sitting down.

'Congratulations,' I say, and thank God I sound normal and not as though I've been inhaling helium. Blood seems to be draining from my limbs and myriad emotions swamp me.

'Thanks,' I can hear the smile in his voice, 'Jaysus, Robs! I'm so excited! I've always wanted to be a Dad!'

'I know you have. You'll be brilliant,'

And he will be too. Pat's always wanted kids and he was fantastic with my half brothers and all his nieces and nephews. It was something of a bone of contention that I wasn't ready to think about children from the instant that the engagement ring was on my finger.

But I hadn't said *'never'*. I'd only said *'not yet'*.

'Thanks. I can hardly wait, so I can't! Jo's over the moon too.'

I make pleased noises but actually I think I might be sick.

'She's going to give up work,' Patrick says, 'And be a full time mammy. I want a rugby team, after all! I bet you're counting your lucky stars now that you escaped? You were always more of a career woman, Robyn. It wouldn't have been your cup of tea. But Jo, well she's not like you. Family means everything to her.'

The long held image in my mind's eye of a little girl with Patrick's eyes and my curly hair dissolves like mist.

'We're going to move out to the country too,' Pat adds, 'I'm earning enough now to buy a little cottage. That was always my dream, remember Robs?'

Oh yes, I remember. Pat always had a longing for the so called simple life and we spent many hours arguing over the pros and cons of moving to the country. Somehow I couldn't imagine swapping Jimmy Choos for chickens and Patrick wouldn't compromise with a mews house in Primrose Hill. Working for *Catch the Bouquet* from the sticks would have been impossible, and the thought of giving up my job and being dependent on Patrick had made my skin prickle with unease. Depending on my father hadn't exactly done my mother any favours.

I force a light note into my voice, 'Barefoot and pregnant. Lucky Jo!'

He laughs, 'She's driving me mad with property papers. It's like living with Kirsty Allsopp!'

'So you're really moving to the country?'

'I'm more traditional than I thought,' admits Pat, 'I really want a country upbringing for our baby and Jo being pregnant has totally changed everything. We're going to get married by the end of the year so that we're Mr. and Mrs. McNicholas by the time the baby comes. Jaysus! My mammy would never forgive me if it was born out of Holy Wedlock.'

I can't listen to any more of this.

'I'm really thrilled for you both. Look, Pat, I'd love to talk some more but I've got to go! I'm about to be rear ended here!' and I ring off, but not before Pat's had time to make a smutty comment about my backside.

The rain is still falling, the traffic is still swishing past and the patrolman is still muttering under Dolly's bonnet, but I hardly register any of this. Instead Patrick's words buzz around my brain like insistent wasps.

I'm not jealous but part of me, the part that really did love Pat once, wants to throw her head back and howl. Why not me? Why wasn't I good enough? What was wrong with me? Why her?

'Ms. Hood,' the AA man calls, 'I'm really sorry but you're going to need a new radiator,' He slams the bonnet shut, 'I'll relay you home.'

I open my mouth to speak but no sound comes out. The whole scene dips and swims alarmingly. The headlamps of passing cars shimmer and brake lights are shimmering rubies.

The patrolman stares at me in alarm.

'Don't cry, love! It's only a radiator. You can fix the car if you really must. It can be mended.'

But I can only shake my head. Everything's changed. Everyone's moving on; Si, Faye, Gideon and now even Patrick.

Besides, I don't think my heart will ever be properly mended.

Chapter Eleven

'She's not going to make it! She's tachycardic and her stats are dropping!'

I'm curled up on the sofa eating Dairy Milk and drowning my sorrows with Blossom Hill while I watch *Casualty*. Staying in and watching people die is a pretty odd way to spend a Saturday evening but it beats having to think about my own life. As yet another train crash/bomb blast/terrorist attack takes place on screen I try to feel thankful for my own lot. Things could be worse: I could live in Holby.

After a long journey home in the recovery van I abandoned Dolly at a garage and then endured another lecture from the patrolman before he finally dropped me off. My bad mood grew blacker with every step I stomped up the path, rising to Shakespearean proportions as I dragged myself up the steps to my flat, slamming the front door behind me. Feeling madder than King Lear I dripped tears and rainwater onto the floor as I peeled off my sodden clothes and contemplated the sodden mass that used to be my coat. One very hot bath and Chinese takeaway later I'm feeling warm again but I still can't escape the feeling that life is moving on without me.

How many other twenty-nine year olds are sitting in watching television on a Saturday night? Not many, I bet. Everyone I know is out and about having a social life. Faye and Simon are at a Christmas party, Bradley and Julia have gone clubbing and Gideon and James are at the opera. I'm all alone apart from Poppy who's opted to stay on suicide watch. She's pretty rubbish at it mind you because all she's done is launch herself onto the sofa and fall sound sleep.

Robyn Hood: the girl who has no social life, can't keep a fiancé and even sends animals to sleep! It would be funny if it wasn't so tragic.

On my lap is a spiral note pad. I'm going to make a list and sort my life out. I saw this woman on Oprah – the kind of Oprah I enjoy rather than Gideon's variety – who was talking all about positive thinking. Cosmic Ordering it was called. Apparently the Universe is like a great big Next Directory, you make a list of everything you want, ask for it and bingo! Along it all comes, only without the £3.50 delivery charge and the bill, hopefully. Well, my ears had pricked up. I'm a world class catalogue shopper; Next, Argos, Littlewoods, you name it and I've probably tried it. So this should work perfectly!

As I watch the A & E team try to resuscitate blood stained patients I scrawl my list of requests. I've narrowed it down to four, which was harder than it sounds, but I don't want to be greedy. Even so, I think I've pretty much sussed the definitive list of my heart's desires.

Lists are great, aren't they? I'm really good at writing lists. I make hundreds of them, detailing all the work I have to do, household chores that need completing and things I need to buy from Waitrose.

Yes! I'm fantastic at making lists of things to do.

Sadly though I'm not *quite* so fantastic at crossing off the things I've done.

Or, if I'm honest, doing them!

But today I must knuckle down and take things seriously. I'm nearly thirty and it's time I took control of my life. No more brooding about Patrick, no more messy finances and no more waiting for things to happen. I'm going to be proactive.

Now, just how shall I go about this? I chew the pen thoughtfully. It's all very exciting really. If I don't think about the gap on my ring finger and the sad sense that all my dreams have evaporated, of course.

My new life starts today! This is my chance to be the new improved Robyn Hood! Independent! Single! Thin!

Once I've polished off this Dairy Milk, obviously.

I look at my list.

1. *Turnover at least 30K with Perfect Day*
2. *Find fabulous new man, preferably one who isn't an Irish Comedian*
3. *Go Swing Dancing*
4. *Be patient with my mother.*

There! I have a life plan. Number one is on track. Winning the tender to plan Saffron's wedding has really raised my profile and *Perfect Day* has been hired for three other weddings since. Hopefully I'll be able to use my switch card soon without holding my breath and praying.

Number two is a bit harder, maybe that would be more logical after step number three? After all, this is already in hand. Jonathan's booked me in for the Swing Dancing and the classes start in the New Year, so actually I can link in the exercise with point number three which is very handy. I must admit I'm not looking forward to going on my own but hopefully somebody will partner me when I get there. Maybe that could even link into point number two?

The power of positive thinking!

Now for number four. Hmm, maybe I shouldn't ask too much of the Universe at such an early stage? Something that tricky should probably be left to advanced Cosmic Orderees surely? Perhaps I'll just work on numbers one to four and think about my mother at a later stage? Or maybe I should order myself a social life?

I'm just contemplating swapping point number four for something totally shallow like bigger boobs or thinner thighs when the tinny tone of my mobile pipes up. It must be Simon, I think as I delve under the detritus on the bed, ringing to say that the meal's over and do I want to meet him and Faye for a drink? I'll slap on some make up, pin up my hair and grab my Oyster card. Then up to the West End I'll go, no longer nearly thirty and social life less.

What a relief. This Cosmic Ordering stuff is amazing. Perhaps I'll order George Clooney next...

After a few frantic seconds trying to locate the phone I eventually find it buried beneath my chocolate. I glance at the glowing fluorescent screen and am taken aback to see the name 'Jonathan'.

For a brief moment my finger freezes over

the green *accept call button.* Jonathan and I text most days, light hearted messages or pictures of things that we each think the other will appreciate, and I always look forward to hearing from him. If I'm honest it's a bit of an ego boost to have even a crumb of attention from such an attractive man.

I know, I know, I'm a sad muppet. And I also know he's married. But a harmless text flirtation doesn't count, does it?

But for Jonathan to call is unprecedented. My stomach see saws and my pulse accelerates to *Casualty* levels. Before I can reason with myself my finger presses the button.

'Hey,' I say, 'This is a surprise.'

'A nice one?'

I laugh. 'It's great to hear from you, almost in the flesh!'

'I was texting you,' Jonathan says, and his Bourneville rich voice makes the small hairs rise on my arms, 'but the text was getting so long I was starting to get RSI in my thumb, so I decided it made far more sense to actually call you. Is that OK?'

'Of course,' I say, but I think we both know that a boundary has been crossed.

'The thing is,' he says, 'I'm at a bit of a loose end. Anita's had to work this weekend and I daren't go to the dinner party we're invited to because that would totally screw the numbers so I was wondering if you wanted to hook up?'

I open my mouth but no sound comes out. That's twice today a man has robbed me of speech. I need to get a grip.

'It's probably a stupid idea,' he flounders, 'I expect you've got lots of plans, a woman like you won't be short of offers on a Saturday night. You're all dressed up and ready to go out, aren't you?'

I look down at my tracksuit bottoms and the giant Mr. Blobby slippers that Pat gave me ages ago (they're very warm actually – that's why I didn't bin them along with his letters, cards and engagement ring) and feel glad that people don't use video messaging just yet.

'I'm certainly dressed up,' I say.

'I'm being ridiculous, of course you're going out somewhere exciting, why would you want to hang out with an old fogey lawyer?' Jonathan says. 'You have a fantastic evening. I'll just heat up a meal for one and watch Celebrity Ice Skating or something. I think that's what old people like me are meant to do on a Saturday night. I guess I may as well get used to it.'

He sounds so sad that my heart goes out to him. After all, I know how miserable it is to be stuck on the sofa when the rest of the world is out and about.

'Jonathan, stop right there,' I say firmly, 'As one sad person who's in her pyjamas watching *Casualty* to another I think it's high time we got off our sofas and did something that vaguely resembles having a life. I've had the day from Hell and I could really do with cheering up.'

'Really? You're not just being kind?'

I take a deep breath. 'I've spent ages standing in the pouring rain watching my car overheat, been told it needs life saving surgery that I'll probably have to sell my soul to afford, and to top that my ex fiancé has called to tell me he's expecting a child with the woman he left me for. Can you top that?'

'Err, no,' says Jonathan. 'Not really.'

Nice one Robyn. Open mouth and shove in your feet, why don't you? Now he probably thinks you're crazy.

'Sorry,' I sigh. 'You didn't need to hear all that. Feel free to put the phone down if you think I'm a psycho.'

Jonathan laughs. 'No more of a psycho than me! I was thinking just the same thing after I opened my mouth about being left alone while Anita whizzes off to work again. I think we have a real connection though, Robyn. I feel as if I can tell you anything. Does that sound insane?'

'Actually, it doesn't. You're the only person I've told about Patrick and the baby.'

'Then we have a bond!' Jonathan declares. 'I think we should go out and celebrate our friendship. What do you fancy doing? Have you eaten? Or do you want to go to a club?'

The Chinese is a solid lump in my stomach and call me boring but the thought of bopping until three am with flat stomached teenagers turns me cold. As my gaze falls to my spiral pad I suddenly have a brilliant idea.

'There is something I'd like to do,' I say.

'What did you have in mind?'

'How about going swing dancing? I know of a club in Piccadilly, *Swing the Mood*, that's meant to be brilliant!'

'Swing dancing,' he says slowly. 'Why not? I can't say I've ever tried but it looks great fun. OK, Ms. Hood, you're on!'

I give him the address of 'Swing the Mood' and we agree to meet at ten. Once Jonathan rings off I tear around the flat, trying to straighten my hair, put on makeup and find the perfect outfit.

Calm down, Robyn, I tell myself sternly, you're being ridiculous. This isn't a date, it's just a night dancing with a man, a married man who has never made any secret of the fact that he has a wife whom he adores.

Get a grip. This is not a date. You are not going on a date.

But no matter how often I repeat this mantra a flutter of butterflies rises in my stomach and my heart begins to gallop.

For a non date this is starting to feel scarily like the real thing.

Jonathan kills the engine of his sleek BMW and turns to face me. 'That was a great evening, Robyn. Thanks so much for suggesting it.'

The car is parked underneath a street lamp. Orange light pools through the windows, casting his cheekbones into sharp relief and playing on his full sensual lips. I look away.

'You're welcome,' is all I say. 'It was fun.'

I sense his smile in the darkness, 'It was fantastic! I never knew swing dancing could be like that. You're an amazing dancer, Robyn.'

'You're not so bad yourself,' I tell him. And this isn't idle flattery either. Jonathan is a natural dancer. He's got rhythm and is surprisingly light on his feet for such a tall athletic man. From the moment we arrived we barely left the dance floor. I loved the way he lifted me as though I was feather light, his strong hands clasping my waist as he slowly lowered me to earth, sliding my body against his, before scooping me up again to whirl me across the room. This man was born to dance, no two ways about it.

'Thanks,' Jonathan says again. 'I had a brilliant time.'

Silence swells between us like a living thing. I'm very aware his body is only inches away, the long lean thigh stretching across the seat is near enough to brush mine, his fingers resting on the gear stick are so close that I could easily reach out and hold them.

But I'm not going to. Swing dancing is fun and flirty and foxy, it's true, and it would be ridiculously easy to get swept away in the emotion of the moment. I tuck my hands underneath my legs though, just in case.

Jonathan clears his throat. 'Can I ask you something?'

'Of course. What is it?'

'This evening really made me feel alive. So I was wondering whether...'

'Whether what?'

'Whether you'd mind if I joined you at the Swing Dancing class? If you'd rather I didn't then please, just say, but I think we could have a lot of fun. We danced well together, didn't we?'

'We did,' I agree.

'So what do you say?' Jonathan turn to face me, his eyes are dark in the gloom but they hold mine with such power that my heartbeat increases, 'Would it be OK with you if I came along too?'

Would it? I've had a fantastic time and Jonathan has been brilliant company. I haven't felt this special and sparkly for a very long time and I've enjoyed every second I've spent with him. But is that actually a good thing?

'And I think we could be really good friends,' he adds. 'We've got so much in common, Robyn. It would be great to spend more time with you and get to know you better.'

'Know me better? How?'

'As a friend,' he says swiftly. 'Nothing funny, I promise. It's just that I think you and I could have a lot of fun. No more sitting at home on Saturday evenings! We can hang out. As friends.'

'It would be more than OK,' I decide. 'It would be lovely to have you come along too.'

'Great!' Jonathan says, 'I'll pop over to the adult education centre on Monday and sign up. Thanks, Robyn.'

'You don't need to thank me,'

'Yes, I do. You've made me feel happy, and for that I need to thank you more than you'll ever know.'

And then he leans across and brushes my lips with his. It's a chaste kiss, a friendly kiss even, but deep in the pit of my stomach something delicious uncurls itself, stretches and yawns.

Once he drives off I sit on the steps of the house and watching the tail lights fade away. My finger tips touch my lips. I can still feel the feathery touch of his lips.

Jonathan Broadhead is my friend. I can deal with that, of course I can. Men and women can he friends. Haven't Simon and I been friends for years without any problems.

Except I never fancied Simon.

And as I sit in the darkness, my breath rising into the air and the frost icing the lawn, I have to admit that I do find Jonathan attractive, very attractive indeed.

But I can handle that.

Can't I?

Chapter Twelve

March

'Turn left! Mum! Turn left now!'

My mother ignores me and the car sails past the huge pillars and wrought iron gates.

'Mum! That was the entrance to *Ketton Place!*'

'Nonsense,' says my mother, flipping down the sun visor and checking her lipstick in the mirror. 'It can't be. The SatNav would have said something.'

My mother's faith in the TomTom Simon and Faye bought me for Christmas is absolute. Never mind it sent us the wrong way for six junctions of the M4 before calmly telling us to turn around; she won't have a word said against it.

'That sign said *Ketton Place!*' I twist my neck to try and read the sign but it's gone in a blur as my mother does her best Formula

One impression. 'We're going the wrong way.'

'Robyn, you worry too much,' my mother says, dropping a gear and screeching around a corner. 'You certainly don't get that from my side of the family. Just relax, darling. We'll find it.'

'We had found it!'

'And as for your temper, that's pure George. You really should get some anger management therapy. You're far too stressed.'

'Only when I'm with you,' I mutter.

I'm perfectly entitled to be stressed today. I'm meeting Saffron at Davie Scott's Wiltshire mansion to discuss the wedding plans. She's hinted that her famous father will be sitting in on some of our discussions which make my nerves jangle so loudly I can practically hear them. So when Dolly refused to start this morning I nearly went into orbit. Of course Fate decided to flip a v and none of my friends were available to rescue me so in the end I was forced to call my mother and ask for her help.

Actually, I'd only asked if I could borrow her car. The last thing I need today is mum in my right ear for two hours, criticising the plans I've made, suggesting all sorts of improvements and winding me up so much that I start to chime. But once Mum learned exactly why I wanted to borrow her Golf GTI nothing could have kept her from coming too.

'Don't you realise how exciting this is?' she'd screeched down the phone. 'Davie Scott is really reclusive these days. Nobody gets an invite to *Ketton* anymore. Not like in the sixties! Davie's parties were legendary; the Stones, Marianne Faithful, Twiggy, even Profumo visited. Everyone who was anyone went!'

'I'm going there to work.'

'Not if you haven't got any transport.'

'Mum! That's blackmail!'

'What a nasty way of putting it,' my mother had said. 'I'm offering to give up a day of my precious time to chauffeur you to Wiltshire and you call it blackmail. Well, it's up to you, Robyn.'

I'd been silent. I desperately wanted to make this meeting but the thought of my mother reliving her youth and trying to flirt with Davie Scott made me feel quite giddy with horror.

'Oh darling, please.' Sensing my indecision Mum went for the kill. 'Hester has never stopped bragging about dating Davie. Wouldn't it be marvellous if I could tell her how well everything is going for *Perfect Day* and make her a teeny weeny bit jealous at the same time?'

Hester has been unbearable for months. I haven't actively caught her rumour mongering but several of my contacts in the wedding planning business have told me she's been pretty unpleasant about *Perfect Day*. Hester always was a bad loser.

'She's supposed to be your friend, mum.'

'She is,' said my mother. 'But *you're* my daughter.'

Touched, in the head probably, I'd given in which is why three hours later I'm lost somewhere south of Salisbury with my Kamikaze diver of a mother and a SatNav with no sense of direction. It doesn't help that Gideon's set the voice on the TomTom to that of Yoda from *Star Wars* and that I have no idea how to change it back.

Why do boys always have to fiddle with gadgets? Why can't they just leave things alone?

'A junction there is,' says the SatNav from its perch on the dash board. 'Turn left you will.'

'See!' crows my mother, yanking at the steering wheel. 'I told you.'

'Told me what?'

'Told you we were going in the right direction. This has to be the entrance to *Ketton Place*.'

Does it? I look out of the window and feel alarmed. We're now bumping along a pot holed track more suited to a massive four by four. The Golf lumbers over the ruts and nearly drowns in a deep puddle. Dark swathes of bushes press in upon the track, blocking out the light and scraping the sides of the car and thick tufts of wild grass grow down the centre of the track, small islands in deep puddles.

'Last night I dreamed I went to Manderley again,' I mutter, through teeth that rattle as the car bounces over the pot holes.

'Nearly there!' says my mother, ever the optimist.

'This doesn't look much like a drive.'

'Nonsense,' Mum taps the SatNav with a scarlet nail. 'We're definitely going the right way.'

Whatever Davie Scott spends his millions on it isn't the upkeep of the drive, I think, clinging on to the door handle for grim death as my boobs bounce around with more energy than the Andrex puppy. I wish Saffron had warned me to come in a Land Rover.

'There!' cries Mum triumphantly as we round a bend in the drive. 'The house! Now take it all back about my navigation!'

'We're coming out of the woods,' I point out. 'Don't you think that's a bit odd? Maybe that road leading up to the house is the actual drive?'

'Oh be picky then. Honestly Robyn, you're never satisfied. You don't get that from my side of the family. You must get that from–'

'My father. I know.' I bury my face in my hands, 'You've told me a million times before.'

But my mother isn't listening to me, she's too busy exclaiming over the house and trying to pull up without running over any of the dogs that have come bounding out to greet us, all wagging tails and lolling pink tongues.

Ketton Place is certainly beautiful. The medieval manor sits amid rolling parkland and trees like a sultana reclining on green velvet cushions. The mellow stone walls glow warm in the morning sunlight and small diamond paned windows twinkle from thick green ivy, like friendly winking eyes.

Opening the car door I slide my legs out in what I hope is an elegant manner in keeping with my surroundings.

'Robyn!' The front door swings open and Saffron runs down the steps to meet me, a smile stretched across her face. 'I'm so glad you're here. And you've got someone with you?'

'I'm Robyn's mother,' my mum stretches out her hand and shakes Saffron's with great enthusiasm. 'Anna Dexter. I run an interior design company. In fact, I was only just saying to Robyn that I could come in very useful sourcing fabrics for your wedding.'

I *knew* she'd do this. Maybe I should give up wedding planning and become a psychic instead?

'It's lovely to meet you,' Saffron kisses her cheek. 'Goodness, did you come through the woods? I didn't know that track was still passable.'

The poor scratched car looks as though it's having a mud wrap treatment but my mother shrugs. 'We love taking the scenic route, don't we darling?'

'Love it,' I agree.

'Come on in,' Saffron smiles, leading us through the dogs that surround us like a furry sea. 'Out the way Henry! Down Florence!'

We follow her up the steps and through the front door. And what a front door it is too, at least ten feet high and six feet wide. Inside Ketton Place is even more impressive. The black and red tiled floor gleams and above my head the ceiling is swirling with plaster cherubs and painted beasts of mythology. It's stunning.

But my mother is transfixed by a different beast entirely, one from rock mythology, because Davie Scott himself is in the hall, resplendent in tight leather trousers and purple snakeskin boots as he reads the Racing Post in front of a roaring fire.

'Dad,' Saffron says. 'This is Robyn Hood, my wedding planner, remember?'

'Of course, I do,' Davie shakes his shaggy mane of salt and pepper hair and rolls his eyes. 'My daughter thinks I'm a forgetful old geriatric.'

'Nice to meet you,' I say, as my hand is

pumped vigorously by the legend himself.

'And I'm Robyn's mother,' says my mum, elbowing me out the way, 'Anna Dexter,'

Davie's bushy eyebrows shoot into his hair. 'Never! You're far too young surely? I'd have thought you were sisters.'

My mother giggles and tosses her hair. 'You're too kind.'

Oh God. My mother is flirting with my client's father. The shame of it. I knew it was a mistake to bring her along.

'I love your house,' she simpers. 'It's beautiful.'

'The perfect setting for you,' says Davie gallantly. He puts the Racing Post onto a table and offers my mother his arm. 'Would you like a tour?'

Does Jordan like pink? My mother is hanging from his arm in a split second, transported back to the sixties quicker than you can say 'time machine'.

'I'd love one!'

'Then come this way,' says Davie. 'Saffron!' he calls over his shoulder. 'Keep an eye on the eleven fifteen at Newmarket, will you babe? Foxy Lady is running at fifteen to one. Racing,' he explains to my star struck mother. 'It's my passion. Or rather it's one of them.'

Then he sweeps her out of the hall like a leather-clad Rhett Butler.

'Sorry!' says Saffron at exactly the same

moment that I do. Then we're both laughing.

'Parents!' grins Saffron, 'They can be so embarrassing. Dad still thinks he's the sexiest man in pop.'

'My mother seems to agree,' I say ruefully. 'I'm so sorry!'

'Don't be,' Saffron says. 'At least it gets him out my hair for a minute. He's so determined to give me the wedding of my dreams that he's starting to drive me mad. I'm all for him being involved but it's still my wedding and there's no way I'm having his band play at the reception. Can you imagine the press response? They'd go crazy if *Blue Smoke* regrouped.'

'I think they're going to go crazy anyway,' I point out. 'That was one of the things I want to think about today.'

'Don't look so worried. I'm an old hand at outwitting the press. We'll come up with something to put them off the scent. I'm really looking forward to today, Robyn. I can't wait to start thinking about the dress.'

'It's a shame Fergus can't make it.' I'm disappointed not to be meeting Saffron's fiancé. 'I've got lots of questions for him. I really wanted his take on the dress code.'

She pulls a face. 'Fergus is always working. At least it means he'll be able to keep me in style I suppose! Anyway, I've lined up the next best thing. Matt Knowles is going to pop over so hopefully he'll be able to answer some of your questions.'

Matt Knowles is the Best Man. I make a mental note to ask him about the speeches and rings as well as to pass an opinion on the morning suits and waistcoats.

'Can you give me ten minutes or so?' Saffron peers at her Blackberry. 'I've just had an e mail from the office and I need to call them. Do you want me to ring for refreshments or something?'

I shake my head. 'I'm fine for now.' Golden sunlight, tinged with spring's promise, streams in through the windows and turns Saffron's hair to flame. 'It's a lovely day. Is it OK if I go outside and stretch my legs?'

'Sure. I'll try not to be long. Then we can really crack on with the planning.'

Leaving Saffron to make her calls I push open the heavy door and make my way across the drive. With every scrunch of my boots on the gravel I feel the tension of the morning slip away. It's a perfect spring day. The parkland in front of the mansion is carpeted in daffodils as though Wordsworth's poem has relocated and in the paddocks Davie Scott's racehorses graze peacefully, as leggy and as beautiful as any sixties model he might have dated.

I walk round the house, admiring the manicured flowerbeds and hanging baskets brimming with bright primroses. Then I turn into a walled garden and almost trip over a man sprawled across the path. For a second I think he's collapsed and am frantically trying to dredge up my meagre medical knowledge, most of it gleaned from my *Casualty* viewing, when I realise he's snapping away with a camera.

'Give me a second,' he says. 'I just need another couple of shots.'

'Shots?' I echo. 'Of what?'

'Well, not vodka! It's way too early for alcohol although,' he adds thoughtfully, 'that might help get me though the next hour or so. I'm actually just taking some pictures of worms, they're the most amazing colours.'

I shudder. 'I'd need more than a shot of vodka to go anywhere near worms. I'd need the whole bottle.'

'Don't diss worms,' the man says sternly. 'Apparently they're very intelligent and they're nutritious too, or so I'm told. Feel free to put your prejudices aside and have a look.'

I follow his gaze to where several of the bricks lining the path have been pushed over to reveal the squirming mass he's photographing. Gross! Why would anyone take pictures of worms and woodlice? It's the still equivalent of video nasty if you ask me.

What a weirdo!

'Aren't they fascinating?' the weirdo says over his shoulder. 'Look at the way they've made their own little ecosystem.'

'I'd rather not. I've had a horror of worms since Steven Buckingham put one down my neck when I was six.'

'What boys do to get attention! Come on, be brave. Just look at the way the light plays on the woodlice shells. Aren't they amazing?' He takes one more photo then jumps to his feet. 'Sorry to get in your way. I just couldn't resist taking some pictures. When I was back packing in Australia I was fascinated by the insects. I even had a special portfolio for them.'

'Surely there are nicer things to take pictures of?'

'You know, there's always beauty to be found in the most surprising places.' The man brushes bits of twig and moss from his jeans and runs a hand through his tangled curls. 'You just need to have an open mind and to know where to look.'

I smile in spite of my aversion to the pink wriggling creatures. 'How profound! So even creepy crawlies are beautiful?'

'I think so but they're not to everyone's taste I suppose.' He pushes the bricks back into place with the toe of his boot. Then he smiles at me, a pleasant smile in a pleasant face. Lines fan out from his eyes suggesting he smiles a lot and the freckles dusting his nose give him a merry appearance. 'Anyway, sorry to get underfoot. You can carry on now, unless you want to see some more? There's a couple of slow worms by the cold frames.'

'Insects and now snakes?'

'Slow worms are lizards actually,' he grins.

I glance at my watch. 'I'll have to pass on the slow worms I'm afraid. I'm supposed to be in a meeting with Saffron Scott.'

'Ah! So you're the wedding planner! I'd better pass on the slow worms too in that case.' He holds his hand out. 'I'm Matt Knowles, the best man. You must be Robyn Hood. I was expecting green tights and arrows at the very least!'

Great. Another comedian in the making, that's all I need.

'Very funny,' I say, forcing myself to shake his hand even though it's probably been prodding all sorts of yukky insects. At least I understand now why he's been lying on his tummy taking pictures – Matt Knowles is a professional photographer and I've often seen his work in the *Sunday Times Magazine* or *National Geographic*. I've been drawn to his name more recently because I'd known he was Fergus's best man.

'You did that feature on children in Basra, didn't you?' I recall. 'Those photos were amazing. They really haunted me.'

Matt flushes. 'Thanks. I just hope I managed to make people think about the suffering of the Iraqi people. That was the point anyway. I like my work to be thought provoking. I'm going to go to Africa soon to do something to raise HIV awareness.'

'Africa. Wow. You must travel a lot.'

'I do,' nods Matt, 'which is fun but makes it hard to put down roots. It drove my last girlfriend nuts. She got sick of it in the end so I settled for an iguana instead.'

'An iguana? Instead of a girlfriend?' I stare at Matt in horror. Worms and lizards? What a lovely combination. The girlfriend had a lucky escape if you ask me!

'Don't look so surprised! Max, that's my iguana, is fantastic. He's house trained too, before you ask, and he's great company. He knows all my secrets and never breathes a word.'

What do I say to this? I'm struggling with a vision of Matt snuggled up on the sofa to watch *EastEnders* with a scaly reptile crouching on his shoulder. Eugh! Here's more proof, as if I needed it, that any single man over thirty has to have something wrong with him.

'Anyway, I'll catch you in a bit,' Matt says, hooking his thumbs into the belt of his jeans. 'I'd better grab a shower after grubbing about with worms. Nice to meet you, Robyn.'

'You too,' I say, and make my way back to the house trying very hard to banish an image of Matt in the shower using his iguana as a loofah. Sometimes it's a real curse having a vivid imagination!

'There you are, Robyn,' says my mother reproachfully when I eventually join her and Saffron in a cosy panelled study. 'Where have you been?'

'Just getting some air,' I say, sitting down next to them. 'Sorry, Saffron. I didn't mean to keep you waiting.'

'You didn't keep me waiting at all,' says Saffron. 'I've been having a lovely chat with your mother. She's been telling me all about her interior design business.'

'Oh?' I think I can be forgiven for not jumping for joy here.

Saffron nods. 'Anna's got some marvellous plans for the wedding! She's been telling me all about her ideas.'

'I bet she has.' I try to catch my mother's eye but Mum is suddenly fascinated by her tea cup and won't look at me.

'Anna thought she could provide all the linen for the wedding at a discount price, in return for having her business featured in *Scorching!* Isn't that a brilliant idea?' cries Saffron, genuinely delighted.

'Brilliant,' I say so acidly it's a miracle my tongue doesn't shrivel. 'Well done, mum.'

'Thank you, darling,' beams my mother, the irony sliding from her like grease from Teflon. 'I've got lots of ideas for the wedding actually! I was only saying to Saffron a minute ago how wonderful it must be to plan a real white wedding. I'm only too happy to get involved in every aspect, after all,' she gives me a sharp look, 'it's not as if I ever got to plan your wedding is it, darling?'

Too right she didn't. If mum had been given free rein I'd have been going up the aisle in the kind of frock that even Barbie wouldn't be seen dead in. I'd kept her strictly at arm's length, thank you very much.

'I didn't know you were married,' says Saffron in surprise.

'I'm not,' I suppose we may as well get this over with. 'I was engaged once, to the comedian, Patrick McNicholas, but we broke it off.'

Saffron slaps her head with the palm of her hand. 'Robyn, I'm so sorry for being tactless.'

'Don't worry. It's ancient history.'

'Patrick's having a child with his new partner,' chimes in mum, ever the soul of discretion.

Poor Saffron looks mortified. 'I didn't mean to make you feel awkward.'

'Don't be silly,' I give her my best *I'm over it* smile. 'We've both moved on.'

'And we need to get a move on with this wedding,' says Saffron, tactfully. 'Can we start with the flowers? I loved the gerberas you sourced.'

'Gerberas!' exclaims my mother like Lady Bracknell when contemplating handbags. 'Surely not?'

“What’s wrong with gerberas?’ I say.

My mother wrinkles her nose. ‘They’re so vulgar, darling. Such nasty bright colours.’

‘Today’s brides want bold and interesting pairings of colours,’ I snap.

‘That’s hardly the thing for a subtle 1920s theme I would have thought. You want something more sophisticated. Maybe some hand tied bouquets of cream roses and baby’s breath for simple elegance?’

‘Hmm,’ says Saffron thoughtfully, ‘maybe.’

‘After all,’ says my mother, ‘we want to make this day really special for you and Fergus. Every detail has to be perfect, doesn’t it Robyn?’

I can hardly argue with this. And besides, my mother has actually made a good point. I just wish she’d made it in a way that didn’t make me feel about twelve again. Mum can be so overbearing sometimes

‘I really want everything to be just right,’ says Saffron.

‘The wedding will be perfect,’ I promise.

‘Right down to every last detail,’ adds my mother. ‘Just leave it to me! I can see it now! I’ll match the table cloths and napkins *exactly* to the ribbons and flowers in your bouquet. I’ll even do the seat covers too!’

I dig my nails into my palms and resist the temptation to tell my mother that planning the wedding involves slightly more than matching linen because I know my words would be totally crushing. Mum's only trying to help in her own pushy way and if I snap at her I'll end up feeling like a sulky little girl. But I don't know how I'm going to get through the next hour or so without screaming if she's going stick her proverbial oar in every two seconds.

Luckily I'm prevented from smothering my mother with her Chloe Paddington bag by Matt's arrival. At least I think it's Matt. The tatty jeans and tee shirt have been replaced with a duck egg blue shirt and black chinos and his hair is smooth from the shower.

'Matt!' says Saffron in delight. 'There you are! This is Robyn my wedding planner.'

'We met earlier in the garden,' Matt tells Saffron. 'Hello again.'

'And this is Robyn's mother, Mrs. Dexter.'

'Hi,' Matt shakes my mother's hand. 'Pleased to meet you Mrs. Dexter.'

'Call me Anna,' purrs mum.

'Anna, then,' says Matt, plonking himself next to Saffron on the sofa and flicking through the file of fabric samples.

'I was thinking about the purple and orange waistcoats that Robyn found in Liberty's,' says Saffron, 'What do you reckon, Matt?'

'Oh no, I don't think so!' cries my mother. 'What were you thinking Robyn? They're far too garish! You need something much more subtle! How about a delicate mauve? I'm sure I have just the fabric in my shop.'

That's it. I'm going to have to nip this in the bud before I hit her over the head with my sample book.

'This is Saffron's decision, mum, not yours!'

So butt out, I add under my breath.

Mum crosses her arms. 'I was just making a suggestion, Robyn. There's no need to get snappy with me. I'm only trying to help.'

'I think the purple's a fantastic choice. Robyn clearly gets her wonderful taste in fabric from you, Anna,' Matt says gently. 'You must have taught her so much.' He catches my eye over the top of my mother's head and winks. 'I really admire that. It takes a truly confident woman to allow her protégée to have some autonomy.'

Mum looks mollified. 'I suppose it does.'

'But you're here to guide her,' adds Matt.

'That's true,' says my mother, 'I taught her all she knows.'

'I can see that,' he nods. 'The purple and orange is such a sophisticated and elegant choice. That's your influence, isn't it? Admit it.'

Mum's cheeks are an exact match for a Mac Donald's strawberry thickshake.

'Well, I don't like to take the credit,' she simpers. 'Robyn has her own ideas too, you know.'

Too flipping right I do, when I can get a

word in edgeways!

'I'm looking forward to seeing them,' Matt says, but the words are spoken to me and I can't help admiring the way he's charmed mum into a rare silence. I'm grateful to him because now I can actually get on with my job and start to make some firm decisions.

'My iguana would look good in purple,' Matt continues thoughtfully. 'It'd go well with his green skin.'

Saffron swats him playfully with a fabric sample. 'Can you be serious for five minutes? Max is not invited, OK?'

'Thank God,' I mutter. Matching a lizard to my table settings is one step too far, even for a devoted wedding planner like me.

While Saffron describes the exact cut of the top coats that she's set her heart on my mobile bleeps at me. It's Jonathan, sending a really sweet text to say he hopes my big meeting goes well.

It's nice that I'm in his thoughts. He's been in mine too a lot recently. Maybe more that he really should be...

Typical. The one decent, iguana less guy out there and he's taken.

Just my luck.

Chapter Thirteen

It's become a bit of a habit that on Saturdays Gideon, James and I head out to brunch. We've found a fab café in Portobello where they serve the most amazing smoked salmon and cream cheese bagels and after being towed along by Poppy for several miles we're normally able to justify the calories. There's something blissfully restful about sinking into a battered leather sofa, sipping a latte and flicking through the papers for an hour or so while the world goes on by outside the steamy café windows.

I'm especially looking forward to a bit of chilling out time this morning because the last two days have been a whirlwind of activity. Thanks to Matt flattering my mother into submission the rest of my meeting with Saffron went like a dream and we managed to get loads of planning done. We've decided on a colour scheme, the invitations have been ordered and I even think we may have found the perfect venue. I've hardly stopped working since mum delivered me back to Ladbroke Grove and I'm even waking up in the middle of the night reaching for my jotter as inspiration strikes.

I just know this wedding is going to be fantastic.

If I don't die of exhaustion first of course!

Anyway, at ten o'clock on Saturday morning I'm still lying in bed. After a night of crazy dreams and much scribbling on my jotter I'm drifting in and out of sleep, all cosy and warm in my duvet and listening to the rain pattering against the window. I'd happily stay here all day except a flurry of impatient texts from Gideon buzzes me into consciousness like insistent SMS wasps.

'At last,' Gideon says when I finally drag myself down to his flat. 'I was starting to think I'd have to send out the search and rescue team.'

'Poppy with a cask of brandy around her neck would have done just fine,' I smile, patting Poppy who's hurling herself against my legs as though she hasn't seen me for months.

'I'm not letting you any where near my brandy,' calls James from the kitchen. 'Not after the damage you did to the whisky.'

'More like the damage your whisky did to me,' I shudder. 'That was the hangover from Hell.'

'I've no sympathy,' James says sternly. 'A girl who drinks twelve year old Macallan like it's juice deserves all she gets.'

'Talking of juice and all things brunch,' Gideon interrupts. 'Can we get going?'

'Let me get dressed,' James wanders into their sitting room in his stripy dressing gown. 'I won't be long, I promise. Have a coffee while you wait. I've put the machine on.'

'Why is everyone so slow today?' grumbles Gideon.

'You look like I feel,' I say to the bleary eyed James.

He smothers a yawn. 'I'm shattered. Last night was really busy.'

Gideon winks at me. 'He just can't keep up with the demands of a young and virile toy boy!'

'Chance would be a fine thing.' James rubs his eyes. 'It's Afghan hounds giving birth at two am with complications and their hysterical owners that I can't handle.'

'My very own James Herriot,' Gideon ruffles his partner's hair affectionately. 'He works so hard. The daring boy is always delivering lambs and putting his arm up cow's bottoms.'

James rolls his eyes. 'Not in Ladbroke Grove. Hamsters with depression and obese Labradors are about the height of excitement at our vets' practice. It's all very tame I'm afraid.'

'Well, you're my hero, darling,' Gideon tells him. 'Now get a move on before I die of starvation!'

'I'll just grab a quick shower then I'll be right with you,' James promises as he heads to the bathroom. 'Help yourself to coffee, Robyn.'

'I'll have one while you're there,' Gideon says, settling onto the sofa, all black leather and chrome and about as comfy as a bed of nails. 'Two sugars, angel.'

'What did your last slave die of?'

'You shouldn't ask questions like that unless you really want to know the answer!'

'On second thoughts I'll stick to making coffee.' I peel myself off the black leather and pad into the kitchen. Gideon and James adore cooking and their kitchen contains more gadgets and electronic equipment than the bridge of the Starship Enterprise. The bespoke units are crammed with organic produce, fresh herbs hang from the ceiling and their expensive Gaggia Achille coffee machine hisses at me like a wild cat from its perch on the black marble worktop. I poke it and jump when hot water spits onto my hand. I need a degree in engineering to suss this monstrosity out.

'Where's the Nescafé?' I call.

'Heathen! I wouldn't touch such muck!'

'I know there's a jar somewhere,' I say. 'I've seen it.'

I open up a cupboard. Unlike the higgledy piggledy chaos of my kitchen cupboards – always a bone of contention between me and Pat who's surprisingly anal for someone who makes his living cracking jokes –

Gideon's are a study in organised tidiness.

'These cupboards are scary. You need to get out more,' I say when Gideon joins me.

'And you need a map to negotiate your way round a kitchen,' he retorts, placing his hands on my shoulders and guiding me to a seat at the reclaimed pine table. 'Sit down and let Uncle Gideon take charge.'

I don't need asking twice. That coffee machine looks lethal and I quite like my hands without third degree burns, thank you very much.

Gideon places a thimble sized cup of inky coffee in front of me. 'Get that down your neck.'

I take a sip and nearly shoot into orbit. 'Bloody Hell! That's strong.'

'Triple expresso,' Gideon knocks his back without so much as a flicker. 'Just the thing to get you kick started.'

'Kick started? I don't think I'll sleep for a week after this. I'll be whizzing around the floor at Swing Dancing class on Monday. Poor Jonathan won't be able to keep up.'

'Ah yes,' Gideon leans back in his chair and regards me thoughtfully through narrowed brown eyes. 'And how is the dashing Mr. Broadhead?'

'He's fine.' I stare down at the grain of the table.

'Just fine?'

Gideon's the only person I've told about

the Swing Dancing class and the fact that Jonathan Broadhead's fast becoming a very important fixture in my life, Jonathan and I are just good friends but recently I've found myself day dreaming about how things might have been if he wasn't married. Sometimes when Jonathan places his hands around my waist and holds me tightly against his chest I feel the beating of his heart and I could swear it races in time with mine. Just the faintest brush of his fingers against the side of my breast as he lifts me for a jive is enough to make my legs turn into over cooked spaghetti and his sweet smile is the last thing I see before I close my eyes at night. It could all be in my imagination but lately I've started to suspect Jonathan feels the same regret that I do. He texts me at least twice a day, sweet messages that show I'm in his thoughts, and he always makes me smile. I wonder if he's day dreaming too?

Normally I'd be straight on the phone to Faye to discuss my feelings for a guy. Or we'd sit at her kitchen table and work our way through a bottle of wine, putting the world to rights until shadows crept across the slate floor and the room began to spin. But something holds me back from discussing my growing feelings for Jonathan with Faye. I guess I'm afraid she won't approve because Jonathan's married. She'll tell me I can't get involved with a man who's already taken and she won't care that Jonathan's wife has no interest in her husband whatsoever. Faye is a black and white kind of a person and when it comes to Jonathan I guess I'm looking for someone to tell me there's nothing wrong with exploring the grey areas, someone who understands how it feels to hover on the edge of something dangerous.

What does Faye understand about being a single almost thirty something woman? She never has to buy meals for one or listen to her mother tell her that her ovaries are withering away. Faye doesn't have to worry about going speed dating and neither has she had to watch the man she once loved settle down with another woman. She's found her Prince Charming and doesn't have to kiss frogs anymore. And unlike my princes hers don't have a nasty habit of turning into toads...

So there's no point trying to talk to Faye about my growing feelings for Jonathan. She'll disapprove and she simply won't get it but Gideon is, for all his affectations and theatricals, a really good listener and he never judges. Things haven't always been easy for him and James so he understands better than most that nothing in life is clear cut. *Every man for themselves*, was Gideon's flippant response when I mentioned Anita Broadhead, which if I'm honest was a more agreeable response to what I know in my heart Faye would say.

‘Wakey, wakey!’ Gideon snaps his fingers under my nose. ‘Earth to Robyn! I was asking you about the sexy dancing lawyer?’

‘Sorry Gids!’ I drag my thoughts away from the thorny issue of the morality of having feelings for a married man. ‘Jonathan’s fine, more than fine actually. He’s the most amazing dancer. I’ve never known anyone who’s such a natural. Honestly, Gideon it’s like he’s been dancing all his life. When he takes me in his arms and moves me around the dance floor I feel like I’m flying.’

‘Blimey,’ says Gideon.

‘Our dance teacher reckons he’s really talented and she thinks we make such a good dance pair she’s entered us for a couple of competitions. She says we’ve got real chemistry and that if we put in the practice we could even win.’

Gideon’s eyes are saucers. ‘Chemistry? As in sexual chemistry?’

‘Of course not! Don’t be so ridiculous!’ my face flames. ‘We’re just friends.

‘Don’t give me that bollocks! I’ve watched *Strictly Come Dancing* for long enough to know there’s always more to it than just the dance moves. Didn’t that news reader run off with her dance partner?’

Er, yes actually. And the tabloids had had a field day with the sports presenter who’d had a steamy affair with his dance partner. Not that I’ve been researching this or anything. I just happened to be online and at a loose end...

'You're doing it again!' cries Gideon. 'Speak to me. I'm real!'

'Oh Gids,' I bury my face in my hands. 'I really don't know what to think. Jonathan's fun. He's attractive. He's a fantastic dancer and he makes me feel like the prefect woman. What can I say? He's married and we're just friends; that's all.'

'Friends? Yeah, right.'

'Yes! Friends! Like you and I are friends!'

'That's utter bollocks!' says Gideon cheerfully. 'It's nothing like you and me. Don't take it personally darling but I've never wanted to shag you.'

'Likewise.'

'But I bet you've thought about shagging the divine Mr. Broadhead, haven't you?'

'Of course not!'

'Rubbish,' says Gideon. 'Of course you have if he's half as gorgeous as you keep telling me he is.'

I study the table top and wait for my face to cool down. Bloody Gideon. He is to tact what I am to rocket science. Last night Jonathan and I met up and went to a swing dancing club. We had a great time and when he dropped me home he brushed a gossamer soft kiss across my lips. My stomach had filled with a flutter of butterflies and I'd wanted nothing more than to melt into his arms and feel his body against mine. I'd been so shocked at this that I'd stepped back hastily only to see my own feelings of surprise and desire mirrored in his eyes. The attraction between us is growing. It's palpable and intoxicating and dangerously mutual.

'He's married, Gids,' is all I say.

Gideon shrugs. 'And where's the wife?'

'She's at work most of the time. She's a seriously important biochemist and doing some vital research into genetic illnesses. Jonathan says her career is everything to her.' He'd looked so sad when he said this that my heart had gone out to him.

'I'm such good company my wife prefers hanging out with microbes,' he'd sighed.

'You're great company,' I'd told him and the smile that lit up his face could have powered the National Grid for a month.

'She should be more considerate of her husband if you ask me,' Gideon says, pouring himself another coffee. 'People aren't toys that can be picked up and put down at will. They have needs and feelings and if this Jonathan's wife is so careless that she neglects him then she only has herself to blame if someone else comes along and takes her place.'

'But they're married!'

'That's just a piece of paper. Marriage is a partnership and it doesn't sound as though this Jonathan has a very supportive partner,' says Gideon. 'Maybe she's seeing somebody else?'

I hadn't thought of this. It makes me feel better.

'Do you think she could be?'

'Who knows? Anything's possible isn't it? All I know is that *you're* not married, Robyn, so what are you worried about? Let Jonathan do the soul searching. You haven't done anything to feel ashamed about have you?'

'No,' I say slowly, 'I suppose not.'

'Well then, stop looking so miserable. Why don't you just enjoy yourself? It's about time you had a bit of fun after Knob End.'

'Gideon!'

'Sorry, darling.' He looks nothing of the sort. 'I meant after Patrick. Just don't get hurt, will you? Stay a bit detached and just enjoy a lovely fun fling. It's the least you deserve.'

'You're right! I do deserve some fun.' This is a novel thought and I discover I rather like it. I can just hang out with Jonathan and have some excitement without the hassle of guilt or commitment. That way I can't get too involved and I can't get hurt either because I'll have remained emotionally detached. He won't he able to let me down or break my heart like Patrick did either because I won't be expecting anything from him except for some fun. It's perfect! Why didn't I think of this before?

'You're a genius,' I tell Gideon.

'It has been said,' he agrees, 'although the words *in bed* normally follow that statement.'

I slosh him on the arm and am about to make a sarcastic comment when my mobile phone rings. The screen says *Jonathan* and my heart bounces into my throat like an India rubber ball. Maybe being detached isn't quite as easy as Gideon thinks it is?

And actually what does Gideon know? He and James are one of the most married couples in the world...

'Hi!' says Jonathan, when I take the call. 'I hope I haven't woken you up?'

'Of course not,' I say and am horrified because my voice sounds like it needs oiling. I take a deep breath and try to slow my break dancing pulse. 'I've been up for hours!'

Gideon mouths 'Liar!' and then tactfully removes himself to the sitting room, where I know he'll be pretending to read *The Guardian* but with his ears out on elastic.

'I was just talking about you,' I say to Jonathan.

'Really? Nice things I hope?'

'Of course! Everything about you is nice.'

'Thanks, that's good to hear,' Jonathan says softly. Goose bumps ripple across my arms in a delicious tide. 'I feel the same way about you, Robyn.'

'Great,' I say. Great? What sort of lame response is that? Why can't I come out with something a bit more meaningful than flipping great? What is it about Jonathan Broadhead that leaves my tongue in more knots than a macramé workshop?

'Listen,' says Jonathan, not seeming bothered that my semantics have all the grace of an elephant. 'I've got a suggestion. You're under no obligation to say yes but I think it could be a whole lot of fun.'

The images that flit through my imagination make my cheeks hot.

'My wife's abandoned me,' Jonathan continues, a sad note creeping into his voice. 'She's gone to a conference in the USA at short notice. All very high powered stuff, of course, and I really can't blame her for wanting to go.'

'Of course not,' I agree, although the way he says it makes me feel that actually I can blame Anita.

'So I'm at a loose end and I was wondering if you'd like to spend the day together? We could go for lunch and maybe have a walk somewhere? And I hear there's a wonderful exhibition of wedding dresses at the V and A.'

'Jonathan!' I laugh, delighted. 'You remember me telling you about it!'

'Of course I do!' Jonathan says indignantly. 'I remember everything you say, Robyn.' He pauses. 'Sorry. I probably shouldn't have said that, should I?'

'No,' I say. 'But I'm glad you did.'

For a moment we're both silent.

'So,' he says finally, 'I know meeting up outside of dance class is kind of unmarked territory but what do you think? Do you fancy a spot of lunch at Covent Garden and a mooch around the market before hitting the V and A? I promise I'll be the perfect gentleman.'

'I don't doubt it for a moment!' I laugh, 'But I'm supposed to be having brunch with my friends.'

'Don't worry,' shrieks the eavesdropping Gideon from the sitting room. 'We can go anytime!'

'I heard that!' Jonathan chuckles. 'Looks like your friends are happy to trust you to me.'

'Of course they are,' I smile. If I trust my instincts than I can't go wrong, can I?

'Good,' says Jonathan. 'I promise you'll have a wonderful afternoon, Robyn.'

We make arrangements to meet in the covered market and then ring off. I place my hand over my heart and sure enough it's galloping faster than Red Rum on the final furlong. We might just be meeting up as friends but we both know something has changed.

And pretty soon I think we'll both know what this means.

Chapter Fourteen

April

'What's the matter, Robyn?' Jonathan looks worried. 'Don't you like the sea bass? Would you rather try my bream?'

I look up from my plate where I've been making swirly patterns in the lemon butter sauce. Jonathan's surprised me with a lunch reservation at *Le Poisson Bleu*, an exclusive fish restaurant in Sussex run by the latest foul mouthed celebrity chef and it probably isn't the best time to tell him I only like fish if it's come to my plate courtesy of Captain Birdseye.

'I'm not telling you where we're going, it's a surprise!' he'd insisted this morning when he'd pulled up really early in his BMW. 'I'm sworn to secrecy! Now come along, Miss Hood! Get out of the house and into the car!'

'My mother told me never to get into cars with strange men,' I'd called from my window.

Jonathan had pulled an offended face. 'I'm not that strange, and besides I'm not the one who's showing my Snoopy pyjamas to the world! I can't say it gets much stranger than that!'

Damn it! Why couldn't he have surprised me with a bit more warning? Given me time to have found a flowing negligee from somewhere and at least attempt to drag a comb through my bog brush hair? And had I even taken my make up off last night?

'Where are we going?'

'It's a mystery,' he'd said, his eyes crinkling up against the bright morning sunshine. 'But I know you'll love it. Come on, Robs, live a little!'

'Yes, for God's sake live a little and get in the bloody car!' Gideon had added, poking his head out of his sash window and glaring blearily up at me. 'Then the rest of us might stand a chance of getting a Sunday lie in!'

Well, how can a girl argue with that? I'd got dressed in record time, snapping on my best lacy black bra and by some miracle finding the matching knickers in my underwear draw. Not that they needed to match, obviously. It just never hurts to match in case, does it?

In case I get run over, obviously.

I'd pulled on my flared jeans and red skinny rib polo neck, yanked my hair into a high pony tail and pulled on my favourite platform boots. A slick of lip gloss and swoop of jet black mascara later and I was good to go. Reminding myself Jonathan was just a friend and therefore it didn't matter if he saw me without my full war paint – after all I never bothered to glam up for Simon – I tore down the stairs and outside into the fresh April morning.

Jonathan had popped the hood down and cranked up his iPod and as we whizzed down to the Sussex coast we bonded over a shared love of Glen Miller and the Rat Pack. We'd sung all the way to the picturesque seaside town of Leddingmouth and the pitch of our voices seemed to blend seamlessly together. How could I be so totally in harmony with a man I hardly knew?

I've been seeing Jonathan outside of class for several weeks and the more time we spend together the more it seems we have in common. From our love of the fifties to a shared delight in pottering around Camden Market we just fit together so easily. He also has to be one of the most thoughtful men I've ever met, constantly surprising me with his ideas and enthusiasm. We've walked along the Thames at Cliveden, had a picnic of crusty French stick, brie and wine in Hyde Park and have spent hours just talking. He's been nothing but proper and gentlemanly but sometimes when his fingers brush mine or when he places his hand in the small of my back to guide me to a table I feel the sexual tension fizzing between us like sherbet.

We'd had a perfect morning wandering around Leddingmouth, eating ice cream, trawling the antique shops and exploring the castle. Then Jonathan had announced we were having lunch at *Le Poisson Bleu*. The waiting list to dine there is about one hundred years and I've no idea how Jonathan's managed to wangle a reservation at such short notice so it doesn't really seem the time or the place to tell him the only way I like fish is smothered in two thousand calories' worth of batter and accompanied by lovely greasy chips. The thing on my plate looks more like an extra from Jaws than dinner. And more to the point where's the ketchup?

'Are you OK, Robyn?' Jonathan asks. 'Are you feeling ill? You look very pale.'

'I guess I'm just not particularly hungry,' I say lamely.

'That's a pity. Save yourself for the dessert. Apparently the crème brulée is legendary.'

I surrender my cutlery with gratitude and wipe the lemon sauce from my mouth with a heavy blue napkin. I know the monstrosity on my plate has probably cost more than my week's earnings but I just can't stomach it. I'm such an ungrateful cow and Jonathan's always so generous. Last week we went to the ballet and then had a fantastic meal and he insisted on paying for everything. I don't think I've ever felt so spoiled. Yesterday he surprised me with a trip to Richmond where we watched the ducks bobbing in the sunshine and ate a pub lunch down by the waterfront. We hardly stopped chatting all day and I loved every second of our date.

Did I say date? Duh, that was silly. These aren't dates in the romantic sense of the word. Of course not. We're just two friends hanging out and enjoying each other's company.

'You don't like the food, do you?' says Jonathan.

I'd much rather have gone to the *Happy Plaice* at the end of the quay and eaten chips out of paper while strolling by the sea. I expect that makes me really boring. Anita probably loves eating in restaurants like this and can dissect her fish with more skill than a surgeon.

'It's really unusual,' I hedge.

'What do you think of the restaurant?' His ocean blue eyes hold my gaze. 'The décor's really something, isn't it?'

It certainly is. The small restaurant, exclusive to the point of only being able to seat a dozen couples at a push, has been designed at great expense to look like the interior of a boat. Only not your usual nets and brass type of look, but more like the first class accommodation on the Titanic. It's not a happy comparison and I'm starting to feel more than a little seasick.

'It's great,' I agree feebly.

Jonathan's lips twitch. 'You fibber! It's bloody awful!'

'I'm starting to worry that we'll sink at any minute,' I confess.

'When Celine Dion starts singing it's time to leave!' laughs Jonathan, pushing his plate away. 'Robyn, I'm so sorry! I really wanted to impress you but this restaurant's a disaster. I think there are fewer bones in Highgate Cemetery than in my fish.'

'You don't need to impress me.' I say, surprised. 'I like you just the way you are.'

'Maybe I don't need to but perhaps I want to? You're an amazing woman Robyn. I can't believe you'd even give me the time of day. What have I got to offer you?'

'Don't be silly! I love spending time with you. You don't need to offer me anything.'

'But maybe I wish I could? Maybe I want ... oh Christ, Robyn,' Jonathan buries his face in his hands. 'Maybe I want things that I know I can't have? That I shouldn't have?'

My pulse is ER high. 'Such as?'

'I love spending time with you,' Jonathan says slowly. 'I love your laughter and your kindness, dancing with you and holding you close. I don't think I've been as happy for a very long time as I am when I'm with you. Maybe I'd like to spend a whole lot more time with you? Be even closer to you? Be,' he pauses and reaches for my hand, 'more than just your friend?'

His eyes meet mine and the emotion in them takes my breath away.

I'm lost for words – which doesn't happen very often.

'Come on,' he stands up and pushes back his chair, shattering an atmosphere so heavy it could double as concrete. 'I've got an idea.'

'What are you doing?'

Jonathan places a pile of notes on the table then reaches out and, still holding my hand, pulls me after him. Diners look up from their meals, cutlery chinking against bone china, before returning to their meals with studied British politeness.

'Right,' says Jonathan once we're outside. 'How does fish and chips sound? Eaten out of the paper with lots of salt and vinegar while we sit on the harbour wall?'

'You're a mind reader! I can't think of anything nicer.'

Jonathan's cool blue gaze sweeps boldly from my face to my body and then holds mine. 'Oh I can think of something far nicer,' he says hoarsely. 'But fish and chips will have to do.'

The world seems to pause and suddenly I'm not aware of anything else except the closeness of the man next to me, his eyes dark with desire and his body only inches from mine. My breathing feels harsh and my heart's doing a techno beat in my chest. Any moment now Fatboy Slim will come along and sample it for his latest single.

What is going on?

Jonathan breaks the spell. 'Cod and chips?'

And then simply we're back to normal again. Whatever normal is now after the things he's almost said. There's a whole sub text running beneath our conversation as we eat and I know deep down that we've turned a corner, but I say nothing. As Gideon pointed out Jonathan is the one with the soul searching to do, not me. Right?

We munch our chips on the harbour wall, tossing the crispy remains to the gulls which squawk and argue in the water below like quarrelsome children. When the sun slips behind a cloud and needles of cold rain prickle our faces we beat a hasty retreat to the Leddingmouth Arms where we spend the next few hours sampling the local real ale and listening to a folk band.

'This is heaven,' says Jonathan, leaning back in his seat. 'A pint, a simple pub and great company. I can't remember when I last felt so contented.'

'It's been a fantastic day,' I say. 'Thank you so much for bringing me.'

'You're thanking me?' Jonathan shakes his head. A lock of glossy dark hair falls across one of his chiselled cheek bones and it takes all the self restraint I have not to reach out and touch it.

I must have drunk more of that local ale than I'd realised.

'Don't you realise how I feel about you?' asks Jonathan. 'I've been trying to tell you all afternoon but I've made a mess of it haven't I?'

'You've been around the houses more than Phil and Kirstie,' I smile.

'Shall I try again?' Jonathan looks up at me from under those thick jet lashes and it's such a little boy look of mingled hope and fear that my heart melts, 'Can I be honest with you Robyn?'

This is the point where I should tell him to stop. I should remind him he's married and that he has a wife. That's what I *should* do. But I find my powers of speech have been stolen not because we are speaking above the din of a very loud band but because Jonathan's lips are only inches from mine.

All the weeks of dreaming and longing are finally taking their toll on me. I feel a pang of need so sharp it's almost a physical pain. I want to turn my head and kiss his lips and bury my hands in his liquorice dark hair. I'm dying for Jonathan to kiss me; my whole body's trembling like a finely tuned violin string. What's the point of pretending? I've never been much good at acting. I'd always longed to play Mary or an angel in the school nativity play but an invariably ended up as a shepherd with a tea towel on my head while other girls got the tinsel and the glory. Twenty years on and minus the silly headwear I'm still about as likely to receive an Oscar as I am to visit the moon. What's the use in kidding ourselves we're just friends? I've never met someone who's so much on my wave length or who turns my bones to blancmange.

Whether it's the strong local ale or whether Gideon's words last week about having some fun have had more impact than I realise I don't know. But I do know this: when Jonathan leans forward and brushes my lips with his I don't pull back.

My first thought is that this is nothing like kissing Patrick. It's not nearly as aggressive for a start; Jonathan's lips are soft and gently move over mine like the smallest of ripples on a lake and I enjoy the sensation of smoothly shaven skin against mine rather than Pat's dark stubble. I almost cry out with loss when he breaks away.

Jonathan is pale. 'I'm sorry! I didn't mean to do that!'

I take a shaky breath. His kiss has rocked me to my very core.

'Don't apologise,' I tell him, 'unless you really didn't want to.'

'Didn't want to? Are you serious? Of course I wanted to,' he rakes a hand through his dark hair. 'Jesus Robyn, I've wanted to do that since the moment I first saw you. You have no idea.'

'I think I do,' I say.

'All those times at swing dancing it's been torture. Holding you close but not being able to touch you and kiss you is agony. Robyn, I can't help myself, I really can't. I'm crazy about you.'

I stare at him. His eyes are almost black with emotion. The sleek corporate lawyer has vanished and in his place is a man of such raw passion that I'm overwhelmed.

I reach across the table to touch his hand only I'm trembling so much that I knock a pint glass over and drench us both in potent beer.

'Oh God! I'm so sorry, Jonathan!'

'Don't be,' Jonathan tries to staunch the flow with a beer mat but only succeeds in drenching himself further. 'A cold shower is exactly what I need! I think we ought to go home.'

'You're right!' I agree hastily. 'I think I've had far too much to drink. We'll probably be really embarrassed in the morning. All the fresh air has gone to our heads. I understand.'

Jonathan's hand reaches out across the table and he traces the pale blue veins on the inside of my wrist with his forefinger. It's such a gentle touch in such an innocent spot that I'm staggered by the jolt of pure sexual energy that zings through my bloodstream. Suddenly my sweater is not the only part of me that's damp.

'Robyn,' he says hoarsely. 'I mean every word. I'm crazy about you; sober, after a beer and even if I'm blind drunk. It doesn't make any difference. I know I shouldn't feel this way but I can't help it. Do you feel the same, Robyn? Do you?'

I slide my hand from beneath his, pick up my bag and without saying a word weave my way, a little unsteadily but hey that ale was strong, out of the pub and into the dark night. My feelings are churning like a washing machine on spin cycle and I have to lean my hands against the harbour wall and take a few big swallows of air to calm myself. Then I stare out into the dark chasm of the sea and port and starboard lights of trawlers that ride the distant horizon. I feel as adrift as those boats far out at sea, with no friendly guiding moon to show them the way home.

How do I feel? There's a tsunami of emotions tearing through me. Excitement, desire, guilt to name but three, and I love every second of being in his company. Jonathan's funny and sexy and he surfs my wavelength but he's only my friend. That's all he can ever be, isn't it?

Or is that all he can be if I decide that's as far as it goes?

'Robyn?' Jonathan is standing behind me. 'Are you all right? I didn't mean to offend you. I wouldn't do that for the world.'

I turn slowly. In the shadows he is marble

pale, his eyes dark and haunted and his body is taut with emotion.

'Please, forget everything I said if it's upset you,' Jonathan says softly.

When I was a child I once dived from the highest board at our local swimming pool. Even all these years on I can still remember how it felt to be poised on the brink with that great sweep of nothingness between me and oblivion, the terror and the excitement all one great mingled tide as I bounced on the balls of my feet and jumped. And nearly twenty years later I feel those exact emotions again.

'I don't want to forget what you said,' I whisper. 'I liked hearing it because, God help me, I feel exactly the same way.'

He says nothing but the wide grin that splits his face practically from ear to ear speaks volumes. Without a word he draws me to him and kisses me and kisses me and kisses me until I think my mouth will fall off.

And I forget about everything else except holding him close and kissing him back for a very, very long time.

Which is probably just as well.

Chapter Fifteen

'Are you sure you want to see this bill, Robyn?' Keith the mechanic holds a large print out in his oily hands. 'You might want to sit down first.'

I shake my head. 'Just get it over with so I can sell my soul to Barclaycard.'

I'm back in the garage because, surprise surprise, Dolly has decided to conk out on me again. She was courteous enough to do so outside my flat this time so I haven't had to plead with the AA to rescue me or defect to the RAC but I'm sure it's only a matter of time. Luckily Keith and the gang at 'Marvellous Mechanics' know me so well by now they were happy to tow Dolly away. I'm probably their best customer and I reckon my bills alone have financed Keith's divorce and his latest on the pull trip to Ibiza.

He pushes the bill across the counter. 'How about a brandy?'

I open the bill and it's a good job I'm leaning against the counter because otherwise I'd be a heap on the floor. 'I'll need the whole bottle!' I gasp. 'Bloody Hell, Keith. What have you done? Made her bionic?'

'It's the six million dollar car all right.'

Keith clicks his tongue in disapproval. 'You could have bought yourself something newer ten times over by now.'

'I need an oxygen tank to even contemplate a bill this high. Can I pay in Monopoly money?' I say as I glance down the bill. How many noughts?

Keith waggles his eyebrows suggestively. 'You can pay in kind if you like.'

Er ... no. I don't like. Not that there's anything wrong with Keith. If men with gold chains and more body hair than King Kong are your thing I'm sure he's great, but he's certainly not my type. He's funny, and a laugh and a seriously good mechanic but I'm not going there. Ever.

'Sorry,' I tell him, 'but I've got a rule about mercy shagging.'

Keith pulls a mock offended face. 'I'll just have to take cash then. Luckily I'm not into skinny birds.'

'Keith! For saying that I could *almost* change my mind. Say it again, go on!'

'Say what?'

'The s-word!'

'Skinny?'

'That's it! The most beautiful thing a man can say to any woman.'

'I don't know why you women have such a thing about your weight. Men don't like skinny birds. We like a bit of meat to hold on to.'

'Nicely put,' I say, but my sarcasm's lost on Keith. And anyway it's well known amongst the lads at the garage that Keith has a bit of a thing for the larger woman. The apprentice who'd complained that the Beth Ditto calendar was putting him off his sandwiches had been sacked on the spot.

He swipes my credit card. 'You never know Robyn, if you ate a bit more and put on a stone or two I could almost fancy you.'

'I really must join a gym.' I retort.

As the machine whirrs and buzzes (thank you baby Jesus) there's a corresponding buzzing in my bag. Fishing out my mobile I feel a momentary pang of disappointment when I see a number I don't recognise. I'd really hoped it was Jonathan. I haven't seen him since he dropped me home in the small hours of Monday morning and I really want to talk to him. Fleeting texts are all very well but I *need* to see him. If he wants to say he's made a mistake by kissing me then I'd rather he told me now. And do I think *I've* made a mistake? To be honest I'm not sure and I won't be until I see him again.

Why, oh why, does it have to he so complicated?

'I'll call you,' he'd murmured when he dropped me at the flat, brushing a soft kiss across my lips. And then he'd driven away into the darkness, leaving me standing on the door step with my heart doing belly flops and my body aching for him. It's been two days now and my emotions feel like they've been poured into a blender and whizzed around on high speed.

'Are you going to get that or what?' Keith's voice slices through my thoughts.

'Oh! Yes!' in a fumble of fingers and thumbs I manage to press the accept button.

'Hello?' I say, in my best wedding planner voice. '*Perfect Day*. Robyn speaking. How may I help you?'

'G'day Robs! It's Julia here?'

'Julia, hi!' motioning to Keith that I need to take this call I take a seat in the reception area. 'How are you and Bradley?'

'Cool,' says Julia, and I can picture her smiling like a tanned and toothy sunbeam. 'Did you manage to get a deal on the dress?'

I'm having so much fun planning Bradley and Julia's wedding. Being on a really tight budget, about fifty pence in total, it's the antithesis of Saffron's do but none the poorer for it. In fact working in such contrast has really helped keep my A list wedding in perspective. Last week Saffron was having hysterics because the ribbons to tie the bouquets were a different shade of purple to the waistcoats whereas Julia was planting seeds to grow the sunflowers that she wants to give each of her guests. The dress is another polar opposite. No Vera Wangs or Stella McCartneys for Jules. She found her dream dress in one of my favourite Camden vintage boutiques.

'Jeez!' She'd clutched my arm so tightly that I'd have bruises for days. 'Look at that dress, Robyn. Isn't it fab?'

I'd followed her gaze across the street to the window of a small boutique. Sure enough in the window was a mannequin sporting a 1970s flowery strapless hippie style dress in a migraine inducing riot of colours.

'It's purple.' I said.

'And orange and white!' Julia said breathlessly. 'And look at the gorgeous belt they've teamed it with! And that big floppy hat! Can't you just see me in that?'

Actually I could. With her flawless caramel skin and tumbling golden hair she would look stunning, all glossy good health like a corn fed Connemara pony.

'And it will go a treat with the Oz theme,' Julia had added, grabbing my hand and towing me across the road in order to get a closer look. 'Let's try it.'

So Julia had tried it and she'd looked stunning. The only problem was that the price was fifty pounds above her budget and the shop owner was away that day so I couldn't use my relationship as one of their top customers in order to blag us a deal. I'd promised to call the very next morning to see what I could do and poor Julia has been on tenterhooks ever since.

'Well?' she demands down the phone.

'What did she say?'

'She said,' I pause like one of the X Factor judges, dragging out the tension until Jules is practically screaming, 'you can have it for two hundred pounds!'

'Yes!' I can imagine her punching the air in delight and tearing round the room. 'Yes! Yes! I love you Robyn! You're the best!'

'Thanks,' I laugh. 'If only all my customers were as impressed!'

I ring off, smiling to myself because Julia's good temper is so contagious. Someone really ought to bottle whatever it is they give to Aussies that makes them so good humoured. I'd buy a gallon of it for Hester, that's for sure.

I'm just about to collect the keys for Dolly when I have a total brainwave. Stacked in the workshop are empty oil drums which could make perfect barbeques for the reception at Brad and Julia's wedding. That will save a fortune on hiring caterers and I'm sure there won't be any shortage of cooks because most of the guests are Australian and could probably barbeque in their sleep.

'Keith,' I shout into the inspection pit, 'can I have a favour?'

'It's too late for my body,' he calls back. 'You missed the window.'

'Oh tragedy!' I sigh. 'In that case I guess I'll just have to settle for a couple of oil drums instead!'

Chapter Sixteen

I'm just laying on the sofa, eating my way though the broken biscuits at the bottom of the tin (because everybody knows they don't count) and thinking that I really ought to do some house work when Jonathan calls.

'Mmmph!' I say, spraying crumbs everywhere.

'Robyn? Is that you?'

I swallow the biscuits frantically and end up coughing. 'Sorry! I wasn't practising Klingon or anything, I was eating some biscuits.'

Oh nice one, Robyn. Very sophisticated. That'll really impress him. I bet Anita doesn't lie around stuffing her face with carbs.

'Right,' he says and then there's an awkward silence. What do you talk about to a man who's recently kissed your lips raw? I hardly think we can go back to discussing the weather or house prices.

'Listen, Robyn,' Jonathan says finally, his voice low and insistent. 'I have to see you. I can't go on like this. If I don't talk to you soon I'll go crazy.'

'Oh.' I reply. I'm not sure what to say because I'm rather shocked by the desperation in his voice.

'Can I come over?'

I glance around the flat. It looks as though it's been burgled. Actually if it had I wouldn't be able to tell. My ironing pile could rival K2 and the washing up is threatening to become an environmental hazard. Newspapers trail across the carpet and Poppy's hair coats every conceivable surface. How long will it take to clear this lot, whiz a hoover round, shave my legs and turn myself into a sex goddess? An hour? Two?

Let's play it safe and say three.

'Of course you can come over,' I tell him, 'Just give me-'

'Great! I'll be with you as soon as I can!' says Jonathan and click! he rings off.

I stare aghast at the receiver. I'm very flattered he's so keen to see me but this is ridiculous. And how far is Muswell Hill from Ladbroke Grove? Thirty minutes at the most?

OK Robyn, do not, I repeat, do not panic. Take a deep breath and–

It's too late. I'm panicking!

I tear around my flat like the Tasmanian Devil on speed, hurling dirty washing up into the glory hole under the sink and stuffing as much laundry into the tumble drier and washing machine as I can manage. I plump cushions and shake out throws, light scented candles and tip bleach down the loo, and I drag the Dyson out of retirement.

Three laps of the flat later, a whisk around the surfaces with a duster and voila! Goodbye *Steptoe and Son* hello Hyacinth Bucket!

I collapse onto the sofa. I hope Jonathan really is coming round to talk because I'm so exhausted from this cleaning frenzy that I don't think I have the energy for anything else. Although, it might be nice not to smell of bleach just in case. Maybe I should have a shower? Eau de *Cillit Bang* probably isn't going to rival Chanel any time soon.

Dashing into the bathroom I turn on the shower, screeching when the icy jets prickle across my back. Then I exfoliate my body to within an inch of its life and smother my hair in deep conditioner. Oh Lord! Should I bleach my upper lip? Wax my eyebrows? And what about my nails? After lugging oil drums around all afternoon my hands are as oily as Keith's (although less hairy, thank goodness!) I haven't got time to do it all. No wonder Victoria Beckham abandoned her solo career. Looking good is a full time job!

To shave or not to shave? That is the question. I don't want to look like I've tried too hard. And if I don't shave them it will make it easier to avoid temptation for temptation is what Jonathan Broadhead is, no two ways about it. Six foot of lean, raven haired utterly addictive temptation. I'm not sure if I want to risk getting involved with him. He may be sexy, and funny and more scrumptious than Dairy Milk but I really should stop this before we both get too involved. I don't care what Gideon said about just having fun. That's all very well in theory but in practice I think I could be in serious danger of falling head over heels for Jonathan. I'm going to have to tell him that this ... that whatever it is between us has got to end.

All the same, I tell myself as I slip into my Amanda Wakeley wrap dress, it doesn't hurt to look good while I tell him.

When Jonathan arrives the flat smells of Jo Malone's orange blossom and the lamps throw inviting shadows across the sitting room. Astrud Gilberto is singing in the background and I've swapped my Mills and Boon for an edifying novel. White wine and beer are chilling in the fridge and kettle chips are decanted into bowls. The scene is set and as I go to open the door I feel calm and in control.

Or at least I do until Jonathan strides into my flat with all the sleek power and beauty of a panther. I look at the hard contours of the body beneath the Armani suit and feel my resolutions melting. He's so beautiful and I want him so much it's all I can do not to hurl myself at him.

Frailty thy name is Robyn!

'Would you like a drink?' I say.

Jonathan loosens his tie with a forefinger. 'A beer would be great.'

I fetch two Budweisers from the fridge and crack them open, racking my brains for something to say.

'How was work?' we both blurt.

'Sorry!' I smile, handing him the drink. 'You first.'

'Work was fine,' Jonathan says, leaning against the mantle piece while his foot taps the floor to some internal rhythm. 'Pretty busy. How about you?'

This is hideous, Normally Jonathan and I natter away without any awkwardness. There's a lump in my throat. Have we broken our friendship? Stretched and twisted it until it can no longer snap back to what it was but remains forever in a new ugly shape?

'Fine,' I mutter, while my eyes sting with tears. 'I got the car fixed.'

'Oh Robs!' Jonathan's lips twitch into a smile. 'Not again? How much was it this time?'

I halve the original number and then divide it by three and when I tell him Jonathan winces.

'I love that car!' I protest. 'She's worth every penny.'

'I know you do. But she must be held together with a wing and a prayer by now.' Jonathan starts to pace around the room. He strays over to my desk and picks up a picture of Hester.

'And what's this?' he asks turning it round

to reveal the Hitler moustache and horns that I'd doodled on in a moment of rage. 'Did you do this, you bad girl?'

'Oops!' I raise my hands. 'Guilty as charged! Actually, I thought it rather suited her!'

Jonathan laughs and for a moment the tension slides from his face. Then he shakes his head and sighs. 'Robyn, you make me laugh like no one else.'

'But? Come on Jonathan, say what you've been dying to say since you first charged through the door. I'm a big girl, I can take it.'

He looks me straight in the eye. 'I love my wife, Robyn, I really do but it's complicated.'

I nod but I don't speak. If he says that Anita doesn't understand him I swear I'll grab him by his Turnbull and Asser collar and hurl him down the stairs. I'm so not going to make this easy for him. I want him so badly that my throat is knotted with unshed tears but this has to be Jonathan's decision. He's the one who's willingly pursued our relationship to this crisis point, the one who drove me to Leddingmouth and told me he's crazy about me.

And he's the one who's married.

Jonathan's eyes slide away from mine, to the tips of his bespoke shoes. 'I don't think we should see each other any more.'

It's a statement not a question so why do I

get the distinct impression he's asking for my permission to leave or to stay? It's the first time his self assurance has really dropped. The arrogance has evaporated and as he looks down at me I'm shocked to see his eyes are bright with tears. In all the weeks I've known him this handsome, clever polished man has never been as beautiful to me as he is in this moment of vulnerability.

All I need to do is agree with him, walk him to the door and say goodbye. That would be it. Over. Simple and quick. We'd never see each other again and it could be as though nothing had ever happened. He can patch things up with Anita and I'll ... I'll...

What will I do? What if Jonathan Broadhead is The One? My last chance of happiness? My last hope of moving to Couple Town with Faye and Simon and Pat and Jo? But how can I have my fairy tale at the expense of some one else? What sort of woman would I be if I talked him out of doing what we both know is the right thing?

The answer to that is a woman I couldn't live with.

I follow him to the door. 'You're a good man Jonathan Broadhead,' I tell him, 'Anita is so lucky to have you.'

As I say her name the little prickle of guilt that's needled me for the past two days goes, which would be good news except that it's replaced by a dart of envy.

Jonathan smiles thinly and walks slowly to the door, his shoulders sagging as though under some invisible weight. He's half out of the door when he holds out his hand as though to say 'I'm so sorry about all this mess' and I take it.

Which as it turns out is a big mistake.

There's no pretending that this is a goodbye peck on the check. As soon as our faces move towards one another his hand slips around my waist and he pulls me to him.

'Oh God,' he groans, burying his face in the hollow of my throat, 'I just can't do it Robyn, I just can't let you go!'

I'm about to pull away, to whisper 'We can't' or some other such cliché but he grabs hold of me hungrily, desire turning his eyes blue gas flames, and no matter how much I tell myself I should I can't rip my gaze from his.

With a groan Jonathan kicks the door shut and we fall back onto the sofa, tearing at each other's clothes and gasping in shock and delight as a million delicious sensations shiver across our bodies.

'Oh Robyn,' groans Jonathan. 'Have you any idea what you do to me?'

And as his hands move lower I forget about protesting and concentrate instead on finding out.

I suppose I ought to say how awkward everything is and how we bash our teeth together and feel embarrassed. But although I have many faults, eating chocolate in bed for one and fancying Captain Kirk for another, I'm not a fibber and I have to say that sex with Jonathan is totally and utterly amazing. For the first time in my life I don't fret about my cellulite or try desperately to suck in my stomach because I can't think of anything else but being as close to him as possible. My hands tear at his trousers, which he kicks impatiently to the floor, before I wind my fingers into his hair and kiss him more and more desperately until we break apart, laughing and breathless. The he kisses me softly, murmuring lots of nonsense about how beautiful I am and how much he adores me.

I'm in heaven.

Later, as I lie trembling and warm in the crook of his arm, I think to myself that this really is it. There's no going back now for either of us, no denying that we're involved, no justifying spending time together with explanations of swing dancing and friendship.

Jonathan and I are lovers.

And already I have a suspicion keeping my heart detached, in order to have the no strings fun so highly recommended by Gideon, is not going to be as easy as I'd thought. In fact I don't think it's going to be easy at all.

Chapter Seventeen

'This is it!' I look up in triumph. 'Australian Mud Cake! I knew there was something with an Aussie theme in one of your books!'

Faye and I are sitting at her kitchen table and have spent the last hour working our way through a bottle of White Burgundy and pile of her cookery books. By agreeing to make the wedding cake Faye is the latest of my friends to be roped into Brad and Julia's Aussie themed wedding, a wedding which is starting to keep me up at night because no matter how I try I simply cannot make the finances work. Fulfilling all Julia's dreams on a budget that barely matches my yearly L K Bennet suit allowance makes splitting the atom look easy.

'Australian Mud Cake?' Fay's brow crinkles. 'Are you sure, Robs? I don't think that was one of my finest creations. Si reckoned it should have been renamed Cow Pat Cake.'

'Si is a total Philistine when it comes to baking. Believe me I know, I saw him live off Fray Bentos for a year! This cake is *exactly* what Brad and Jules are after. Look,' I slide the book across the table, 'It's perfect.'

'But that's from *Things to bake on a Rainy Day,'* Faye says. 'Isn't that a bit of a bad omen? I thought Julia had her heart set on a sun soaked Australian vibe?'

'Mmm,' I flip through the next book thoughtfully. 'That's another problem. How am I going to pull off Bondi Beach weather in the middle of a British summer?'

'You'll do it, Robs, if anyone can. You've always loved a challenge.'

'This wedding is more than a challenge,' I sigh, taking a big gulp of wine. 'It's almost impossible. Every day Jules phones with a new idea. She wants the kind of wedding that Jordan would envy but for about fifty pence. Hester would pop a blood vessel.'

'You can do it babes,' says Faye. 'You've always been creative.'

'But there's creative and there's needing to be a bloody magician! Faye, I've got no budget to play with whatsoever and I've still got to find a venue for the reception.'

'Can't you tell Julia that she needs to up the budget?'

I shake my head. 'She and Bradley are really pushed for cash. They've promised to pay for his mum and sister to come over from Australia for the wedding. Besides, I've promised them that I'll sort everything out. I can't let them down, Faye.'

'You won't let them down, babes, you'll think of something, I know you will. You're a brilliant wedding planner,' says Faye loyally. 'I'll get my thinking cap on and I'm sure between us we'll come up with a venue. I'll make the cake in the shape of Sydney Opera House and with white chocolate icing. It can be my present to them, so you can cross that off the list.'

'Are you sure?'

'Of course I am!' Faye takes the cookery book and turns the corner of the page down. 'Anything to help my best friend out. And besides, if you've got one less thing to do and worry about maybe we'll see a bit more of you?'

I feel a stab of guilt that would give Lady Macbeth a run for her money. After weeks of playing answer phone frisbee I've finally made it over to see Faye. It's not that I haven't wanted to visit my best friend it's just every moment I haven't been working has been taken up with seeing Jonathan. My heart is constantly flipping over with excitement and my nervous system is so awash with adrenaline I'm probably over the limit! I don't think I've been this consumed with desire for someone since I was a teenager! It's ridiculous and wonderful and terrifying all at the same time to realise I'm falling head over heels for him. Last night Jonathan stayed over – Anita is at yet another conference – and it was amazing. Not just the sex, although that's fantastic, but just being able to hold each other close and drift into sleep before waking up as rosy sunshine was spilling into my bedroom and making love to the sound of the birds singing their little hearts out in the plane trees outside.

'What are you smiling about?'

'Nothing!' I drag my thoughts away from last night. 'I was miles away!'

'You certainly were.' Faye's eyes narrow thoughtfully. 'You had a really soppy look on your face. Go on, you may as well tell me. Who is he?'

Don't you just hate it when your best friends can read you like a book? And since mine probably has a title like something by Jackie Collins I think I'd rather Faye didn't turn the page. I still haven't told Faye about my affair with Jonathan. I feel guilty for not confiding in her but I have a nasty feeling she won't approve. Being a married woman Faye's bound to take Anita's side, which is ridiculous really when we don't even know Anita. I'm doing my best to put Anita to the back of my mind and the last thing I want is Faye arguing the case from her point of view.

'Nobody!' If I wasn't already off to Hell for seeing a married man I'd certainly be on my way for all the fibs I've told to my best friend lately. 'I was thinking about the wedding.'

'Yeah right. Come on, Robyn, who is he? Someone you've met on the swing dancing course?'

I blush right down to my toe nails. 'Faye! Give me a break. Why can't you just leave me bolted to my shelf? I quite like it up here you know! I don't need a man.'

'Rubbish!' says Faye cheerfully. 'I know you, remember? Tell me about this course. There's got to be someone special, surely? Don't you have to dance really close together? Is there nobody there you fancy?'

This is hideous. I really don't want to lie outright to my best friend but how can I tell her the truth? If in doubt change the subject. One trick I learned from Patrick that may actually pay off.

'I'm starving.' I jump up and pad over to the fridge. 'Have you got anything to eat?'

Fay looks at me as though I'm crackers. 'I'm a professional cook. Of course I have. Help yourself.'

I open the fridge door and as always I'm amazed at the contrast between the contents of a couples' fridge and my own single girl's variety. My pink Smeg contains several bottles of white wine, a Lush face pack and some wilting celery whereas Faye's is groaning with yummy things. Parma ham and melon jostle for pole position with creamy Dolcelatte and a rich home made chocolate mousse. Faye makes Nigella Lawson look like an amateur.

'How are you not the size of a house?' I wonder, selecting some stilton and a jar of caramelised onion jam.

'Spinning classes,' says Faye. 'They're Hell but they certainly burn fat. Anyway, you're looking pretty trim yourself lately. Is that the dancing?'

I'd better not tell her that energetic sex with Jonathan is the best work out yet.

'Swing Dancing is great exercise,' I say, as I rummage in the breadbin and pull out some of Faye's own ciabatta.

'Well, it seems to be doing you the world of good, you're looking great.' Faye tactfully drops the subject of men. She knows something's up but she's not one to pry. Thank goodness.

'Thanks. My teacher says I've really improved.'

'Si says you're entering a competition. You must be getting really good.'

'I wouldn't go that far!' I laugh, 'But apparently I have a really good chance of being placed.'

'That's brilliant babes!' Faye is genuinely delighted for me. 'When is it? Maybe Si and I could come and give you some support?'

Oh God! No way! If Faye sees Jonathan and I dancing together she'll know in an instant exactly what's going on. She cannot see us dance at that competition! She just can't!

Luckily God hears my panicked pleas for as I slice the bread I glance up at the cork board Faye's pinned above the work surface.

On it is a collage of recipes snipped from magazines, pictures of gap toothed nieces and nephews and various take away menus. But what catches my eye this time are two tickets to a wine tasting event. There's nothing unusual about this, Si's always enjoyed good wine, but luckily for me this event's the same night at the dance contest.

'That's a shame,' says Faye, when I point this out. 'I'd love to see you dance. Who's your partner?'

'It depends who's at the class. We often take it in turns to swap partners,' I fudge, because this is true in a way. Lots of the other dancers do chop and change their partners, it's just Jonathan and I who always dance together.

'Kinky! That makes our wine tasting group sound really boring.'

'I'd rather be bored than trundled across the dance floor by a guy who makes Keith the Mechanic look like Fred Astaire! It really isn't as glamorous as it seems,' I say as I return to the table with the spoils of my trip to the fridge.

'Maybe so but it's certainly put a spring in your step. I haven't seen you look so happy and sparkly for ages. When you do meet a guy he won't be able to resist, believe me.' Faye hacks off a wedge of stilton and munches thoughtfully. 'Any fit guys involved in Saffron's wedding?'

'Faye Harvey! You are obsessed! Butt out of my love life!'

'Sorry!' grins Faye. 'Si's so busy working I have to get my excitement somewhere.' She says this in a light-hearted way but for a second something akin to sadness flickers in her eyes. Then it's gone and she's smiling at me. 'Only kidding! I love being an old married woman. It's just that sometimes I miss the excitement of all those possibilities waiting to be discovered.'

'You wouldn't want to be single and nearly thirty,' I say. 'Believe me, there really aren't any opportunities, I should know! All the good men are taken and the ones left over are single for a very good reason. You were just asking me about single guys involved with Saffron Scott's wedding? Let's take the Best Man Matt as example to test this theory. He's single. Talented. Good with my mother.'

'Marry him quick!'

I grimace. 'He's a bit odd. He spent ages telling me all about his pet iguana and what fantastic company it is. Apparently it even sleeps on his pillow.'

'No way!'

'OK, I may have made that up,' I admit, 'but he watches television with Max, that's his iguana, on his shoulder. He told me that himself. And he was very keen for Max to wear a purple bow and be a member of the wedding party!'

Faye's bottom jaw is practically in the wine cellar. 'He *was* joking right?'

'I'm not sure. But I tell you what, I'm not about to take the chance that he's not kidding. Can you imagine an iguana on the loose at my wedding?'

'Not really,' says Faye. 'What do iguanas do? Are they savage?'

'I haven't a clue and I want to keep it that way. And he kept cracking jokes non stop, just like you know bloody who!'

'Patrick doesn't have a monopoly on humour, babe.'

'One wannabe comedian in a lifetime's quite enough, thanks.'

Faye doesn't say anything. She really doesn't get it.

'Don't you see?' I say. 'This proves everything I've been trying to explain about all the single men our age having something wrong with them!'

Faye munches thoughtfully on a chunk of Stilton. 'Some of them must be all right, surely?'

'Not the ones I keep coming across,' I sigh. 'Believe me there's a really good reason why they're all single. So unless I develop a sudden passion for reptiles I really am stuffed!'

'So what about younger men? A nice toy boy you could train up?'

We splutter into our wine.

'I've never really thought about it,' I say

once I've got my breath back from laughing so hard.

'Forget younger men. That was a stupid idea. You can't possibly go out with a guy who thinks Fergie is a pop star rather than someone who was once married to Prince Andrew. Just be patient, babes. The right one will come along.'

But what if he already has? For a split second I'm seriously tempted to tell Faye about Jonathan Broadhead because it seems really wrong to keep something this important from her. Gideon's great but at the end of the day he's still a bloke. I'd really like a woman's opinion on the subject. But I know Faye will disapprove horribly and she'll try and make me see things from Anita's point of view and at the moment I'm trying very hard indeed to put all thoughts of Anita as far out of mind as possible. Besides, why should Anita have a wonderful man like Jonathan when she clearly doesn't give two hoots about him?

'What if the right one can't be with me?' I wonder aloud

'Then never fear,' grins Faye. 'I hear iguanas make wonderful companions and they look great in purple!'

We both burst into fits of giggles, laughing until our sides ache and the tears run down our cheeks. The situation really is hopeless; if I don't laugh I'll probably cry. Thank goodness I've met Jonathan or I think I'd be seriously tempted to give up all hope entirely, buy myself a cat and go quietly bonkers on my own.

'So this is what goes on while I'm toiling away at work!' Simon strolls into the kitchen, dumps his briefcase by the table and drops a kiss onto Faye's head. 'How the other half lives! What are you two cackling about?'

'Men of course,' wheezes Faye. 'What else could be such an endless cause of amusement'?'

'Oh Lord,' Si rolls his eyes and gestures theatrically towards the empty wine glasses. 'Shall I go away?'

'No, you don't count,' I tell him. 'You're an honorary girl.'

'I am not!' Si plops himself down next to Faye and loosens his collar by running his finger around the inside. 'I'll have you know I'm all man! Especially when it counts.'

'Putting out the bins you mean?' I ask.

'Ignore her, honey,' Si says to Faye, resting his head on her shoulder. 'Robyn knows I was Uni's answer to Brad Pitt.'

'Si, you must have misheard that. I think the expression was arm pit? Referring to that rather embarrassing eco phase when you refused to use soap?'

'I was saving the planet!'

'With all the Greenhouse gases and methane vapours you were giving off you were probably single handedly responsible *for* the hole in the ozone layer!'

'Women like men with an environmental conscience,' protests Simon. 'Faye does.'

'Luckily for you,' I laugh, 'because the rest of us preferred soap!'

'Faye can scrub me clean whenever she likes,' Simon deadpans.

'Right, that's enough dirty talk!' I pull a mock horrified face. 'Maybe I should go so that you guys can be alone?'

'Don't be silly,' says Faye. 'Stay for dinner, I've made a casserole, there's loads. We'd love you to stay, wouldn't we Si?

'Of course,' says Si. 'Especially if you do the washing up afterwards. Only joking! You know we've got a dishwasher!'

Faye thumps him on the arm. 'Ignore him Robyn. Stay and eat, please.'

I know they both mean it but I also know Si has been working really long hours recently and the last thing they really need is me being all green and hairy when they could do with some time alone. Faye is probably desperate to curl up with Simon and I'm sure he feels the same but they're both sensitive enough to consider the feelings of their sad single friend. Couples like them make me feel there's some hope for marriage and long term relationships after all. It's enough to make my inner cynic pack her bags.

But later on as I sit in the back of a taxi

speeding across London towards the small bespoke Hotel where Jonathan is waiting for me I look across the dark waters of the Thames and try to ignore the question that nags at my mind like an insistent toothache, the question that's asking me why, if I believe so much in marriage, I am racing across the ink dark city to give myself heart and soul to a man who is very married indeed?

And even more than that, a man who has never tried to deny *that* marriage or the fact that he loves and misses his wife.

Chapter Eighteen

Is there anyone in the world who enjoys family gatherings? Much as I love my family I can think of more restful ways of spending my day off – running the Marathon or scaling Everest for example would both be a breeze in comparison.

It's a lovely sunny Sunday but instead of sunbathing on my tiny roof terrace and sipping cold white wine – which believe me I really need after the week I've had – I'm at the christening of my cousin's umpteenth baby. It's not that I have a problem with my cousin Annabelle or that I don't love my family to bits but I'm really tired after a hectic week and it's hard work having to be sparkling and entertaining when what I'd actually love to do is collapse in a heap somewhere. I've chatted to my aunt about the garden, played football with my little brothers and entertained people over lunch by telling them the story of how I stopped the press following Saffron to her latest dress fitting. Actually this story's funnier in the retelling because at the time I was terrified I may have blown Saffron's exclusivity deal with *Scorching*.

I'd been really careful to keep the identity of the designer a secret so when we'd been about to leave the designer's studio I'd been horrified to see a swarm of paps waiting. It was only by throwing a coat over my mother's head and racing with her to the car and diverting their attention from Saffron that we'd managed to get away with it. I'm no Miss Marple but it seemed a strange coincidence that Hester's latest celebrity client was also having a fitting with the same designer. Hester would think nothing of wrecking Saffron's special day if it meant she could ruin *Perfect Day* at the same time. I don't need to be a genius either to figure out how Hester gets her information. My mother couldn't keep a secret if her life depended on it and she just can't help boasting. I'd only agreed to take her along because she'd insisted she needed to see the wedding dress if she was to co-ordinate the table linen properly. From now on I'm telling her nothing.

Unless, of course, I want it to go straight to Hester...

'Robyn's getting married,' announces my Great Aunt Ethel across the finger buffet.

Heads swivel. Several older relatives stop mid chew and my dad looks stunned.

'Really?' I'm rather insulted my dad sounds so amazed. It's not *that* unlikely, is it?

'No, dad, of course I'm not,' I say firmly. I raise my voice several decibels. 'I said I'm arranging a wedding, auntie! Not getting married.'

'Well, you'd better get a move on, my girl,' she says. 'You're getting on a bit now. Isn't it time you had a little one of your own?'

'There's plenty of time for that,' dad points out. 'Robyn's far too busy with her business to think about having a family yet.'

'Are you a lesbian?' asks one of my teenage cousins, his eyes out on stalks.

Dad cuffs him gently. 'Robyn just hasn't met the right man yet.'

Sometimes I *almost* wish I were a lesbian. Women are so much kinder to each other than men, aren't they? It would be really nice to hang out with someone who exactly understood period pains, didn't find farting hilarious and who wouldn't leave the loo seat up for me to fall down in the middle of the night.

But enough of Patrick already!

'Hello,' smiles my cousin Annabelle, joining us with the latest baby all milky and sleepy in her arms. 'Are you having a good time?'

'This is what you need,' my great aunt tells me sternly as she takes baby Charlie in her arms.

Oh goody. Now we can talk about my childless state rather than my husbandless one. While my great aunt bounces Charlie up and down and everyone coos over him I retrieve my buzzing mobile from my little rosebud bag and flip it open. It's a text from Jonathan.

Bored and missing u! Am texting from the bathroom and thinking about escaping down the wisteria!

I smile but a small hand clutches my heart and squeezes it tightly. For a moment I imagine how different today would be if I'd been able to share it with the man I think I'm falling in love with. If I had Jonathan by my side nobody would be pitying me for my sad single state and making comments about my running out of time. If only he could be here as my partner.

If only, the two saddest words in the English language. But I can't complain, I knew exactly what I was getting into when I started seeing Jonathan. Of course he can't be here.

I just never thought it would feel like such

a cliché. Or quite so lonely.

'Do you want to hold Charlie?' asks Annabelle.

For a minute I think about telling her that if I want to hold something pink and squishy I'll go to the nearest fishing shop and buy some maggots. Why is it that people with kids have all the zeal of religious fanatics when it comes to converting their friends to the dark side? Is it because if they have to suffer broken nights, leaking boobs and puke on their clothes then the rest of us should too? Or is it, I wonder as I look at the soft curve of Charlie's check and his perfect rosebud lips, because having a baby really is the most wonderful experience in the world?

Will I ever be in a position where I'll be able to find out for myself?

Annabelle, dad and Great Auntie Ethel are looking at me expectantly. If I turn down the chance to hold little Charlie I'll be right up there with Rose West and Myra Hindley in the gallery of totally unnatural women. Taking a deep breath and hoping desperately Charlie doesn't chose the next five minute to empty his stomach over my new Chloe jacket, I hold out my arms.

'I'd love to.'

Annabelle passes the sleeping baby over and I settle his little head into the crook of my arm. Dark eyelashes flutter against his cheek and he makes a little whimper before settling back to sleep. He's all warm and sleepy and heavy in my arms.

'You're a natural,' says dad.

Annabelle nods. 'He doesn't go to everyone, Robyn.'

I feel ridiculously chuffed. Little Charlie is happy and contented in my arms. I'm not a failure as a woman after all. Take that everyone!

I drop a kiss onto the baby's cheek. My goodness, how impossibly soft his skin is! If Clinique could match this they'd make a fortune. He smells gorgeous too, a sweet milky smell mingled with baby powder, and he feels all plump and cuddly. Something deep inside me starts to melt.

'He's lovely, Annabelle,' I tell my cousin. 'You're really lucky.'

I'm taken aback to discover I mean every word. Oh Lord. I hope this isn't my biological alarm clock starting to ring. I'd put it on snooze when I was in my early twenties and I've been hoping it stays that way. Getting broody is so not an option. Can you imagine how complicated that would make everything?

Honour and duty satisfied I pass the baby back and watch him snuggle back into Annabelle's arms as she carries him over to the next group of relatives who coo and fuss obligingly.

'It's hard to believe you were like that

once,' dad sighs. 'I don't know where the years have gone, Robyn, I really don't.'

'You weren't there for most of them,' I point out. 'To be fair I was lucky if I saw you once a month.'

Dad picks up two glasses of champagne. 'Let's go and sit on the lawn. I can keep an eye on the boys from there and Great Auntie can't earwig.'

It is amazing just how much a very old and supposedly very deaf person *can* hear. One Christmas Auntie Ethel had horrified Pat by telling him she'd heard very word of his naughty telephone conversation to me. Pat had blanched and since I'd received no such call I'd just put it down to senility. But two years on I'm not so sure.

Dad and I sit on a bench beneath a beech tree and watch my brothers kicking a ball around. Tom and Tim are only eleven but already they've lost their baby features and are starting to grow into the men they'll become. With their mops of curly brown hair and peat soft eyes I see in them the resemblance to myself and to my father and it both saddens and comforts me. I'm sad because these little brothers are a remote part of my life but at the same time I love spending time with them and having a chance, albeit a belated one, to be a big sister. It's also strange to see my father in role as an active parent, not something I often experienced as a child being more often than not left in the car with a packet of crisps while dad propped up the bar/placed a bet/saw his latest girlfriend.

I sip my drink thoughtfully. Will Tom and Tim grow up to be no good cheating scumbags (my mother's expression) like my father? Or has dad really changed enough to bring them up as decent human beings who respect women?

'I won't make the same mistakes with them, you know,' dad says.

'Sorry?'

He nods towards the boys. 'I missed out on your childhood, Robyn. And I'm truly sorry for that. I'm sorry for hurting Anna too, not that she'll ever accept an apology.'

'Why should she, dad?' I shake my head. 'You broke her heart and left us in the lurch. How could anyone get over that?'

'We were too young. We should never have got married; it was bound to end in tears. Anna and I should have been a fling that burned itself out except...'

'Go on, dad, you can say it, except she got pregnant with me. I know I wasn't exactly planned.'

'But no less wanted,' dad covers my hand with his and I'm taken aback to notice the hairs that speckle it are now grey. 'You mustn't ever think that. Once we knew you were coming you were wanted, very much.

But I was only twenty-two, Robyn, and an immature twenty-two at that. I didn't know how to handle the responsibility,' he pauses, 'or Anna's moods. But I didn't question things because in those days you just got married. There were no unmarried mothers. It was a different world.'

'So you married her, big deal dad. Why do that and then cheat on mum?'

Dad looks down at the lawn. 'I'm not proud of myself, Robyn. I know there's no excuse for what I did so I'm not going to start making one now. All I can say is I felt trapped and I wanted an escape, not from you but from all the responsibility of trying to be a dad and a husband. That was why I messed around. I was looking for a way out.'

Tim kicks a football to Hannah.

'Goal!' he yells, punching the air with a fist. 'Did you see my goal, Dad?'

'It was brilliant!' calls Dad. 'David Beckham had better watch out!'

Tears tighten the back of my throat. 'So what's changed? Why's it different with the boys and Hannah?'

Why wasn't I enough to make you happy and keep you and mum together?

'I suppose it's because Hannah's the one for me.' He waves at Hannah who blows him a kiss before kicking the ball back to the squealing boys. 'Which sounds cheesy, I know, but it's true. I'm not saying she's better than your mum, darling, but she's a very different person and we have common ground. That means a lot, you know.'

I look him in the eye. 'Did you love mum?'

He sighs. 'Of course I did. What I had with Anna was the kind of passion that only comes once in a life time but sometimes that isn't enough. You can love someone with all your heart but know deep down that being together is never going to work out.'

I look at Hannah with her sensible bob and gentle face. There's no comparison to my mother. The two women make chalk and cheese look alike.

Maybe this is what would have happened to me if I hadn't found out about Patrick and Jo in time to call off our wedding? Would I have become as distrusting as my mother, moving from one man to the next always hoping one day someone might come along who will make everything all right? Maybe the relationship I have with Jonathan is actually ideal because both of us know exactly where we stand and can't get ever be hurt or disappointed?

It still doesn't stop me missing him, though.

'I'm sorry I let you down.' says dad. He looks so sad and tired as he says this that something in me relents a little.

I squeeze his hand. 'It's OK Dad, that's the past. I love spending time with you and

Hannah and the boys. It's lovely having little brothers.'

'They love you to bits,' dad smiles. 'It's Robyn this and Robyn that all day long. But I worry about you, sweetheart. You looked really sad today, and I don't think it was just thinking about the past, was it? Are you working too hard?'

'I'm flat out with Saffron Scott's wedding and my budget wedding is starting to spiral out of control,' I say quickly because I really don't want my father to start poking into the truth. Not that I'm sure what the truth is exactly, only that holding Charlie and being with my family has stirred up some very strange feelings.

'Is that the Aussie wedding?'

I nod, 'I have a very ambitious bride with a very tiny budget. At the minute I'm trying to find a venue for the reception, which is easier said than done.'

Dad jumps to his feet. 'Robyn, come with me a minute, there's someone I want you to meet. Someone who owes me a few favours.'

Perplexed I follow him across the lawn and onto the lichen speckled terrace. Dad is given to sudden impulses, of which I'm a prime example, and I'm used to his sudden enthusiasms by now.

'Adam,' says my father to a tall man with a face that droops just like Deputy Dog's, 'this is my daughter, Robyn.'

'Hi Robyn.' Adam turns away from the group of guests he's been chatting to and shakes my hand. His is moist and it's all I can do not to instantly wipe mine on my skirt.

'Adam's a friend of ours,' dad explains. 'He owns a conservatory and marquee company and put this one up for the christening.'

'It's called *Wicked Windows*,' Adam tells me proudly. 'We've just been commissioned to provide a glass exhibition house and marquee close to Hyde Park.'

'That's great,' I say politely.

But dad looks as though he's about to pop with excitement. 'Don't you see, Robyn? You could have the Aussie wedding in the marquee!

'Dad!' I laugh. 'You can't go around offering other peoples' marquees as wedding venues! Sorry Adam, please excuse my father!'

'It's a great idea,' dad says stubbornly.

He's right, it's brilliant but since I don't know Adam from ... well Adam, I don't feel comfortable inviting Julia and her entire wedding into his marquee.

'It's only standing empty before the exhibition opens,' says Adam, 'which seems a bit of a waste, now I come to think about it. You're more than welcome to use it if the dates fit.'

'Really?' My heart starts to rise like a hot air balloon. 'Are you sure?'

'Totally,' Adam assures me. 'I owe George

a favour anyway, he and Hannah took my tribe last weekend so my wife and I could go to Venice, and this is the least I can do. In fact I'm delighted to be able to help.' He opens his wallet and hands me a business card. 'Give me a call in the week and I'll see what I can do. If not that marquee then I'm bound to have another you could use.'

I'm so over the moon that I need oxygen and without thinking twice I hug both dad and Adam, spilling their drinks and scuffing the toes of my new Christian Louboutin Mary Janes, but who cares! I've got Jules and Bradley a venue!

Once I've replenished the drinks and buffed the toes of my shoes with my sleeve I wander along the terrace until I find a quiet spot. Leaning my elbows on the stone balcony I take a few deep breaths before fishing out my mobile phone and texting Jonathan. I'm so excited about finding this venue and I can't think of anyone I'd rather share my news with. Jonathan has had to listen to me stressing about Julia's wedding for weeks now so the least I can do is put him out of his misery.

But they say a watched mobile never beeps and after about ten minutes I give up waiting for a reply. Jonathan's probably too busy with Anita's family to text me back. He'll reply when he gets a minute, I'm sure.

Somehow though this thought doesn't

make me feel much better. I crumble lichen between my fingers and watch the other guests chatting and laughing on the lawn. Dad has joined in the football game, only now he and the twins are taking on Adam and his three children to lots of laughing and cries of 'Off side!' while Annabelle's husband pushes his eldest child on the swing while she bottle feeds the baby.

Am I the only single and childless person in the world? Is being able to eat toast in bed and read all night if I feel like it really compensation for the ache inside me, dull an insistent like emotional toothache?

But then I wonder, as little Charlie is sick all over Annabelle's beautiful John Rocha dress, do I actually have the perfect relationship? I have no mess, no ties and no fuss over family duties with Jonathan, only the best bits of being with someone. I have all the excitement, mind blowing sex and the presents that I could desire without the dirty socks on the floor, the ring round the bath and the puking babies.

It's perfect! I'm the luckiest girl in the world to be with a man who's so careful to make me feel like a princess.

And if I do feel undeniably lonely when everyone else leaves in pairs, or holding the hands of their yawning children, then it's a small price to pay for being with Jonathan.

Isn't it?

Chapter Nineteen

Oh. My. God. Just how much money have I spent today? Honestly, the pile of shopping bags is so high I can't see to the other side of the room. A heap of sage and pink carriers, delicate lingerie wrapped in the softest tissue paper, shoe boxes, brown paper bags with the sweetest pink ribbon handles from my favorite vintage store and my stunning new Emma Hope overnight bag have turned my bed into a shopoholic version of Tracey Emin's. When I met Saffron this morning for some shopping and an afternoon of pampering in The Sanctuary I'd fully prepared for some serious retail therapy, but this is something else.

I suppose the steam coming off my credit card was a little bit of a giveaway...

But what's a girl to do when the man of her dreams, the sexy handsome man who makes her insides turn to ice cream, calls up out of the blue and invites her on a romantic weekend away to Edinburgh? Does she:

a) tell him she's busy and can't make it

b) pack a tatty bag with her usual clothes

c) blow all this month's money on a major pampering session and new clothes

I think we all know the answer to that one girls, don't we?

Never mind, I can happily live on Asda's Value Beans until June if it means I can wear these stunning Gina shoes and the beautiful hand painted 1950s dress I unearthed in a tiny boutique just off Floral Street. In fact I may have to live off beans until Christmas seeing as I also splashed out on a pair of Gina sandals and a Stella McCartney night dress.

Er ... Christmas 2010 that is because I then had to buy a gorgeous Emma Hope overnight bag to pack my beautiful new clothes in. It just didn't seem right to use the tatty old wheelie bag I've had for years. I'm sure Jonathan's used to sweeping up to elegant hotels with stacks of Louis Vuitton luggage for valets to deal with and I can't be letting the side down. Jonathan's always groomed and stylish and I don't feel I have any choice but to do my best to keep up with him so what are a few more zeros on the credit card bill if it means I'm that little bit closer to being his perfect woman?

That probably sounds ridiculous and certainly Jonathan has never said anything to suggest he expects me to he perfect but I can't help feeling I need to always be that extra bit sparkly and special whenever we're together. Much as I love slobbing out in my ancient pyjamas with my hair scooped up in a clip I don't feel I can subject Jonathan to such a sight. With him I need to be always available, always immaculately groomed and always cheerful, the exact antithesis of Anita I suppose, but its bloody hard work. I'm constantly face packing, tweezing and painting my nails and my legs are so hairless they practically squeak when I walk, but it's a full time occupation.

Always beautiful and always happy, that's me. If I was one of Roger Hargreaves' characters I'd be Little Miss Prozac.

And, following today's shopping marathon, Little Miss Overdraft!

'This is my treat,' Saffron had announced when we'd checked into the Sanctuary, 'for all the hard work you've done so far.'

'It's my job!' I'd protested. 'And besides; I'm loving every minute of it!'

'Spending last weekend listening to Dad and the boys jamming is way beyond the call of duty.' Saffron had passed her platinum Amex to the supermodel receptionist. 'My ears are used to it but yours must have been bleeding. Are you sure you're happy to deal with the extra paparazzi attention now *Blue Smoke*'s playing at the reception?'

I'd been waking up in the night panicking about this but there was no way I was going to let Saffron know. She was paying me to deal with all those stresses and, although dealing with massive press interest in the reforming of one of the biggest rock groups of the sixties hadn't originally been part of the equation, I was determined to do exactly that.

'It'll be fine,' I'd said firmly.

'Great!' she smiled, collecting our swipe cards and heading towards the changing room. 'I knew that was what you'd say. I thought we could discuss the guest list after our treatments? Dad really wants Mick and Keith there but I'm not sure. And what about Jerry? Should I invite her too? It's a minefield.'

My chin was nearly on the heated floor.

'But don't worry about that right now.' Saffron passed me a towelling robe, as warm and fluffy as toasted marshmallow. 'Enjoy your flotation tank first. It's meant to be really relaxing.'

But after this bombshell a month in the flotation tank wouldn't have been enough to relax me. Ditto the salt body scrub, the deep cleansing facial and the Indian Head Massage. As Saffron lay by the Koi pool sipping wine and chatting excitedly about the expanding guest list my heart had flipped and flopped like the big orange fish beside us. If Hester got wind of this there would be Hell to pay. I'd have to be sharper than Gideon's entire Sabatier collection to stay ahead of her. Well, I'd wanted a challenge!

Be careful what you ask for...

After kissing Saffron goodbye it had been almost a shock to find myself back amidst the bustling afternoon crowds in the piazza. A bit light headed from the wine and the pampering, at least that was my excuse, I'd found myself wandering into Coco de Mer and gasping over delicate wisps of lace and silk that cost more than my usual mortgage payment. Some of the items made my face flame and others made my mind, and presumably other parts of the anatomy, boggle.

Maybe I ought to get out more? I'd thought, flipping through a rail of whips. I'd obviously been living a very dull life, although hopefully that was all about to change now I was seeing Jonathan. And a whole weekend together too! I could hardly wait. It was just going to be so perfect. I could picture us eating a lazy breakfast in bed, licking croissant crumbs from our fingers and sharing kisses sweeter than any pain au chocolate before exploring the city hand in hand. It was going to be Heaven!

Eventually I'd plumped for sweetest pink Bo Peep frilly knickers and matching bra. They were probably the most modest garments in the shop but when I tried them on I loved the way they moulded to my body and made my boobs look like two perfect scoops of vanilla ice cream. It was worth every penny to feel that sexy and I'd passed my card over with out thinking twice. Besides, I regularly spent that much on Dolly so it was high time I had a treat!

As I pack my new lingerie into the Emma Hope bag excitement fizzes through my blood stream. I can hardly wait to be alone with Jonathan. This weekend is going to be perfect. Although neither of us has said anything we both know going away as a couple moves our relationship to a whole new level and takes something that began as a bit of fun onto a far more serious footing. Where we go from here I don't know but I'm looking forward to finding out.

My mobile interrupts my thoughts (why did I let Gideon put Crazy Frog on it?) and I go into a tail spin when I can't find it just in case Jonathan's calling to say he's outside. It wouldn't be the first time, Oh Lord! I haven't got any makeup on and I'm sure my body is still covered in salt. Locating my mobile beneath a pile of pink and sage tissue paper my heart sinks when I realise it's Faye. I've ignored two calls already today. If I disregard anymore she'll start to get suspicious because I'm normally super glued to my mobile.

'Babe! Where've you been?' asks Faye when I answer. 'I've been calling you all day!'

'Sorry, hon,' I fold my new Agnes B cardigan carefully and drop it into the bag. 'I went to The Sanctuary with Saffron. They don't let you have phones on in there.'

That's not *strictly* lying, is it?

'I was starting to think you were hiding from me.'

'Don't be daft! I'm flat out with weddings, that's all.'

'Si and I were only saying earlier that we've hardly seen you lately, so I had an idea. How about you come over tomorrow and have dinner with us? I'll cook that lemon chicken dish you like so much. Then we'll kick Si out and have a girly night in while he sees the rugby boys? We can watch *Titanic* and blub without him making sarky comments! Sounds good, huh?'

She's right. It does sound good. Hanging out with Faye and Simon used to he one of my favourite ways to spend time when I was single and since I'm still single as far as Faye's concerned it's becoming increasingly difficult to make excuses.

'That sounds lovely,' I say. 'I'd love to come...'

'But?'

'I'm not here this weekend, babes. I'm going away.'

'Are you?' Faye sounds taken aback. 'You didn't say. Where are you going?'

Oh God. I am such a crap liar. I must never, ever play poker. If I spontaneously combust now, leaving nothing but a smoking pair of Gina sandals on my fluffy white rug then I only have myself to blame.

'I'm going to a Wedding Fayre,' I say, crossing fingers, toes and basically everything crossable. 'It's in Edinburgh so I'm flying up first thing tomorrow.'

'That sounds fun.' Faye pauses for a moment. 'Si's busy on Saturday. Maybe I could come with you? We could do the wedding stuff and then have a good trawl round the city. The shops are supposed to be fantastic.'

She's not wrong. Every second since Jonathan invited me to join him, which hasn't been spent beautifying and shopping, has been spent surfing the net and finding out as much as I can about Edinburgh. It looks an amazing city; from the castle that dominates the urban skyline to the chic wine bars to the streets of funky boutiques and antique shops, and I can hardly wait to start exploring.

But with Jonathan. Not Faye.

'I miss you Robyn,' she says, 'It would be fun to catch up.'

Oh God. It's official. I'm a bigger cow than Ermintrude.

'I'm so sorry, babes, but I'm going with a client. We've booked a room and everything. I'd have loved you to come otherwise.'

'Oh. Right.' For a second there's something really bleak in Faye's voice. Then I wonder if I've imagined it when she says briskly, 'I'll just have to tell Si he can't go into the office again and drag him to Ikea or something then, won't I?

'Good luck,' I shudder. 'You and every other couple in London!'

At least Faye is in an *official* couple. She doesn't really need me when she has Si to keep her company. And if Faye goes to Ikea with Si she won't have to hide behind the bookshelves if they meet someone they know, will she? Some of us don't have any choice except to go to the other end of the country in order to be together.

We ring off and I return to my packing but somehow my metallic bag doesn't glow quite so brightly and the beautiful lingerie looks obvious rather than delicately sexy. I cover it up with some tissue paper and sigh.

Why does everything have to be so complicated?

Chapter Twenty

OK. Here's a handy hint for anyone who ever goes on a romantic mini break with her lover: unless masochism is your thing do not, I repeat do not, wear your brand new sexy lingerie for the journey. Put all ideas of mile high clubs or kissing passionately in cabs out of your mind because believe me it will not happen. You'll be in far too much agony.

I spent ages this morning straightening my hair, applying my make up and of course cantilevering my cleavage into my beautiful new bra. The knickers too were a miracle of engineering and while waiting for Jonathan to collect me I'd admired my raised rear end in the hall mirror. Eat your heart out J-Lo! I'd never felt so sexy in all my life! I could hardly wait for Jonathan to unwrap me.

But six hours later it's a very different story. This underwear is strictly designed with seduction in mind which probably means it isn't normally worn for long. Not quite the thing for a two hour delay at Heathrow, an hour and a half plane journey and then a crawl through the lunch time traffic into Edinburgh. Sitting next to Jonathan in the taxi I'm trying hard to pretend the under wire isn't about to puncture my lungs and that the boning is severely restricting my breathing. Breathing's over rated in my opinion. But ouch! I wince as the taxi humps over a speed hump, only a man could have designed such a heinous piece of torture.

Gingerly rearranging my tortured torso I try to smile and poor Jonathan looks alarmed by the manic grimace I shoot in his direction. God, it even hurts to smile. In fact it's agony to do anything which remotely resembles being alive. I take my hat off to those Victorian women with their hour glass figures. No wonder they were always having hysterics and fainting. Having a body like this is seriously hard work.

'Are you OK?' Jonathan asks.

'I'm just excited,' I tell him. 'I can never sit still when I'm excited.'

'Those are two of the things I love about you.' Jonathan takes my hand in his. 'I love your energy and enthusiasm.'

Energy and enthusiasm? That would give Si hysterics after all the times he had to drag me out of bed to get to my lectures. I'm the girl who makes arthritic slugs look active. I must have done a better job than I'd realised of being the bright, shiny and always up for fun Robyn.

And hold on! Did he just say that my energy and enthusiasm were two of the things he *loves* about me? Is Jonathan saying that he *loves* me?

'Oh look!' Jonathan says hastily, probably realising that he's dropped an entire TV show of Clangers. 'Here we are. The Balburnie Boutique Hotel. What do you think?'

I think I want to get out of my underwear, but that's a bit forward seeing as we've just arrived!

'It's gorgeous!' I breathe, because it really is. Our cab has pulled up in a cobbled street full of stunning Georgian Houses. Set back from the road in its own private garden is our hotel, a beautiful honey hued mansion house with sash windows like demure downcast eyes and window boxes that spill nasturtiums and greenery.

'I knew you'd love it.' Jonathan pays the cab driver. 'It's a great place to stay.'

'You've stayed here before?'

'A couple of times. It's pretty special. And it will be perfect for you – we're only a stroll away from some of Edinburgh's best shopping.'

As I try to manoeuvre myself out of the cab, which is easier said than done when you have to walk like a Thunderbirds puppet, I try hard to ignore the questions forming in my mind. Questions like *who did he come here with?* And *did he come here with Anita?*

Questions which if I'm honest I'd rather not know the answers to at the moment.

We check in at reception and a porter escorts us up a sweeping staircase. As I follow I take in the understated elegance and imagine what a lovely setting for a wedding this could be. Just the sort of place I'd love for my own wedding...

Yeah. Right, Robyn.

'The Burns Suite,' the porter announces proudly, turning the key. 'It's one of our finest suites and it has a wonderful view of the city.'

Jonathan plucks a twenty pound note from his wallet and the porter practically falls over himself to help us further before backing out of the room.

'Alone at last!' Jonathan grins, 'What do you think of the room? Will it do?'

Will it do? Nobody has ever taken me to a place like this before. When Pat was touring the comedy circuit, in the hand to mouth days before *Nosh*, we thought we were lucky to make it to a Travelodge, but this is something else! The room is light and airy, feminine yet tasteful in a manner that probably cost thousands of pounds to create, and which speaks of a calm and understated luxury. Champagne's cooling in an ice bucket by the bed, flowers are strewn across the counterpane and filmy lace curtains are fluttering in the warm breeze.

'It's perfect!' I breathe.

I kick off my shoes and pad across the thick pile of the carpet and lean on the broad window ledge. The view is absolutely stunning, from my vantage point I can see across the formal courtyard garden and over the higgledy piggledy chimneypots right across to the castle perched upon its volcanic crag. Then past the river and across the miles to the glittering silver ribbon of the Firth of Forth.

I turn and smile at him. 'This is wonderful Jonathan! I can't wait to explore the city. There's so much to see I hardly know where to start!'

'I've a confession to make,' says Jonathan as he uncorks the champagne. He pours a brimming glass and hands it to me. 'I've arranged a couple of meetings for this afternoon. You don't mind do you? I am supposed to be working after all, sexy and distracting as you are!'

'Oh.' My euphoria pops away like the champagne bubbles in perfect sync with my dreams of our lovely afternoon wandering through the ancient city.

'Don't look so disappointed, angel, I'll make it up to you, I promise.' He puts the bottle down and presses kisses onto the top of my head. 'I'd much rather be with you than shut in a room with a stuffy load of old lawyers. Believe me, I'll be thinking about you for every single second, thinking about holding you and touching you and having you in my arms all night long.' His voice is hoarse. 'I've thought about nothing but you all week.'

He folds me into his arms and I feel the corded muscles of his arms tighten as he presses me against his chest, my breasts in their torturous bra squashed against his beautiful Turnbull and Asser shirt. It's not quite the romantic scenario I was hoping for because I can hardly breathe. Has anyone ever been killed by their under wire before?

'Jonathan,' I gasp, 'I-'

'Don't say anything.' He stares into my eyes with the burning intensity of a Barbara Cartland hero. 'Just let me hold you. God, you're the most sexy woman I've ever seen.'

Trussed up in my lingerie I feel about as sexy as a turkey dished up for Christmas lunch, but who am I to argue? Besides I've paid a fortune for these scraps of lace so I may as well get my money's worth. And I can't wait to get them off, although maybe not for the reasons I'd originally intended!

'I think we need to freshen up after the flight,' murmurs Jonathan, kicking open a door concealed in the wall to reveal a bathroom of Wembley Stadium proportions. In the corner is a huge bath with beautiful golden taps surrounded by gilt-framed mirrors. Piles of thick fluffy white bath towels wait for the lucky bathers while pots of expensive bath oils beg to be poured into hot water.

Jonathan lowers me carefully onto the soft carpet, gently running his hands up and down my body while I shiver in delight. He loosens my hair and spreads it around me before moving his hands lower. Jonathan knows exactly how to turn me on and my heart is doing a clog dance. He has to be the most beautiful man who's ever breathed oxygen. And he wants *me*. That in itself is a massive turn on.

'I think we need to try that bath, don't you?' he whispers, those dark navy eyes sparkling above me.

'Absolutely,' I agree, not daring to move a

muscle. Those knickers are tighter than I thought and it's not easy trying to look sexy and suck in your stomach at the same time.

'Well then,' Jonathan's hands were suddenly inside my dress, underneath the scaffolding of the evil bra and caressing my nipples, 'we'd better get you out of those dirty clothes.'

I gasp as he pulls the dress from me. His hands tenderly skim my skin and as desire ripples through me I reach out for him, my lips and tongue exploring and teasing. Somehow we manage to wrestle his clothes off too and Jonathan stands before me like a beautiful Greek statue, so muscled and as hard as marble. Laughing he picks me up and lowers me onto him, his strong arms clasping me tightly and sliding me down his body. I cling to him and curl my legs around his waist, loving the feeling of being so close to him.

I lose track of time as we move together around the bathroom, clawing, gasping and holding each other desperately. Eventually, up to my neck in bubbles of Floris, my knuckles turning white as I grip the edge of the bath, ripple after ripple of pure pleasure that make me cry out, followed seconds later by Jonathan's shout of triumph. Then we slump against the porcelain and slop water all over the carpet.

This man is amazing and more addictive than any Class A drug. They probably have entire therapy sessions at the Priory dedicated to Jonathan Broadhead.

I hope I don't have to check myself in too soon!

'Well, Miss Hood,' Jonathan bites my shoulder playfully. 'I must remember to take you to Edinburgh again.'

'You haven't taken me to Edinburgh yet.' I point out. 'We never even got round to lunch.' As if in agreement my stomach rumbles.

'Oh angel,' Jonathan's already reaching out for a towel. 'I'm sorry, but I can't possibly have lunch now, I'm way off schedule.' He drops a kiss onto the top of my head. 'We'll have to take a rain cheek on that one I'm afraid. Dinner later though! I know the most fantastic restaurant off William Street.'

He's out of the bath now and stalking across the room. I watch rivulets of water trickle down the smooth skin and race over his tight buttocks and feel a twinge of loss. Jonathan's mind is miles away from me now, racing towards contracts and clauses and other lawyery stuff. As my knowledge of the law is gleaned from *Ally McBeal* I'm a bit vague but I can tell when a man is thinking about other things. I'm on ice like the champagne.

'Feel free to order whatever you like from room service,' he continues as he slips into a crested bathrobe and pads into the bedroom. 'Put it all on my bill.'

I close my eyes. Why do I suddenly feel as though I ought to be waiting to be paid? It must be the Catholic guilt thing that comes of spending my formative years in a convent school. Feminism Robyn! I tell myself firmly as I hear Jonathan gathering his things together. Women chained themselves to railings so you can be here now, sexually satisfied and independent. What exactly are you expecting him to do? Declare undying love and cancel all his meetings just because he's made love to you?

This is the downside of being a hopeless romantic.

'I'll be back at six,' Jonathan reappears in a fresh suit.

'You're going right now?' I can't keep the disappointment from my voice. I'd pictured a nice cosy lunch, followed by a romantic stroll in the city. Hanging out alone in the hotel suite hadn't quite figured in my plans.

He strokes my cheek tenderly. Just one look from those eyes and I'm lost.

'I'll be as quick as I can, OK?'

'Ok,' I let him kiss me and tell myself I don't mind but in fact I'm starting to feel like one of those Bond girls who once shagged by Bond is left alone to await a grisly fate. I half expect to see a string dripping poison appear above me in wait for my post coital snooze.

'You're fantastic.' Jonathan flicks his

tongue against mine just long enough to turn me on again. 'I'll be back soon.'

He gives me a kiss so toe curlingly sexy that I sigh in delight. This is more like it! Just as I reach for him, to tease and hopefully to persuade him to jump back into the lukewarm water, there's a polite but sharp knock at the door.

'Mr. Broadhead? Your car's here.'

'Christ!' Jonathan pulls away and grins sheepishly. 'What are you trying to do to me? I was almost–' He sits back on his heels. 'Are you trying to make me miss my car?'

I smile, feeling every inch like Joan Collins in her Dynasty heyday, and blow some frothy bubble bath at him. But this seems to make him a little impatient as he brushes it from his lapel and springs to his feet.

'I can't miss this meeting, not even for you, Robyn Hood,' he tells me sternly whilst simultaneously combing his hair in the large and very steamed up mirror. He seems to be taking an awful long time to do it, but then I'm used to Pat (who always looked like he'd just woken up) and Si (who has an allergic reaction to combs). I guess if I was as beautiful as Jonathan I'd preen myself too. Perhaps Narcissus had a point?

'I'll have to shoot,' straightening his tie as he goes Jonathan turns in the doorway to smile. 'Have a lovely afternoon, Robs.'

And then he's gone.

I clamber out the bath and pad across the carpet feeling like an extra from a spaghetti western. Wrapping myself in a fluffy bathrobe I wander into the bedroom, pour a glass of bubbly and pause by the dressing table. What I see makes me groan. Rather than the tumbling-haired, sexy-eyed goddess that I'd imagined I see instead a piggy-eyed Medusa lookalike with sausage pink skin and makeup halfway down her face, Very attractive. Not. Feeling my confidence draining away with the bath water I flop onto the bed. I wonder if Anita ever looks this rough?

I'm not going to let myself go there.

In reality Jonathan spends all of Friday and a good chunk of Saturday working and I explore Edinburgh on my own. There's lots to look at from the funky boutiques in William Street to Princes Street where Karen Millen and Jo Malone are vying for my purse. But, apart from the fact that I've already flexed my flexible friend a bit too far this week, it isn't the same on my own. Everywhere I look I see people all coupled up in a totally licit way; holding hands as they peer into antique shop windows or sipping lattes at pavement cafés and it makes me ache inside. This wasn't what I'd had in mind at all when I'd packed my bag with such excitement. Being all alone in this beautiful romantic city really sucks.

Things perk up on Saturday afternoon though because Jonathan finally tears himself away from meetings and we spend a happy couple of hours wandering around galleries and exploring the city. We have so much fun together that I manage to put aside the complications of our situation, complications which seem to be more apparent with every day that passes, and am content to just enjoy the moment. Hand in hand we stroll around the castle and steal kisses like teenagers before returning to the hotel for a blissful hour before trying out the bath again and getting ready to go out for dinner.

And what a dinner it is! Jonathan has certainly spared no expense and has reserved a table at Le Sept, one of the most exclusive restaurants in the city. I feel like a princess in my beautiful new dress and Gina shoes and he's so attentive and generous that I'm consumed with guilt for being so put out that he was working earlier. Nothing is too much and everything he does has one sole aim, which is to please me. How could I have been so ungrateful? I'm so lucky to be able to spend any time with him at all.

Stuffed, warm and rather sleepy I push my plate away and place my hands on my full stomach.

'That was amazing. I don't think I'll eat again for about a month though!'

'Mmm,' Jonathan swirls his port thoughtfully. 'Every time I eat here it just gets better.'

'You've come here before?'

He nods. 'A couple of times, that's why I made a reservation for this evening. I knew how good it was, Robyn, and nothing but the best for you.'

It's on the tip of my tongue to ask him exactly who he's been here with but I'm scared as to what the answer might be. I don't really have the right to be upset if he's been here with Anita because I've always known he's married. Some of the gloss slides off the day as her wraith slips in between us. I take a sip of blood red port and try to rationalise with myself. Jonathan's married. He was always married. Nothing's changed. A small knot of unease tightens in my stomach.

Once the bill's paid we step outside into the velvet soft night, Jonathan takes my hand and we walk slowly along the road. My hand's warm and snug in his and it feels so right to be together like this that I push my worries aside.

'Excuse me, sir. Buy a rose for the lady?'

A flower seller appears at Jonathan's elbow carrying a basket in which nestle four velvety red roses. I cringe inwardly. The last thing I want is for Jonathan to be put on the spot. Everyone knows the symbolism of a red rose, after all!

Jonathan raises his eyebrows. 'Just the

one? I think she's worth a lot more than that.' He reaches into his jacket and plucking out his wallet hands the flower seller four twenty pound notes. 'I'll have them all!'

'Jonathan! Don't he silly!' I protest, but loving this overblown romantic gesture nonetheless. 'One rose will do!'

'Indeed it will not,' says Jonathan, gathering the roses into a bouquet. 'I've left you alone far too much this weekend, Robyn, and this is just the first of many ways that I'm going to make it up to you.'

'You're mad,' I say, burying my face in the soft petals.

'Mad about you,' murmurs Jonathan. 'But I think you already know that, don't you?'

Jonathan undoes his silk tie and uses it to lash the stems together, then he hands me the flowers with a flourish. I feel like a heroine in a romantic novel and I practically float across pavement.

Well either that or the Gina shoes are higher than I'd realised!

In any case no one has ever made me feel this special in my life. I look up at Jonathan's sculpted and handsome face and my heart constricts with the oddest pang. Could he really be the one?

I'm still pondering this question as I step aside to allow a crowd of suited men and women pass us by. Their faces are flushed with good humour and alcohol as they call to each other. Then, to my surprise, I realize they're waving to Jonathan. Instinctively I hide the roses behind my back.

'Jonathan!' shrills a woman with a sharp steel grey bob and a red gash of a mouth. 'Fancy seeing you here! I thought you were having an early night?'

'Yes, you great pussy!' hollers another, all red cheeked and glittery-eyed. 'After wrestling that contract all morning you said you were too exhausted for a night out.'

'Amanda. Clive,' Jonathan's fingers slip away from mine and he air kisses the woman and shakes hands with her companion. 'What a lovely surprise to see you here. These guys are from the legal team I was working with today,' he adds to me.

'More of a surprise to see you,' remarks Amanda and her eyes, cold as sea washed glass, flicker over me. 'And this is?'

I stick out my right hand and shake her hand. 'I'm Robyn. Robyn Hood.'

And if any of them makes a crack about my name I'll shove my roses so far up their backsides they'll be sneezing petals for a month!

'Robyn's my events manager,' says Jonathan smoothly. 'She's joined me for this evening seeing as I'm at a loose end.'

'How very kind of her,' says Amanda, but as she looks at me I get the distinct feeling she knows *exactly* what I've joined him for and suddenly all the roses and expensive hotels and wonderful romantic afternoons seem cheap. 'An events organiser?'

'Apparently so.' I mutter.

Jonathan chats easily to the other lawyers for a few minutes before they continue on their noisy way.

'Phew,' he says. 'That was close.'

I bite my lip. 'Jonathan, why did you say that?'

'Say what?' he tries to take my hand again but I keep the fingers curled up in my palm.

'Tell them that I'm your events manager?'

Jonathan looks puzzled. 'But that's exactly what you do. Events manager is a perfectly honest description of your job, isn't it? What did you want me to say?'

I stare up at his handsome face, the jet black lashes, the sapphire eyes and those strong kissable lips and all of a sudden I feel uncertain.

Where exactly is this relationship going?

And more to the point where do I want it to go?

Chapter Twenty-One

June

Why is it that on days when you need everything to go smoothly Fate always decides to give you the finger? So far today I've had a bill from the Inland Revenue, a rogue red sock has turned my whites an alluring shade of salmon pink and just to really make my day Dolly's decided to get a flat tyre on the way back from the supermarket.

'I don't believe it!' I howl, thumping my head against the steering wheel. 'I haven't got time for this!'

I'm supposed to be meeting Saffron and Fergus at *Hush*, a discreet Covent Garden wine bar, to discuss the latest developments with the wedding. Or perhaps that should be to discuss *some* of the latest developments because I've no intention of telling them about my mother's sudden obsession with coir matting. The 'natural' look is all very well but it would make a really unsteady table covering and as for the burns on the guests' elbows ... it doesn't bear thinking about.

Well, no way is mum having her way on this. I might feel a bit guilty about throwing a few red herrings in her direction in order to put Hester off the scent but there's nothing wrong with the white linen and purple damask we've already selected. Nothing wrong with it at all apart from the fact mum has a store room full of coir matting that she bought on a whim and is absolutely desperate to get rid of I'm going to have to put my foot down.

Hard.

But in the meantime I'm stuck at the side of the road with time trickling away, bags full of defrosting food and a car that's going nowhere fast. There's only one thing for it. Much as I hate to admit defeat and fly in the face of feminism (sorry Germaine) I need a man to help me out. Flipping open my mobile I speed dial Jonathan only to be diverted straight to answer phone. This isn't unusual but today it makes me feel really annoyed. Sometimes I can't help feeling Jonathan gets all the good bits of a relationship – the romantic assignations, the sparkly compliant girlfriend and of course the sex – and none of the crappy bits like the food shopping and the flat tyres.

And sometimes I feel really lonely, which is ridiculous. Isn't it?

'Flat tyre?' says Simon, when I phone him. 'Can't you call the AA?'

'They hate me, remember? No more call outs as long as I've got Dolly. I know this is really cheeky, Si, but could you come and help? I'm by Kensall Green Tube.'

'I'd love to, Robs, but I'm snowed under at work right now.'

'On Saturday?' I'm taken aback.

He sighs. 'Afraid so, things are crazy here. Can you change the wheel if I talk you through it?'

'Maybe,' I say doubtfully. I've seen Keith change wheels so maybe I could have a go. On the other hand I've watched *ER* loads of times too but I'm hardly qualified to do a heart transplant.

'Come on, Robs,' says Si. 'Whatever happened to girl power?'

I'm not sure I ever had any to be honest but maybe it's time I got some? Besides, how hard can changing a wheel really be?

The answer to this question is pretty darn hard actually. As I tuck the mobile under my chin and struggle with jacks and nuts and gloopy black oil I start to see Keith in a whole new light. I break two nails trying to lift my spare wheel from its hidey hole and almost weep when I smear grime all over my lovely Alice Temperley shift dress. By the time the wheel's changed I'm as hot in the June sunshine as the melting tarmac and running seriously behind schedule. I tighten the nuts as instructed by Simon and collapse against the bonnet.

'Easy, wasn't it?' says Simon cheerfully

from his air conditioned office.

'Quite frankly, no. Splitting the atom was probably simpler.'

He laughs. 'Look, babes, I've got to get on. Fancy popping over later and catching up properly? I can give you a lesson in car maintenance!'

'Tempting though that sounds I'm busy tonight,' I say. At least I hope I am. I'm still waiting for Jonathan to confirm. Anita's supposed to be going to Frankfurt for a conference but when we last spoke he wasn't sure if she was flying tonight or first thing tomorrow.

'Maybe another time,' Si doesn't give me the third degree thank God but I still feel bad. I really do mean to make the time to see him and Faye but it's so hard when I never know for certain what's happening with Jonathan.

Simon rings off and I drive home, praying for all I'm worth that I've put the wheel on right and don't end up a splat of Robyn jam on the A40. Luckily Fate is on my side this once and I make it back in one piece. By now I'm running so late that I only have time for a quick shower and have to forgo washing and straightening my hair. In the humidity my curls have gone wild so I scoop my hair into a quick up do and shove in some glittery clips to hold it all in place. Then I slick on some lipstick and mascara, slip into my floaty Ghost dress and the Gina sandals I bought for my Scottish trip and dash for the tube. With any luck I should just about make it to *Hush* in time.

But luck it seems is off on her holidays because there's a signal failure on the Piccadilly line and by the time I emerge from the fetid depths of Covent Garden Tube my dress is sticking limply to my limbs and springy spirals of hair are escaping from the clips. I feel sticky and gritty and out of sorts. I'm really late and I hate being late. It looks so unprofessional.

Outside the heat's intensified and the piazza has a Mediterranean feel as tourists, bright as butterflies in summer clothes, throng the streets and soak up the rays while lunching at pavement cafés. Chatter and laughter fill the air and I feel some of my tension slip away. By the time I enter the air conditioned bar I'm smiling again. No wonder people in warm climates are more relaxed and happy than the British. It's really hard to be grumpy on a lovely sunny day.

'Robyn!' A tall blonde man waves at me from the bar. 'Over here!'

'Fergus!' I weave my way to his side. 'I'm so sorry I'm late. I've had the day from Hell and its only lunchtime!'

'Don't worry, I've only just got here myself,' Fergus kisses my cheek. 'Saffron can't make it at all so you're one better than her.

There's been some crisis at work apparently and she went tearing off to *Scorching*. So you're stuck with me, I'm afraid. Hope I'm good enough.'

'You're more than good enough, Fergus! It's your wedding too.'

'True,' he smiles. 'But just in case you needed some extra input I've managed to rope Matt into joining us.'

'Matt?' I echo.

'My best man? You met him I think?'

'I certainly did,' I say grimly. Matt had done a brilliant job of distracting my mother, so a million Brownie points there, but his constant joking around had really been wearing. Saffron and mum might have found him hilarious but some of us had had work today.

'Talking about me?' Right on cue here's Matt now, his blue eyes crinkling as he smiles at us.

'Robyn was wondering if you've got the iguana with you,' says Fergus.

'Certainly not!' Matt pulls a mock offended face. 'He's not old enough to drink.'

'But we are,' says Fergus. 'What would you like, Robyn?'

'I'd love a martini,' I say. 'But are you guys sure you wouldn't rather reschedule for another time when Saffron's available? I really don't mind if you've got other things you'd rather do.'

'Much as I'd love to be on the golf course

Saffron would kill me if I skipped this meeting,' Fergus laughs. 'There's urgent place settings and vow writing to discuss apparently, and Matt's desperate to find out more about his Best Man's duties.'

'Any excuse to have a drink,' says Matt.

'So I'll get the beers in,' says Fergus. 'Martini for you, Robyn. Matt?'

'A Bud for me please,' Matt decides. 'Shall we grab a table?'

As we make our way through the busy bar Matt rests his hand in the small of my back and I'm surprised to discover I like this gesture. It's gentlemanly rather than sexual though, there's nothing sleazy about Matt, but his hand is firm and warm against my body. Now he's not grubbing around in the dirt looking at insects he's actually quite attractive.

It isn't disloyal to Jonathan to think this, is it? I'm just admiring Matt the same way I'd admire a nice pair of shoes or a painting; appreciating his attractive qualities doesn't mean I love Jonathan any less.

'What are you thinking about?' asks Matt.

Thank goodness he can't read my mind!

'Are you thinking about the wedding?'

'Of course!' That's not a technically a lie. Matt's the best man so I *was* thinking about the wedding in a roundabout way.

'I'm really looking forward to it,' Matt says. 'I'm working really hard on my speech, there's a couple of good sheep jokes I thought I'd use and a mother-in-law one. What do you reckon?'

'Uh, well, it depends on the jokes,' I begin before the twinkle in his eyes gives it away. 'Very funny, Matt!'

'Sorry,' Matt doesn't look anything of the kind. 'You're just such fun to tease, Robyn. I love the way you blush when you try not to be embarrassed.'

'I'm not blushing. My cheeks are flushed from the heat. It's eighty degrees today.'

'And about minus eighty degrees in this air con,' Matt gives me that lopsided smile.

Yes, how I can feel hot in the arctic air con is one of life's great mysteries. I glare at Matt, wishing he'd let up on the kidding around. I'm not very good at being teased these days and neither do I appreciate the constant jokes. Another Patrick in the making is the last thing I need from a Best Man. Feeling annoyed I tune out Matt's jokey retelling of a friend's stag night traumas and busy myself by checking my mobile phone for messages. While Matt chats away merrily I scroll through all the sweet texts from Jonathan that I've saved. I can't wait to see him later.

Fergus returns with the drinks and I'm delighted that for all his kidding about wanting to play golf he's actually really keen to discuss the wedding. And it's quite sweet how earnest Matt is about his role as best man. By the time I've worked my way through several drinks my notebook is filled with ideas and avenues to explore and the two men seem more clued up about their duties. Matt's looking forward to planning the stag night but, thank goodness, has agreed to hold it a week before the wedding. That's a big relief because I'm already certain he'll come up with something crazy. I did a wedding last year where some jokers put the bridegroom on the Eurostar as a joke. Flying to Paris to rescue him had been above the call of duty but proof that I'm dedicated to my job! The best man had footed the cost for that.

Half way through telling this story as a warning to Matt I get a phone call that makes my heart plummet. It's the photographer friend of Gideon who's promised to take the photos at Brad and Julia's wedding calling to say he's been offered paid work on the same day. Although I totally understand why he's letting me down it's a huge blow. I'd really hoped to get Brad and Jules a great photographer for free because a decent portfolio costs thousands. What little money they did have has long been spoken for.

I snap the phone shut and tug at one of my stray curls. I've got a digital camera so I guess I could have a go but being from the cutting tops of heads off/lopping off feet/leaving the lens cap on school of photography it's a bit of a gamble.

'What's up?' asks Matt. 'And don't say nothing, I can see you're upset. Spill the beans.'

I put the phone down with a sigh. 'I'm arranging a budget wedding for an Australian couple I know and the photographer's just let me down. They're absolutely brassic and since he was going to take the pictures for free as a favour it's going to cause major problems. I'll probably end up taking the pictures myself now.'

'Matt can give you some lessons,' suggests Fergus.

'Any time,' grins Matt.

I shake my head. 'I'm hopeless. It would be like getting Leonardo da Vinci to teach colouring in!'

'I'm rubbish at colouring in, I could never keep inside the lines, but I can take photos, or so I'm told.' Matt leans forward and the afternoon sun turns his hair to a golden halo. 'When's the wedding?'

I name the date and then sigh. 'It's way too soon. I'll never find a replacement now. Back to the drawing board.'

'I'm not working that weekend,' says Matt slowly. 'Why don't I take the pictures for your friends?'

I wait for the punch line or for Matt to crack up and cry, 'Not really! Fooled you!' but he doesn't. In fact he looks serious for the first time all afternoon.

'Seriously,' Matt says. 'I'm not booked for anything else.'

'That's a really kind offer,' I sigh, 'but I don't think they could afford you. They've blown the budget on plane tickets for their folks and food and beer for the barbie reception.'

'They're having a barbie for the reception? There's no way you're keeping me away in that case. When I went travelling I spent six months in Sydney and believe me there's nothing that beats the way Aussies barbeque. I'll do the photographs for free in return for a few burgers.'

As he says this Matt puts on a broad Australian accent and licks his lips. I start to giggle when he goes on to describe the hat with corks he could bring and the Rolf Harris cassette he has somewhere at home.

'I'm sure I could find a couple of kangaroo steaks and some possum sausages to bring along too,' he adds, his wide grin revealing a quirky chipped tooth. 'Ever tried those?'

I pull a face. 'It's a wedding reception, not *I'm a Celebrity get me out of here!*'

'You've not lived until you've tasted a roo burger. Anyway, the offer's there. I'm more than happy to help out.'

I can hardly believe it. A prize winning photographer is volunteering to take the pictures for Brad and Jules free of charge? I can't turn that down.

'I don't want to impose.'

'Don't be silly. Here,' Matt opens his wallet and pulls out a business card. 'There's my number. Call me with the date and I'll make certain to keep that day clear in my diary.'

I pocket the card gratefully.

'I thought you hated doing wedding photography?' says Fergus. 'You told me it's your golden rule to avoid it like the plague.'

Now it's Matt's turn to look rather flustered. Knocking back the dregs of his Bud he gives Fergus a faux glare. 'I only said that to get out of doing your wedding, mate. All those moaning celebrities wanting me to capture their best sides? No thanks.'

'Right,' Fergus says slowly.

Matt gets to his feet. 'Besides, it sounds like a great party and if I can help Robyn's friends in the process so much the better. Is the inquisition over?'

Fergus holds up his hands. 'Sorry.'

Matt shrugs on a rather crumpled linen jacket. 'Give me a ring, Robyn, and we'll fix a time to talk to Brad and Julia about what they'd like.'

'I thought we were on a pub crawl this afternoon? Where are you off to in such a hurry?' asks Fergus

'Nowhere exciting,' says Matt.

'I don't believe you. You're off on a hot date, aren't you?' I tease.

Matt smiles. 'I will end up red and sweaty by the end of it, but I don't think playing squash with my brother counts as a hot date! Why, are you jealous?'

'Jealous! As if!' I squeak before I notice that he's laughing.

'Very funny, Matt.'

'Stop winding Robyn up,' Fergus tells him. 'She's got enough stresses with all the weddings without you making things worse.'

'Sorry,' Matt says, kissing me goodbye, his golden stubble deliciously rough against my skin. 'I just think she looks so sexy when she gets cross. Joke!' he adds quickly. 'You look sexy all the time, Robyn, even when you pull those miserable faces!'

Fergus shakes his head. 'No wonder you're single, mate.'

Matt sighs. 'That's why I stick to insects and iguanas. At least they appreciate me.'

'I'll appreciate you,' I say, because he looks all sad now, 'if you really mean it about taking the wedding pictures for Brad and Jules.'

'I'm forgiven for my teasing am I? I can't help it you know, you make me so nervous, Miss Hood, when you look at me with your serious school marm expression. My mouth goes into overdrive I'm so scared.'

'You should be scared,' I say. 'But I'll let you off without a detention though, if you really mean it about doing those photos.'

Matt grins broadly, and it's like the sunshine has spilled in from the piazza. 'Give me a bell tonight. I mean it. I'm really happy to help you out.'

'I will,' I promise.

'Good.' He looks down at me and those smoky blue eyes are suddenly intense with an emotion I can't quite define. 'I'll be looking forward to your call.'

And even though Matt drives me mad I discover I'm looking forward to making it

Chapter Twenty-Two

July

'And finally, I'd like to propose a toast to the person who made today possible! From finding such a great venue to even arranging Bondi Beach weather, we couldn't have done it without her.' Bradley beams at me. 'To Robyn Hood!'

As everyone raises their cans of Fosters and calls my name my eyes fill with tears. I know I've said it before but I really love weddings, especially the weddings of people I care about and Bradley and Julia's is no exception. I've been thinking about this wedding and ways to make it happen for so long that now the day has finally arrived it all seems a bit surreal. Surreal in a good way though because everything has fallen into place so beautifully. From the moment I opened my curtains and discovered that the British sun had finally realised what it's for I'd a feeling this wedding was going to be perfect and I haven't been disappointed. Julia looks stunning with her long blonde ringlets tumbling onto shoulders as smooth and golden as peaches and Bradley can hardly tear his eyes away

'Well done, Robs,' Simon smiles at me across the table where I'm sitting with him, Faye, James and Gideon. 'This is one brilliant wedding. You've outdone yourself.'

'Do you reckon?'

'I certainly do. Everyone's having a brilliant time. I'm really pleased Brad and Julia let you invite us. That was really kind of them.'

I nod. Julia and Brad insisted that since I've done so much for so little I invited my friends too. Even Poppy's been included and is sporting a bright red bow for the occasion. It's lovely to have them here, sipping drinks in the sunshine and enjoying an event I've worked on for so long. They've had to listen to me stress about it for long enough after all!

'I don't know how you did it on such a tiny budget though,' says Gideon.

That makes two of us.

'She's brilliant, that's how,' Faye says warmly. 'And creative and talented too don't forget. I loved the sand on the marquee floor. That was genius.'

Actually, this wasn't so much genius as desperation. When Adam called mid week and told me the floor wasn't going to be laid for another ten days I'd had to think pretty fast. The idea of a sandy beach floor had come to mind while I was watching *Home and Away*, not so much down to genius as down to a guilty love of Aussie soap.

Still, it doesn't hurt to let my friends think I'm brilliant!

'Thanks, Faye. I'm glad you think it's going OK.'

'More than OK! This is such a happy occasion, everyone's relaxed and having fun. It feels more like a party than a wedding.'

'That's exactly what Brad and Jules wanted,' I say, pleased. 'No formalities or stuffy etiquette, just a big party to celebrate their love for one another.'

Gideon sticks his fingers down his throat and makes vomiting sounds.

'Pack it in!' James wallops him on the arm. 'It's lovely seeing people so much in love. Just look at them.'

We all gaze across to Bradley and Julia who are feeding each other hot dogs and kissing tenderly between mouthfuls. They're totally oblivious to anyone else and as I watch them a sharp claw of jealousy scratches my heart. I can't imagine Jonathan ever being like that with me, not while he's constantly looking over his shoulder just in case someone he knows is nearby, anyway.

'All right,' says Gideon grudgingly, 'it's very sweet.'

'It's more than sweet. It's exactly what love should be. Nothing else matters except being together.' As she speaks Faye's lips go all thin and pinched. 'He'd rather be with Julia than anywhere else.'

'Meanwhile back in real world where people have bills and mortgages to pay,' Simon points out, 'the real world where people have to work pretty bloody hard to keep all the plates spinning'

'There's working hard and then there's living in the office,' snaps Faye.

I meet Gideon's eyes across the table. *What's with them?* says his troubled expression.

Simon runs a hand through his sandy hair. He looks grey and tired. 'I can't exactly imagine Bradley in an office, Faye, especially in chambers.'

'He can look at my briefs any day!' quips Gideon and the peculiar tension melts away but as my friends joke amongst themselves I can't shake off a sense of unease. I've never in all the time I've known Faye and Si as a couple heard a cross word between them but there's definitely an undercurrent today.

'And talking of gorgeous men,' drawls

Gideon, shading his eyes against the bright sun, 'that photographer is divine! Darling, you are so sneaky keeping him to yourself all this time!'

'She certainly is.' Faye fixes me with a beady look and I find myself hoping desperately she doesn't start match making. That would be really embarrassing since I can't explain to her why I'm not interested.

'Don't start,' I warn her.

'Why not? He's really nice! Look how kind he's been about doing this wedding for free.'

She's right. Matt's been a star about doing this wedding. He's in real demand and this is one of his only free weekends between jetting off to far flung locations so it's more than generous of him to have agreed to do the pictures. Underneath the jokey exterior and the strange passion for odd creatures there's actually a pretty decent guy.

'He's been really good to Brad and Jules,' I agree.

Faye snorts. 'What bollocks! It's nothing to do with Brad and Julia. Why don't you give him a chance?'

Because I'm in love with Jonathan Broadhead, I want to scream, but of course I can't. Even though Matt and I have got on better lately, his modesty and generosity proving even if he likes to joke and tease he's nothing like Patrick, he's not my type.

Jonathan is.

Matt's moving through the guests taking pictures, sometimes organising people into groups and sometimes catching them unawares. I've been watching him shoot all day and I'm intrigued by this different side to Matt, this serious side to him as he works which is so different to the flippant joker I'm used to. His intensity, the laughing down turned eyes narrowed as he shoots every frame, is really sexy.

Did I say sexy? I meant impressive!

Matt senses me watching and gives me a crinkly-eyed smile. I smile back at then look away quickly, suddenly fascinated by the flower arrangement on the table.

'Never mind the flipping flowers. Go and talk to Matt!' Faye says, giving me a little push. 'He's really nice, not at all like the joke telling weirdo you made him out to be.'

'He's busy,' I say.

'Crap!' Faye says cheerfully. 'He's taking pictures, not splitting the atom! Stop making excuses. He's a nice guy, you get on with him and you're both single so what's the problem?'

'Nothing.'

Gideon catches my eye and I look away guiltily.

'So go and talk to him. Have some fun for once,' she continues bossily. 'He keeps looking at you. I'm sure he's interested.'

God, I seriously hope not. That's a complication I can do without.

'OK,' I sigh. Not wanting to tangle myself up with any more fibs, deliberate or through omission, so I give in and join Matt.

'Hey,' I say.

'Hey.' Matt takes another picture then lowers his camera. 'This is a great wedding, Robyn. Well done.'

'Thanks.' I suddenly feel really shy. 'Julia looks amazing, doesn't she?'

Matt's looks at me, a slow appreciative look that travels from the tips of my flowery flip flops past my floaty pink gypsy skirt and white strappy top to my face, which is turning the exact hue of my skirt.

'She's not the only one,' he says softly.

'Er, right,' I squeak, sounding like I've been inhaling helium. Why am I so crap at accepting compliments?

'One of your roses is coming unpinned. Here let me.' He reaches out and secures the heavy silk flower. His body is so close yet not close enough to touch and I can smell his skin, warm and spicy in the sunlight.

'Robyn,' he says slowly, 'I was wondering–'

But what Matt's wondering I don't get to find out because at this exact moment Julia joins us with a portly middle aged man in tow.

God! Don't you just hate interruptions?

'This is her,' Julia shrieks, throwing her arms around me. 'I told you all about

Robyn, Uncle Shane, from *Perfect Day* wedding planning? She's the one who's arranged this entire wedding! And hasn't she done a fantastic job?'

As Matt steps back and busies himself with his camera the moment passes which is probably just as well because I don't want things to get complicated. Matt's a great guy but I'm with Jonathan. And I love Jonathan.

'Pleased to meet you, Robyn Hood,' booms Uncle Shane. One huge ham of a hand grips mine and pumps my arm vigorously while sausagey fingers crush mine. 'I'm really impressed with what you did.'

'Thanks.' My hand's released and I wiggle my crushed fingers, relieved to find that none are broken. 'It's been fun even though it was a challenge on such a small budget.'

'That's my niece for you, always has to do things the hard way! I offered to pay for a really flash wedding but would she have it?' He smiles fondly at Julia. 'Would she Hell!'

What?

WHAT!

'Aw, c'mon, Uncle Shane. Don't be like that. Brad and I wanted this to be our day. You know Auntie Nolene wouldn't have been able to resist sticking her bib in. I'd have been going down the aisle dressed like Dame Edna!'

'You may have a point there, dahl. But what's the point of being Managing Director of Regent Hotels if you can't splash the cash a little?'

My chin nearly hits the grass. Regent Hotels is a rapidly growing chain, the latest of whose acquisition is the stunning Mayfair Regent which enjoys the patronage of film stars and rock musicians. Jonathan and I had lunch there a while back and the food was to die for.

'I didn't want a big flashy wedding,' Jules insists. 'This is about me and Bradley. Not PR! Who needs big expensive weddings?'

Er, me actually and the black hole that is my overdraft.

'Look at what Robyn did on a shoestring and then imagine what she could do with a more generous budget,' Matt says. 'Some one with her talent could do wonders.'

'They could indeed,' Uncle Shane agrees. 'Tell you what Robyn, why don't you give me a call on Monday and maybe we can have a talk about trying out your services?'

'That's a great idea!' shrieks Julia, leaping up and down like a loony. 'Say yes, Robs, go on!'

Oh bollocks. I'm dreaming aren't I? I knew all this was too good to be true. In a minute my alarm will start to shrill and I'll wake up to see grey skies and bucketing rain. But in the meantime while I wait I'll just give myself a little pinch in case–

Ouch!

'Well?' Uncle Shane waves a gold business card under my nose. 'What d'you think? Are you interested?'

Does Posh Spice like shopping?

Trying to restrain myself from snatching the card, which is what I feel like doing, I take it slowly and tuck it into my clutch bag but inside I'm whooping with excitement. This is exactly the kind of break I need if I'm to raise the profile of *Perfect Day* and really compete with Hester. She'll be incensed when she finds out about this!

'Come and have some food.' Jules tugs Matt's sleeve, 'You've not eaten a thing yet and Robyn's told me how much you love a good barbie.'

'Those roo burgers are going fast,' warns Uncle Shane.

'Your face, Robyn! Give it a go!' laughs Julia.

'Maybe,' I hedge. Call me pathetic but I really can't face the thought of munching on Skippy.

'Your loss,' she shrugs. 'Come on, I'm famished!'

Julia and her uncle head back to the barbeque where Bradley and his friends are knocking back Fosters and slapping steaks onto the griddle. When he sees his new wife Brad's face lights up like the Oxford Street Christmas lights and he pulls her into his arms.

'They're really happy,' Matt observes. 'It's great to see.'

'I know. They make you believe in marriage and romance, don't they?'

'I never had you down as a cynic. I thought believing in marriage was a pre-requisite in your line of work?'

'It is and I do believe in marriage, it's just sometimes you look at couples years on and you wonder how they ever got together in the first place. You know the type I mean, you see them all the time in restaurants ignoring each other and looking pained.'

Like Jonathan and Anita, I add under my breath. Not that I've ever met Anita let alone seen her with Jonathan, but if Jonathan's with me they can't possibly be happy *together*, can they?

'The way I see it,' says Matt, his forehead creasing thoughtfully, 'marriage is bloody hard work. It's about him not hating her when she moans about the football and her not hating him when he drops his dirty socks on the floor.'

'Don't tell me you drop your socks on the floor!' I screw my nose up in mock disgust.

'No, I never drop my socks, just my pants! Fancy coming over to pick them up?' Matt grins.

'About as much as I'd like to eat my own vomit,' I say.

'Stop playing hard to get, Miss Hood. You

know you're dying to see my iguana.'

I'm not playing, I am hard to get! In fact I'm taken. But of course I can't tell Matt this. Anyway he's only having a laugh with me. This isn't serious flirting.

'That's original at least,' I laugh. 'Beats coming up to see your etchings, I suppose. I know I don't want to see those.'

'You'd love my etchings,' Matt waggles his eyebrows. 'I've been told they're very impressive.'

'No thanks. I'd rather see the iguana! Or even the dirty pants!'

'At last! All my life I've been waiting to meet a girl who'd pick up my dirty laundry. After all, isn't that what love's really about?'

'Shame on you,' I say. 'What ever happened to romance?'

'Dirty laundry is real life,' suddenly Matt looks serious. 'Not like all this flowers and weddings business. Loving someone when the glamour's worn off is what really counts. My parents have been married for over thirty years. They bicker like mad but they still hold hands when they go out and, much as my brother and I pretend to hate it, they kiss like teenagers when they think they're alone.'

'That's lovely. My parents are the complete antithesis of yours. In fact, they're an advert of why *not* to get married.'

'And mine are so happily married that I can't possibly live up to them! If I ever marry I'm going to have to do my best to work at it and make our Golden anniversary.' He gives me a wry grin. 'Being a lazy git that's probably why I'm still single!'

'Let's hope Jules and Bradley make it,' I say, watching the happy couple share a tender kiss. 'Thanks for taking the pictures today, Matt. It was really kind of you to do that for them.'

Matt looks away from the bride and groom and smiles down at me. I find myself thinking how kind his eyes are, all down turned and sleepy and sparkly.

'I didn't do it for Bradley and Julia, Robyn,' he says.

'Really?' My pulse is racing faster than Lewis Hamilton.

'Really.' Matt nods. Then he winks at me. 'I did it for the roo burgers! Come on! Let's grab some before they run out. Last one there's a dingo!'

And off he strides towards the Barbie leaving me staring after him.

Well, you walked right into that one Robyn! What did you *think* he was going to say?

Matt has to be one of the most infuriating men I've ever met! I'm torn between laughing and screaming.

And curiously disappointed.

Chapter Twenty-Three

'That's it! I can't dance another step. I think you've broken my toes!' I collapse onto the dry grass, kick off my flip flops and wiggle my toes. 'Ouch! They're black and blue. I'll probably limp for weeks.'

'What absolute bollocks!' Matt plonks himself down next to me. 'I'm not that bad a dancer. Am I?'

'Put it this way, I'd stick to photography if I were you.'

'And there was I thinking you'd enjoyed dancing with me all night.'

'I did,' I laugh. 'And luckily I have two feet, so it doesn't matter that you've crushed one.'

Matt shakes his head. 'If you only knew how your cruel words hurt me, Miss Hood!'

'And if you only knew how your clumsy feet hurt me, Mr Knowles!'

Injured feet aside this wedding's been more of a success than I could have ever imagined. After the barbeque the dancing began, courtesy of Bradley's friend who regularly runs a karaoke night in the pub, and everyone's had a brilliant time getting on down. I've spent most of the evening dancing with Matt who doesn't appreciate swing dancing at all. There's no comparison to dancing with Jonathan but what Matt lacks in skill he makes up for in enthusiasm. My sides ache from laughing so much.

It's late evening and the reception is still going strong. After a glorious sunset the light has bled from the sky and now Hyde Park is all inky blue and purple shadows. A smile of moon hangs above the buttery light of the marquee and the white fairy lights we festooned the trees with sway gently in the breeze. Strains of music float towards us, mellow and dreamlike above the soft chatter of the remaining guests, and with a contented sigh I flop backwards onto the grass and gaze upwards at the glittery skies.

Whoa! Why is the sky flipping and rolling like that? I only had a couple of beers. OK, maybe a *few* more than a couple but not enough to be drunk, surely? Perhaps a little bit tipsy, but nowhere near as hammered as Jules. When the time had come to depart for Kings Cross to catch a train up north for their hiking honeymoon, Bradley practically had to carry his bride into the taxi. Come to think of it he'd been staggering a bit himself too. I hope they make it to the Isle of Mull.

'Star gazing?' Matt's lying prone too and staring up at the Heavens.

'Mmm.' Better not tell him I actually need

to lie down.

'I love the stars,' Matt says. 'Doesn't it just blow you away to think each one is a sun just like ours? Think of all the possible worlds out there filled with people who are maybe staring up at us right now. It puts everything into context, doesn't it?'

'It certainly does when you put it like that.'

'See those three?' He raises himself onto one elbow and jabs a finger skywards. 'They're part of Orion. They make his belt. And those ones above the trees are part of the plough.'

I look but all I can see are millions and billions of twinkly stars and then one that fizzes past, so fast that I almost miss it.

'Look!' Matt clutches my arm. 'Shooting star! Make a wish!'

I squeeze my eyes shut. I'm going to wish for Jonathan.

Or I think I am but somehow it feels really wrong to wish for someone else's husband and I find myself wishing instead that we do really well at the Swing Dance competition on Wednesday.

I'll get to Heaven yet!

'What did you wish for?' asks Matt.

'Don't be so nosey. Besides, it won't come true if I tell you.'

'Fair enough. But that means I can't tell you either.'

'And what makes you think I want to know?'

Matt chuckles. 'You're a woman? In my experience that means you always want to know what's going on in our sad little man brains.'

Mmm, that's a fair point. I was always wondering what Patrick was thinking about. I probably gave him too much credit for thinking deep and meaningful thoughts when he was probably wondering what was for dinner or who his next conquest would be. Still, I wonder what Matt has wished for?

'I'm not telling you,' he says when I finally crack. 'Not yet anyway.'

Abruptly the atmosphere between us becomes so thick you could cut it with a chain saw and I'm suddenly really aware that I'm lying down in the dark beside a man who is most definitely not my boyfriend.

I sit up quickly. 'I'm starving.'

'You've guessed,' Matt complains. 'I was wishing for some food.'

'The barbeque's long finished but there might be some left overs.'

'Who's talking about burned burgers and cold sausages? Come on,' Matt leaps to his feet. 'I've got a much better idea. Get up, lazy daisy. I'm going to take you on a mystery tour.'

'I can't leave!' I protest. 'I'm the wedding planner.'

'The wedding's finished,' says Matt, smiling down at me. 'It's nearly one a.m. Your work here is done.' He reaches out his hand and pulls me up to face him. 'Time to have our own party.'

I glance towards the marquee. Sure enough the guests are thin on the ground. Faye and Simon left hours ago and Gideon and James have vanished too. Only a few die hard Aussie rellies are left, swigging what remains of the lager and dancing unsteadily to someone murdering 'Nothing Compares to You'. Matt's right. This party is well and truly over.

So we walk together through the London night, so sticky and balmy that we could be in the Caribbean. Holding my flip flops I walk barefoot and even though the burning heat of the day is just a memory the pavements are still warm. As we stroll Matt and I chat about Saffron and Fergus's wedding and he roars with laughter when I tell him about all the red herrings I've fed Hester via my indiscreet mother.

'It's not that mum's vindictive,' I explain as we near the Albert Memorial, 'it's just she's really proud to be involved with this wedding and finds it impossible not to boast. If Hester chooses to believe everything mum tells her than that's her fault.'

'So you reckon Hester thinks that the wedding's going to be held at Ketton Place?'

I cross my fingers. 'That's the idea. With

any luck she'll accidentally tip off the press who'll go haring down there.'

'Well,' whistles Matt. 'Who'd have thought you could be so devious?'

I open my mouth to protest and then close it again. After all I've been fibbing to Faye for weeks now by inventing excuses for standing her up because Jonathan suddenly has a window for me.

'What's up?' Matt asks.

'What you just said, about being devious? I don't want to be that kind of person.'

'Hey,' he gives my bare shoulder a brief squeeze, 'I was only kidding around. Of course you're not devious. You're a lovely person, Robyn, all your friends adore you. The blonde girl, Faye was it? She was singing your praises.'

I sigh. There are some secrets that just have to be kept, aren't there? And seeing Jonathan has to be one of those secrets even if it makes life complicated. I can't tell Faye the truth. Just like I can't tell Matt the real reason why I don't respond to his gentle flirting. I feel like I'm wading through toffee, getting more stuck in my own deceit as the days go by, and I hate it.

'For what it's worth,' Matt adds softly, 'I think you're OK for a girl who doesn't appreciate insects and iguanas.'

I know he's still kidding but I feel my cheeks grow warm. Thank goodness it's dark!

We stroll through the empty park, the dry grass prickly under my bare feet, and for once Matt doesn't fill the silence by cracking jokes. I've come to realise that he only kids about when he's nervous. He's not like Patrick at all. Joking for Matt is a defence mechanism, whereas for Pat it's a big attention grabbing exercise. Matt would rather be behind the camera than showing off in front of it. The two guys couldn't be more different. Besides there's no way Pat could have walked this far and not made a pass at me. Not that I want Matt to make a pass at me! But it kind of high lights the differences between them.

As for Jonathan, he wouldn't be seen dead walking through the park without his shoes. He'd have to be in a smart car being chauffeur-driven back home. I love him dearly but he isn't as spontaneous as Matt, everything has to be planned around Anita I suppose, so it's great fun for me to be crazy and carefree in the warm midsummer night.

I muse on this as we continue to make our way through the park. The air is heavy with night scented stock and the bushes rustle with the secret lives of night time creatures. A lone dog fox strolls past, only feet away from us, fixing me with a yellow-eyed stare and practically posing as Matt takes a picture. Then with a whisk of his white tipped tail he trots away into the purple shadows. Above my head the tree tops are dark sentinels shielding us from the sodium glare of the London skyline and wrapping their wooded arms around the precious parkland. It's a magical night.

Then, looming abruptly out of the darkness, I see the extravagant testimonial of Queen Victoria's love for the husband who'd died so young. However have we reached the Albert Memorial so quickly? The time has just galloped away.

'I've always wanted to look at this more closely,' I tell Matt as we pause to admire it.

'Well here's your chance!' Matt says, his eyes glittering excitedly in the orange street light. 'Stay there! Don't move!'

I watch open mouthed as he wraps his camera bag around his neck and then starts to shimmy up the one hundred foot Albert Memorial. Trust me to end up with a nutter. Either that or he's far more drunk than I realised.

'Matt! What are you doing? Get down! You'll fall!'

'Relax!' Matt's voice floats down to earth from his perch fifty feet up where he's leaning against the stone. 'I'm fine! I've always thought I could get some amazing shots here!'

'It's too dangerous!' I'm at the foot of the monument and crane my neck upwards to where he's happily snapping away.

'It's a Hell of a lot safer than Iraq, at least nobody's going to shoot me here,' he calls back.

'You're mad, Matt Knowles!'

'But isn't it fun!' There's a flash and I realise that now he's taking pictures of me. 'Don't move, that's a *great* view of you! God, you're sexy when you scowl.'

In spite of myself I start to laugh.

'And even sexier when you smile! Come on, smile again! I promise you'll have never seen a profile of yourself like this before!'

Flash! Flash! As I shake my head and plead with him to come down to earth before he breaks his neck Matt shoots frame after frame of me. Wow! A world famous photographer is taking pictures of me!

But then he is drunk.

'I wish you could climb up here,' calls Matt. 'The view's amazing. You'd love it!'

I think this highly unlikely seeing as I sometimes get vertigo looking out of the kitchen window but for a split second I'm tempted. Matt's such a free spirit that I can't help feeling some of his impulsiveness is rubbing off on me too. Otherwise why else would I be barefoot and with my hair all curly and crazy on the edge of Hyde Park at two a.m. with a virtual stranger? Thank goodness Jonathan can't see me looking such a state. Would Jonathan, neat and fastidious Jonathan who always plans things like a military operation still love me if he could see me behaving and looking like a teenager? It hurts my head to think about this and I press my hands to my temples as though trying to squeeze these unwelcome thoughts away.

Eventually Matt clambers down without mishap. We make our way to an all night greasy spoon that he knows and over a massive fry up look through the digital images. The views are amazing and I'm taken aback by the raw power of Matt's talent. The city looks like something out of Arabian Nights, all shimmery and sparkly and magical.

'You're really talented,' I tell him, in between mouthfuls of bacon and eggs, 'These are lovely.'

'So I'm not quite so crazy then?' Matt mops up egg yolk with Mother's Pride and chomps thoughtfully. I love the way he's attacking this basic food with as much enthusiasm as Jonathan does when in an expensive restaurant. There's something really attractive about the way Matt grabs life with both hands and wrestles it to the floor as though each minute might be his last.

Maybe I need to work in a war zone to be a little more appreciative of life's simple pleasures? Not that I suppose they'd have much use for Wedding Planners in a war zone but I'm sure I could do something.

Not sure what though...

'You're still crazy but the photos are great. The Albert Hall looks amazing.' I scroll through the digital images, pausing at the bird's eyes view of me. 'Hey! You can see right down my dress.'

'Can you?' says Matt innocently. 'I didn't notice. I was concentrating on your smile and the way that the light was playing on your face. Look at your cheekbones.'

'Never mind my cheek bones! I look like Jordan. I'm erasing that one,' I say, deleting the close up.

'Spoil sport,' Matt grins.

'And that one, and that one!' I delete the next two frames as well and Matt reaches across to retrieve his camera before I can do any more damage.

'Eat your toast and leave my pictures alone,' he scolds. 'You've erased the best ones!'

'Hardly.'

Matt shakes his blonde curls. 'Look what you've left me with,' he says, passing the camera back over my congealing food, 'What sort of a face is that to pull? You look a right old misery guts.'

I study the picture. My hands are pressed against my temples and my mouth droops at the corners. In the sodium light my eyes are bright with unshed tears.

So, yes, I think it's fair to say I look miserable.

'Lucky the wind didn't change,' teases Matt. 'Whatever were you thinking about? It must have been something terrible to make you look that sad. Were you worrying about Hester?'

I turn the camera off but unfortunately I can't turn off the uneasy gnawing in the pit of my stomach.

Because when Matt took that photo it wasn't Saffron's intricate wedding or Hester Dunnaway that I was thinking about, was it?

It was my increasingly complicated relationship with Jonathan.

Chapter Twenty-Four

It's going absolutely crazy in here. On one side of the dance floor a swing band is playing, the flurries of notes rising above the buzz of conversation and the static from the PA system. Across the shiny parquet tables have been set up so the excited audience can sit and watch the action in comfort while working their way through the odd extravagant cocktail. Their pale faces seem to stretch back for ever until they lose their distinction and are nothing more than shadows. There must be sixty people at least crowded into the audience and all of them watch the floor hungrily. The lights have been lowered and a spot light follows the every movement of one couple who twirl and jive cross the floor with ferocious energy. Opposite them a panel of judges watches impassively, only taking their eyes from the dancers to jot down a note or to exchange an opinion, while to their left the other contestants await their turn. Some are laughing and relaxed while others are green with nerves and dreading their ordeal on the dance floor.

Oh sorry. I think that's just me! Everyone else is having fun.

Remind me why I wanted to do this again? Right now I think I'd rather dig up worms than have to spin and jive in front of judges who'd make Simon Cowell look like a soft touch.

Oh. My. God. This is it. After months of practising fiendishly the swing dance competition has finally arrived and suddenly I'm terrified. Can Jonathan and I really compete with these dancers? I watch the dancing couple execute a complicated cartwheel move and my heart follows suit.

'Relax,' Jonathan pulls me against him and drops a kiss onto the top of my head. 'This is meant to be fun, remember?'

'I know, but they look so professional!'

'And so do you,' he reassures me. 'Your outfit is so damn sexy I feel half inclined to forget this whole competition and drag you off to bed! I don't know if I'll he able to keep my mind on the choreography.'

'You'd better!' I giggle, loving him even more for being able to magic my nerves away.

Jonathan gives me a cheeky grin. 'A skirt that short should be illegal. Let's hope it distracts the opposition. Great outfit, babe.'

I've worked really hard on our outfits and if mum was surprised when I asked to borrow her sewing machine she never said anything. She's probably too busy plotting how to get her Rouge Noired talons into Davie Scott to worry about what I'm up to but at least I've been left to sew in peace. I'm really pleased with what I've come up with; all those nights of going cross-eyed over sequins and stabbing myself with pins have been worth it. I'm wearing a short flared scarlet skirt with a black leotard that I've customised with thousands of red sequins and Jonathan has a matching red waistcoat. His tight black trousers show off his long legs and gym honed thighs while the red sets off his dark good looks to perfection. I only wish my legs were equally long and lean. Still, black tights are slimming, aren't they?

'My skirt isn't that short!' I protest.

'It's perfect,' Jonathan winks, 'and so are you!'

I squeeze his hand and take a deep breath. The music has stopped and the breathless dancers squeeze past us, wreathed with smiles because their ordeal is over. This is it. Months of work distilled into a three minute routine that will hopefully knock the judges dead.

'Couple number six,' announces the compere. 'Robyn Hood and Jonathan Broadhead.'

'Ready?' Jonathan asks taking my hand and smiling down at me. At the far end of the ballroom the tuxedoed band have struck up a Lindy Hop and before I know it we're on the dance floor jiving and whirling and there's no more time to worry. All I can think about are my lollies and kick taps and spins as Jonathan and I twirl across the room in a blur of scarlet glitter.

This might be an in house dance competition but the atmosphere couldn't be more serious if we were on *Strictly Come Dancing*. We're whirling and spinning for all our might in front of the judges who are marking us on the Three Ts – timing, teamwork and technique. Every step has to be perfect, every lift and landing clean and precise if we are to win; there's no room for error. But today is one of those magical days when everything goes perfectly and as Jonathan and I dance it's as though our minds and bodies are in perfect synch. As we showcase our individual choreographed routine we are in perfect harmony. I know his every touch and as we dance we're so close I can almost hear the blood galloping through his veins. When he slides me down his body I feel his heart pounding against mine and as his hand skims my breast my own pulse quickens. Faster and faster we dance and the air between us crackles like the Space Dust I loved to eat as a kid.

I wonder if the judges can hear?

As Jonathan lifts me for the final time and the crowd cheers I smile into the sea of pale faces, almost missing my next move when I notice Faye in the audience watching me.

Oh crap!

The sight of my best friend is the emotional equivalent of having a bucket of cold water thrown over me. Although my feet move automatically through the steps my concentration is shattered as I peer into the audience and pray that I'm mistaken. Faye can't be here. She's off to the wine tasting event tonight with Simon. It's my guilty conscience playing tricks on me, the swing dancing equivalent of Banquo's ghost.

Jonathan moves me into the final Jumping Joe, twirling me round and round with dizzying speed. The faces blur and dip but as I crane my neck there's no mistaking the hideous truth. Faye is indeed seated at a table watching us and the tight set of her lips tells me all I need to know.

'What's wrong?' whispers Jonathan as the

music dies away and the audience erupts into applause. 'I thought that went really well.'

'It did.' I can't see Faye now but I can feel her eyes burning into my back. Possibly smoke is rising. 'Faye's here, Jonathan.'

'Shit!' Jonathan turns pale and drops my hand as though it's a cockroach. 'What did you invite her for? She knows Nita, for Christ's sake.'

'I didn't invite her. She's supposed to be at a wine tasting. It must have been cancelled or something.' I'm needled by his horror of possible discovery. So much for our closeness minutes earlier.

'OK,' Jonathan says, 'let's not panic. She wasn't here before the showcase, was she? So she didn't see us together apart from on the dance floor. She hasn't seen us do anything except for dance so there's nothing to worry about.'

We make our way from the dance floor. Normally Jonathan would pull me close or at the very least hold my hand but now he's a good foot away and even further emotionally. My eyes prickle with tears.

'We'll bluff it out,' decides Jonathan. 'She won't know that there's anything between us.' But a muscle twitches in his cheek and his hands are balled into fists. He couldn't look more guilty or tense if he tried. Besides, Faye's no fool. She'll have worked out there's something going on just by watching us dance.

'Go home, Jonathan,' I say wearily. 'It'll only make things worse if you're here. I'll have to think of a really good reason why I forgot to mention that you were my dance partner.'

This is the part when Jonathan will say enough's enough, we're in this together and it's time everyone knows the truth, right?

Errm, no. Apparently not.

'Good idea,' he agrees swiftly, clearly not realising that this is the point where he's supposed to brush my arguments aside and declare his love for me. 'I'll tell the organisers I've had to pull out of the competition and rush home. I'll call you later, Robyn.'

And that abruptly he's gone, leaving me to face the music. My limbs feel rubbery, as though all the blood has migrated from my body to my guilty flushed face. Forcing my lips into a 100 watt smile I weave through the crowd to join Faye at her table.

'Faye! What are you doing here? I thought you were going wine tasting with Si?'

Faye can barely look at me. 'Si had to work. I thought it might be a nice surprise to come and support you.'

'It was! It is! A lovely surprise, I mean!'

'Please Robyn,' Faye shakes her head slowly, 'no more lies. I saw the look on your face when you noticed me in the audience. You were horrified. How long have you been seeing Jonathan Broadhead?'

'Faye, I'm not-'

'I'm not stupid, Robs. Anyone with half an eye can see you're an item. No wonder you haven't had time for me lately, it all makes sense now. And to think that Si and I were so worried about you working too hard and being lonely! God, you certainly had us fooled.' Her eyes narrow. 'That's who you went to Edinburgh with, isn't it, not a client? God, Robyn. How have you managed to tell all these lies for so long? I never thought you were the type.'

I'm not! It's been impossible trying to remember exactly what I may have said and to whom, a bit like trying to hold all the plot lines of the soaps in your mind.

'It's not like it seems,' I begin.

'Oh, Robyn, please,' Faye sighs, 'It's *exactly* how it seems. How long have you been seeing Anita Broadhead's husband?'

Put so bluntly this sounds terrible, like I should be branded with the scarlet letter or something.

'It's not like that, Faye! We never meant anything to happen but we just couldn't help the way we feel. Jonathan hasn't been happy with Anita for ages. She's far too busy with her career to have any time for him.'

'So it's Anita's fault her husband's a cheat? Oh please.' Faye rolls her eyes. 'You'll be telling me next that his wife doesn't understand him. What a cliché. Honestly Robyn, I thought you had more sense.'

My throat is knotted with tears. 'Jonathan loves me, Faye. He really does. And I love him.'

'Just listen to yourself!' I've never heard Faye sound so scornful. Her top lip curls angrily. 'Love? What total crap. He isn't free to love *you*. He's married! He has no right loving you, if he actually does love you rather than the ego boost and the excitement. This is crazy, Robyn! You're going to end up getting really hurt.'

'Jonathan does love me!' I snap. It's so easy for Faye to sit on her high horse when she hasn't got a clue. Everything is always so straightforward for her, with her perfect life and perfect husband.

'Yeah, right,' Faye snorts. 'Of course he does. I bet he says that to all his bits on the side.'

'I am not his bit on the side, as you so nicely put it. We're together.'

'Oh really? So where is he now? By your side acknowledging your relationship or has he slunk off home to Anita, shaking in his bespoke shoes that I'll tell Si and blow his little secret out of the water?'

Tears spill from my eyes. 'You're supposed to be my friend, Faye. Why are you being so cruel?'

'Friends don't lie to each other, Robyn.

Friends don't pretend to be going away on business or that they're too busy to see one another.'

'I couldn't tell you. I couldn't tell anyone!'

'I bet you told Gideon, though? I thought so,' she adds when I say nothing. 'I can imagine what Gideon would say *"Carpe diem, darling, and what ever other bits you can seize as well."* But what about your judgement, your sense of right and wrong? What ever were you thinking, getting involved with a married man?'

'It's easy for you to say!' I shoot back. 'You have no idea what it's like for me being the token single one when you and every one else are happily coupled up. I feel like Bridget bloody Jones. I never thought I'd fall in love with a married man! I didn't mean to.'

'But that's just it, Jonathan's married. You're supposed to love marriage. At least that's what you're always telling me, or is it just another fib?'

'Of course it isn't!' I cry. 'It's not my fault Jonathan's marriage is on the rocks. That's Anita's fault.'

'Rubbish!' Faye snaps, her eyes glacier cold. 'Anita works her arse off to keep Jonathan in his designer suits and poncy cars. He can't have it both ways. And if you're always there keeping his bed warm and massaging his ego what possible chance does Anita have of ever solving their problems?'

'Why are you taking *her* side? She's not your friend, I am!'

'Because I'm a wife too,' Faye cries. 'I know how hard it is to be married and to put up with someone's moods and annoying habits. What chance does a wife stand when another woman decides to flatter her husband's ego and make him feel eighteen again? When he's seen you bleach your moustache and been to buy your Tampax the mystery is well and truly gone. There's no competing with a woman who spends hours preening and plucking and who always looks perfect.'

I stare at her. Has Faye been spying on me?

'I love him, Faye.'

'I'm sure you do,' she says slowly. 'But it's wrong, Robyn. I thought you were better than that. I thought you had morals.'

'I knew you'd be like this!' I blurt angrily. 'Judgmental and horrible and on Anita's side. That's why I didn't tell you about me and Jonathan. I knew you'd spoil everything.'

'By telling you the truth?' Faye shakes her blonde head. 'That's why you didn't want to tell me, Robyn. You knew exactly what I'd think and deep down you know I'm right. Either way this relationship can't end well. Someone's going to end up hurt.'

'Jonathan won't let me down!'

'He's let his wife down big time. What makes you think you'll be any different?'

'Because he loves me and he wants to be

with me! Trust me on this.'

'Trust you?' Faye echoes. 'How can I ever trust you again after all the lies you've told? How will I ever be able to tell when you're telling the truth? And to think that all the times you told me about just being good friends with Simon I thought I could believe you.'

'What's Si got to do with this?'

'He's married and you're always on the phone to him. Fix my car, Si. The central heating's broken, Si. I can't sort out my taxes, Si. And off he goes to help you out, with me all trusting at home thinking that you're just good friends. How do I know you haven't been carrying on for years with *my* husband?'

'That's a horrible thing to say!'

'Is it?' Faye shrugs.

'Si and are friends. He's like my brother and besides, I'd never, ever do that to you and neither would Si!'

'So you say. But I bet Anita Broadhead thinks she can trust her husband too.'

'It's totally different!'

Faye drains her wine glass and rises from the table. 'Anita's a wife. I'm a wife. How's it any different?'

I'm horrified at the direction our argument is taking. Apart from being distraught because Faye and I have never rowed I can't believe she could really think so poorly of me.

I clutch her arm. 'It's different because I'm your friend!'

Faye shakes my hand off. 'Are you? I'm not so sure anymore. I don't think I want to be friends with someone who knowingly gets involved with a married man.'

She scoops up her bag and turns sharply on her heel, every hair on her blonde head stiff with anger and disappointment. The room blurs because my eyes are swimming with tears.

'But most of all, Robyn,' Faye says over her shoulder, 'real friends don't lie to each other, do they?'

Clutching her bag to her chest she walks away, leaving me reeling from our harsh exchange. Blinking tears away I watch her stride to the door without so much as a backward glance.

Our friendship is in tatters. How on earth has it come to this?

Later that evening I lie on my bed. Eventually dark settles throughout the flat but I can't face switching on the lamps. Instead I watch orange swathes of headlights march relentlessly across the ceiling and listen to the bristling traffic and the distant rumble of tubes.

I've cried so hard since my row with Faye that I don't think I have any tears left to shed. I've worked my way through an entire loo roll trying to dry my eyes and I think my nostrils have sealed themselves shut. I can't believe how judgmental Faye was and the harsh words we've spoken keep replaying themselves in my mind like some horrible tape recording until I feel like screaming. Try as I might I can't press pause so round and around the words go, each time more painful than the last.

Gnawing in the pit of my stomach is a horrible feeling that I don't quite want to acknowledge, but which feels horribly like doubt. Doubt edged with guilt because talking to Faye has made my relationship with Jonathan become real, as though now she knows about us it isn't just a romantic interlude but something else altogether, something complicated, and messy and maybe a little sordid. Faye has managed to make Anita Broadhead real for me rather than a distant and shadowy figure. Before this evening I've either not thought about Anita at all or dismissed her as a cold and emotionless career woman who makes Jonathan unhappy. In other words I've blamed her rather than Jonathan for our affair and done a very good job of convincing myself that she can't really love him.

But Faye has let her in and now she's real I'm starting to feel bad.

I grind my knuckles into my eyes as though to rub out the images I have of Anita home alone wondering where her husband is, or cooking the dinner or loading the washing machine and taking care that the temperature is just right for his shirts. In fact I'm overwhelmed just contemplating the hundreds of every day ordinary tasks she must perform from food shopping to collecting dry cleaning, all the little chores that are part of her life with Jonathan. Faye's right. Anita is his *wife*. They've built a life together and even if it isn't always perfect or romantic it's real.'

I love Jonathan but does he really love me? And maybe more to the point *should* he love me?

Abruptly my mobile phone shrills for the fifth time in as many minutes, flooding the room with ghoulish green light. I don't need to pick it up to know it will be Jonathan. He's been trying to call me all evening but for the first time since we've been together I really don't want to talk to him because what's the point of Jonathan knowing how upset I am when nothing he can say or do will me feel any better? Ironically after months of dreading her calls the only person I want to speak to now is Faye.

And I don't need to be psychic to know she won't be contacting me in a hurry.

Chapter Twenty-Five

August

OK, don't panic, Robyn! Everything's going according to plan and nothing is going to go wrong. Positive thinking, remember? Today's wedding is going to be absolutely perfect.

I've been repeating this mantra to myself for the last three hours as I've whirled around organizing the staff, retrieving runaway bridesmaids and reassuring Saffron that the press haven't found us. I've just about everything crossed that they won't either because it's been a stroke of genius to hold the wedding at the picturesque manor house belonging to Laney Scott, Saffron's third stepmother, rather than at the more obvious Ketton Place. Apart from the fact that Cheyneys Manor is stunning medieval gem with the most perfect rose garden for the pictures and a Great Hall that lends itself brilliantly to the reception I'm even more delighted with this venue because I'm sure the paparazzi will never find us. Cheyneys nestles in the deepest, greenest midst of Buckinghamshire miles from anywhere and a good hour from Ketton Place. I could kiss Laney Scott for offering it to us. Hopefully by the time Hester and the press realize I've thrown them an entire years' quota of red herrings Fergus and Saffron will be married and their exclusive will be safe.

As I make my way down the grand oak staircase, pausing to rearrange the white roses and ivy that festoon the banisters, I smother a yawn. Although it's only ten thirty in the morning I've been on the go since before sunrise and with just under an hour until the ceremony I'm not finished yet. I've pulled on a pink prom style dress and bullied my hair into a chignon in record time because I haven't got a second to waste. Even while I give last minute instructions to the caterers I'm mentally ticking off what I've achieved and running through the list of jobs still to get done.

So far so smooth. Davie Scott and the band have stayed away from the booze, Matt's called to say that he and Fergus are en route to the church, the flowers have been delivered and Saffron is busy getting ready and posing for the *Scorching!* photographers. Even the weather has obliged and as I leave the cool of the house it's almost a shock to feel the heat of the midsummer sun on my face. Not that I have time to stand around enjoying the sunshine!

I walk as fast as I can along the path that leads from the manor house and through the rose garden, my hat swinging in my hand and my sandals crunching on the gravel. Bees drone from the waxy petals and the scent beats anything Chanel could dream up. But best of all at the end of the rose garden is a secret gate which opens up into the churchyard of St. Anthony's, the small Norman church where for centuries the occupants of Cheyneys have worshipped. Saffron can make her way to church without any sneaky cameras getting a shot of her dress or the even more prized picture – Davie Scott in a morning suit and with his flowing grey mane tamed beneath a top hat.

Shutting the gate behind me I wonder how many brides have passed through that gate, their hearts fluttering beneath their corsets as they made their final journeys as single women. My heart is fluttering too because this really is it. The biggest wedding of my career is about to take place. Over six months of planning and dreaming and worrying are all distilled into the next few hours and the future of *Perfect Day* rests on their success. All my other worries, financial and romantic, pale into insignificance, filed under *think about it later.* Nothing matters now apart from Saffron's big day going to plan. Everything has to be perfect.

Mind you if I had to pick a perfect venue for a wedding I'd be hard pushed to find somewhere better than St. Anthony's. The small flint church bathes in golden sunlight, surrounded by velvet smooth lawn and lichen smothered tombstones. Dark yews shade the path and shield the churchyard from the road, tall grasses and wild flowers nod in the soft breeze and the only sounds I can hear are the trembling coos of wood pigeons and the distant buzz of a combine harvester. It's all so quintessentially English that I wouldn't be surprised if Hugh Grant and Helena Bonham Carter sauntered past with a Merchant Ivory film crew in tow.

Maybe, just maybe, I'm going to pull it off?

Inside the church it's cool and shadowy. Dust motes dance and whirl in rainbow hued shards of lights, in perfect time to the gentle voices of the choir who are busily warming up. While I check that the flowers are exactly right and count the order of services I listen to the strains of *Ave Maria* and *Pie Jesu*, my eyes filling as each sweet note floats upwards. This is exactly the kind of music I'd adore to have at my own wedding and exactly the picture perfect church whose aisle I'd love to swish down clad in ivory silk and lace. I'm not sure who'd be waiting for me at the altar though, probably no one at this rate. Jonathan and I have hardly spoken since my row with Faye firstly because I can't put her angry accusations out of my mind and secondly because I suspect Jonathan's terrified that he's about to be found out. I've cried myself to sleep for more nights than I care to count because I'm going to have to choose between them, aren't I? It's becoming more and more apparent that I can't have the man I love and Faye's friendship, so who do I choose? I've been chewing my nails so much over this dilemma that I'm practically down to my elbows. In fact here I go again...

Yuk! False nails are so not conducive to a good chew! What was I thinking opting for an elaborate manicure? Who would really care if the wedding planner had gnawed stumps?

I glance at my watch. Nearly eleven o'clock. The first guests will be arriving soon and then it will be full steam ahead until gone midnight. Maybe I can sit in the sunshine and gather my thoughts for a few moments before everything goes crazy? Pretty soon there'll be bridesmaids to keep in line and a wild sixties rock band to contend with, not to mention my mother who looks like a cross between Joan Collins and a Cheeky Girl in her wedding finery.

Yes, I decide as I make my way to the porch, a few quiet minutes is the least I deserve, especially since I'm on duty and won't be able to sink a few vodkas to calm my nerves. I'll just move that flower arrangement first though. What was the vicar thinking, standing it right on the edge of the font? It could seriously block the view of someone sitting in that pew, like the couple who are just coming in for example.

I heave the heavy vase into my arms and stagger into the shadowy nave just as this elegant couple pass by. They're having a furious discussion about something whilst trying to pretend otherwise. You know the kind of row I mean where couples hiss *darling* at one another while clearly meaning the polar opposite. Not wanting to embarrass them I tuck myself behind the font and pretend to be looking for stray orders of service. Not that this couple show the slightest interest in me. They're far too busy having their whispered row.

'I can't believe you've brought this up now!' The woman hisses to her partner. 'This really isn't the time!'

'It's a wedding,' he grates, 'so I'd have thought it the prefect time.'

My stomach curdles and it's just as well I'm crouched down on the cold floor because otherwise I think I'd have fallen over. I know that voice. Very, very well.

It's Jonathan.

Duh. Of course it's Jonathan. His family are old friends with the Maitlands so I'd known he'd been invited but I'd done a very good job of putting it to the back of my mind, the mental equivalent of the glory hole under the sink where I bung my bank statements and credit card bills until I feel brave enough to deal with them. And of course if this is Jonathan then this tall, very slim Scandinavian looking blonde dressed in a cream shift dress and cream high heeled sandals has to be Anita.

Why didn't Faye tell me she was so beautiful? With her hair piled high to emphasise her long neck and slender shoulders Anita looks more like a supermodel than the bespectacled lab coated scientist of my imaginings. She's simply stunning.

What is Jonathan thinking? There's no way I compare to her, even on a thin day wearing control pants and my best frock. I crouch behind the font and hold my breath. I can't breeze past them now, I'll just have to wait until they take a pew and then make a run for it.

But, unfortunately for me, Jonathan and Anita don't seem to be in any hurry to move.

'I've told you before, Jonathan, this isn't a decision I can rush.' Anita Broadhead looks away from her husband. In the soft candlelight her face is lined with worry. 'I'm not ready. *We're* not ready.'

'So you keep telling me.' Jonathan crosses his arms. 'But you'll never be ready, will you, Nita? There's always an excuse or a reason to put it off. A conference? A paper to deliver? A new post to take up? Maybe you should just be honest for once? Why not admit it isn't what you want?'

'I'm not saying it isn't what I want!'

'So what is it then?' There's ice in Jonathan's voice and I shiver, hating being a voyeur to this private argument. I haven't a clue what they're rowing about but I can see both of them are very upset. The muscle ticking in Jonathan's cheek says he's more than upset; he's incandescent with rage.

'Then what the Hell is wrong with you?' he demands.

'It's not what's wrong with me!' Anita's eyes glitter with unshed tears. 'It's what's wrong with *us*, Jonathan. Things haven't been right for months. All you do is work. You never want to spend time with me anymore and I'm sick and tired of always sitting at home on my own waiting for you to come home!'

What?

'If you said "yes" I swear to God I'd be there for you,' Jonathan says, his voice low and urgent. 'You know I would.'

'Do I? That's too much of a gamble on my part, Jonathan. What if things carried on as they are? It would be a disaster.' She shakes her head. 'The answer has to be no. For now, anyway.'

'For now. For next year. For the next five years,' Jonathan says bitterly. 'Forget I even asked. I shouldn't have bothered. I've always known that your marvellous career comes first. How stupid of me to imagine coming to a wedding would make you think any differently. Some marriage we have.'

Shaking off her hand Jonathan stalks up the aisle and flings himself onto a pew. Anita sighs heavily. 'We still have a marriage though,' she calls softly after him. 'I've never forgotten that, Jonathan, or that I love you. Have you?'

As she follows him to the pew I can silently answer that question. Jonathan has tried very hard indeed to forget both of these things and I've gone out of my way to help him, haven't I? I always knew he was married; it was just easier to pretend otherwise.

Once they're both seated I stand up shakily, blood gushing into my cramped limbs in a torrent of pins and needles. I discover I'm holding a lump of candle wax, dropped from some long forgotten christening, in which I've somehow embedded two pink false nails. I manage to extricate my hands and slip out of the church without either of the Broadheads noticing, although quite frankly they're so wrapped up in their row that a herd of wildebeest could probably rampage through the nave and not attract their attention.

Safely outside I lean against the porch wall and take a slow, deep breath. Although the sun is bright and warm I feel chilled to the bone and my stomach is churning as though I'm on the deck of a cross channel ferry in a Force Nine rather than a peaceful country graveyard. I close my eyes but still see the sadness etched onto Anita's face, sadness caused maybe in no small part by myself. There's no doubt in my mind she loves Jonathan just as much as I do. The sadness in her face when she talked about him never being there for her would melt the coldest of hearts.

Faye tried to tell me Anita Broadhead isn't a career obsessed ice maiden as Jonathan has led me to believe. Her passion for her job is only part of the story and I have a feeling that Jonathan hasn't read me all the chapters.

What have I done?

And more importantly how can I put things right?

Chapter Twenty-Six

'Robyn! I've found you at last! Thank Christ for that!'

I'm yanked from my guilty thoughts about the state of the Broadheads' marriage by Davie Scott all but collapsing in front of me. His breath is coming in big gasps and he holds his hand against his heart while he struggles to speak. My own heart plummets. I *knew* it was all too good to be true. This is the bit where all my plans start to collapse like a house of cards.

'What's happened?' Hideous images flicker through my mind's eyes; Fergus has cold feet, the bride's been taken ill, the paparazzi have Cheyneys under siege...

'Jeez,' Davie puffs. 'I can hardly breathe I'm so fuckin' unfit. I've only run from the house. It's all those sodding drugs I did in my youth.' He gives me a wink. 'And not just my youth either, if I'm honest. Jesus! My heart's going to bloody burst.'

'Take a moment,' I say, alarmed by the grey pallor of his face. I know I'm being selfish here but a dead rock star's the last thing I need. 'Come and sit down in the porch for a second.'

Taking his arm I guide him towards a small bench, shoving swathes of roses and baby's breath aside so that can sit down without ruining his daughter's flower arrangements.

Davie's breath becomes less laboured once he's sitting, thank goodness, because my emergency wedding kit doesn't include a defibrillator and paramedics.

'Feeling better, Davie?'

'Much better,' he nods, giving me the slow appraising grin that I'm reliably informed (too much detail, thanks mum) drives women of a certain age crazy. 'Besides, I can't sit next to a foxy chick like you and be too shattered to enjoy it.'

Foxy chick? I laugh at his sixties slang in

spite of the panic which I'm sure has added to the single grey hair Gideon spotted yesterday.

'Oh behave, Austin!' I quip. 'Now you can breathe do you think you can tell me what prompted this mercy dash?'

'Yeah, sure,' Davie says, delving into the pocket of his morning suit and pulling out a suspicious looking cigarette. 'Let me just have a toke of this first to calm my nerves, then I'll spill the chilli beans, doll.'

'Davie! No way!' I snatch the offending roll up and stuff it into my bag. 'Firstly you nearly collapsed because you couldn't breathe and secondly we're in a Church! You can't have a joint here. I won't have it!'

'Babe, has anyone ever told you that you're smoking hot when you're sexy?' Davie twinkles.

Actually yes. For a second it's a midsummer night again and Matt's laughing down at me from the Albert Memorial, his eyes crinkling with laughter when I cover my cleavage with my clutch bag. Not that I'm thinking about Matt. I'm convinced his joke call about losing the rings is the cause of that horrible first grey hair. Well, Matt'll be laughing on the other side of his face when he finds out he owes me a life time of visits to Nikki Clarke for a colour!

Anyway, back to the aging rock star with his hand on my thigh...

'That old Scott charm might work on my mum,' I tell him sternly as I remove the hand, 'but I'm totally immune. Just remember Saffron's rules, OK? No getting off your face until the wedding is over and you've played your set at the reception. And certainly no chatting up the guests! Now, can you please tell me what disaster is about to befall your only daughter's wedding?'

'Oh yeah, your mum,' to my alarm a dreamy expression flits across his craggy face, 'Now there's a real woman–'

'Davie! Your daughter's wedding! Remember?'

'Sorry!' Davie Scott pulls himself together with a start. 'Where was I? Oh yeah, I remember now, you left your phone in Saffron's bedroom, doll.'

'Oh my God!' I clap my hands to my head. 'How could I have been so careless?'

My mobile's the nerve centre of today's proceedings; everyone from Fergus to the photographer to the jazz band has to be able to contact me on it. I must be stressed not to have noticed the Nokia shaped gap in my bag.

He passes the phone to me. 'I took a call for you, babe, someone called Carolyn? She's in a flap because her car's broken down. She says there's no way she can get a cab big enough to fit her harp in.'

'But she's supposed to be playing while

Fergus and Saffron sign the register! There's no way we can do without her.'

'Maybe I could help out? I'm sure Ricky could play lead guitar,' suggests Davie helpfully.

Now it's my turn to go a nasty shade of putty. The very thought of the tattooed Blue Smoke guitarist twanging away on his electric guitar rather than Carolyn's angelic notes galvanises me into action. If Jimmy Choo could see me sprint back to Cheyneys he'd be amazed – whoever knew a girl could move so fast in four inch heels?

Twenty minutes later Dolly and I screech up outside a rather dull 1930s house. Surely a harpist ought to live somewhere a little more gothic? I think as I hammer on the door. Turrets and a moat at the very least, a pebble dashed semi seems oddly disappointing. Still the scream with which Carolyn greets me is as gothic as anything Bram Stoker could have dreamed up and my blood is well and truly curdled.

'There's no way my harp will fit in that!' she screeches, pointing at Dolly. 'Are you kidding?'

I glance into the hall way where the six foot tall harp looms above her. Bugger! It's far too wide to fit in Dolly. That'll teach me to do my research on harps via Philadelphia adverts!

My thoughts zip to Warp Factor ten

quicker than you can say *Captain Kirk* and before I can think better of it I'm running out into the road and flagging down a passing Transit van. The two lads inside are a bit surprised at first but soon rise to the challenge of being knights in a white shining van and before long they're heaving Carolyn's precious harp into the back.

Well, that and the fact that I've just bribed them with an invite to see *Blue Smoke* play for the first time in fifteen years...

'You're mad!' Carolyn giggles, as we hop after the harp.

'If I am then today's driven me there!' I say.

We hunker down into the van and I settle myself onto a pot of pink paint, luckily the exact dusky rose hue of my dress so if it spills I won't be in too much trouble. 'Where to, darlin'?' The driver asks, turning round and smiling at me.

'Do you know St. Andrews? It's the small church in Cheyneys village, just off the A40.'

'My SatNav does,' he says switching in on. 'Ta da! It's only twenty miles away.

'I know it's a total cheek, but could you please go as fast as you can? We're meant to be at a wedding.'

'And there was me thinking you were two angels straight from Heaven!' He grins, swinging the van onto the road. Carolyn rolls her eyes but I can't help laughing.

'If I am then my halo has well and truly slipped.'

'It's far more fun to be bad,' the van driver grins. 'I'm Jack, by the way and the strong silent one is Andy.'

'All right?' mutters Andy from deep beneath his Burberry cap.

'I'm Robyn and this is Carolyn,' I decide to make idle chit chat to pass the time and to take Carolyn's mind off her poor harp which is bouncing about like Skippy. 'Thanks for helping out.'

'No probs.' Jack cuts up a Mercedes, zooms into the outside lane and gives the finger to the irate driver. 'Twat!'

A very pink Mercedes. Unmistakeable. It's Hester's, and she's driving in the opposite direction. Yay!

I cling onto my pot of paint for grim death while Carolyn flings her arms around the harp.

'You sure the wedding's at Cheyneys?' Jack asks, settling into the fast lane. I try not to notice the speedometer which is hovering just below a hundred. I did, after all, ask him to get us to the church in record time.

'Totally sure,' I say through rattling teeth. 'Why?'

'We've come through Salisbury, where Davie Scott has a pad? Every photographer in Britain must have been trying to get through the one way system, as well as all the die hard fans desperate to see *Blue Smoke*. Fuck me!' Jack shakes his head. 'I can't believe me and Andy are really going to see them play!'

'Only if we get there in one piece,' mutters Carolyn.

'Wait a minute,' I interrupt Jack's excited monologue about what legends *Blue Smoke* are. 'Did you just say there's lots of press on their way to Ketton?'

'Sure did! The news said there'd just been an arrest, some knob tried to break into the grounds of Davie's mansion. Fans and paps are going mental. Every rozzer for miles has been drafted over.'

If I wasn't holding on for grim death I'd be punching the air, leaping up and down and shouting 'Yes!' at the top of my lungs. My ruse worked! The press is eighty miles away without a clue where Saffron and Fergus are really getting married and Hester Dunnaway's plotting has all been for nothing. What I wouldn't give to see the look on her face when she finds out she's been well and truly hoodwinked, and by my mother of all people! After the way she used mum nothing could be sweeter!

The traffic and Fate must be smiling on us and most of the highway police diverted to Ketton Place because Jack makes it to St. Anthony's with minutes to spare, screeching to a halt alongside the village green like something out of the A Team. Wrinkling my nose against the smell of burning rubber I clamber out of the van and run towards the vestry, Andy and Jack hot on my heels with the harp. Moments later Carolyn, cool as the proverbial cucumber, wheels it into position at the side of the chancel just as the Wedding March strikes up on the organ. I collapse onto a pew next to my knights in shining overalls who are staring open mouthed at their rock heroes clad in Armani rather than leather and only inches away.

I *knew* there was a reason I'd allowed myself to be persuaded it was a good idea to let *Blue Smoke* reform at this wedding!

I glance across the nave. Fergus is standing ramrod straight as he awaits the arrival of his bride, every inch the serious groom about to make the most solemn promises of his life. In total contrast his best man is bent double and trying hard to regain his composure.

Honestly! Matt Knowles has to be the most infuriating man I've ever met, which is saying something giving the serious competition for that title. What on earth can be so funny at a time like this? If he's lost the rings I will personally drown him in the font and no sexy lopsided smiles will be able to save him.

Not that I think his lopsided smile is sexy.

'What?' I mouth at him across the church.

Matt dashes tears from his eyes with a snowy cuff.

'Your hands,' he mouths back. 'Matching them to your dress is genius!'

I stare down at my hands and only just stop myself crying out in rage. Yesterday's soothing hand massage, paraffin treatment and frill set of acrylics are totally buried beneath a thick layer of rose pink emulsion. I only hope I haven't touched my face or my hair. There's no time to check now or to flee to the loo and scrub the crusty paint off because Saffron is slowly walking up the aisle. She looks so heart stoppingly lovely that no one will be looking at me anyway.

As we rise to sing *All Things Bright and Beautiful*, pink powder falling from my hands when I open the order of service, I try to organise my thoughts for the reception.

All I need to do is have everyone in the right place at the right time, ensure that Davie and co stay away from the drink/illegal substances/groupies until they've played their set, stop Matt goofing around too much and, of course, avoid the Broadheads. Even more to the point I'm going to need to avoid Faye too. The notion of me, Jonathan and Faye in the same place doesn't exactly make me want to jump for joy. In fact, forget Matt Knowles; maybe I can drown myself in the font?

'Dearly beloved,' begins the vicar, once

the hymn ends, 'we are gathered here today, in the sight of Almighty God...'

Great. Now the service has started I'm well and truly trapped. There'll be no scuttling out of the church to get on with work for me. I'm just going to have to do my best to be as busy as possible. If I rush around and do all the chores, even those I could easily delegate, I should be able to avoid Faye and, even more importantly, Jonathan for the entire day.

Even if afterwards is going to be something else entirely...

Chapter Twenty-Seven

'What happened to the pink hands?'

Matt's soft words, whispered into my ear, almost make me zoom into orbit because the whirl of things to do at the reception has totally absorbed me. From the minute that the happy couple left the church I've been tearing round like a pink prom-dressed Tasmanian Devil making sure everything's fallen into place. Miraculously somehow, in between locating an asthma inhaler for a poorly guest and keeping Davie Scott away from the champagne, I've even managed to nip to the loo and scrub the paint from my hands.

'All gone,' I say, holding up my hands and wiggling my now paint free fingers.

'Let me check.' Mutt slowly takes my left hand and holds it up to the light, turning it gently as though inspecting for left over flecks of emulsion. His fingers are strong and his grasp warm. Denim blue eyes that are narrowed thoughtfully flicker to mine as his forefinger brushes across my palm. 'Yes, totally clean. Shame. That was a particularly novel look. I really liked the pink streaks on your face too.'

'I looked like a girly commando!' I grin. 'Thank goodness no one was looking at me.'

'I was,' Matt says.

Now my face is pink again and I can't blame the paint this time. Get a grip Robyn, it's nothing personal, Matt's always joking and teasing. Extricating my hand from his, I attempt to gain my composure.

'You shouldn't have had time to do anything except focus on your duties!' I scold. 'You're the best man, Mr. Knowles, and your mind should be firmly on the job. Like right now, for example? You should be at the top table with the bride and groom, not gassing with me. We're just about to serve the first course.'

Sure enough as I say this a fleet of immaculate waiters and waitresses parade into the Great Hall, holding aloft trays of fragrant smelling food. For a moment I'm overwhelmed with emotion because everything just looks so perfect. From the shafts of bright sunshine that stream through the latticed windows and dance upon the flagstones to the lines of trestle tables draped with my mother's snowiest linen and piled with creamy roses, the scene is just beautiful. At the top table are Fergus and a radiant Saffron, all flushed cheeks and sparkling eyes, laughing at something Davie has done. Above the light chatter and bubbles of laughter the notes of Carolyn's harp float skywards, the perfect accompaniment to the scene.

A waiter passes by and Matt peers at the tray of entrées, his nose crinkling.

'Robs, what exactly *is* that? It looks like Yorkshire puddings full of gravy and with bits of grass floating in them!'

I laugh because I'd thought exactly the same weeks earlier when Saffron and I finalized the menu.

'They're miniature Yorkshire puddings with herb scented beef jus, you Philistine!'

'I stand corrected!'

'Wait until you try them,' I say. 'I've sampled the menu and it's all to die for.'

'Aren't you going to sit down and eat?' Matt asks, 'You've been working flat out. Surely you should have a break?'

I laugh. The very thought of stopping now mid operation! It *may* look as though I'm sailing through the proceedings like the swans gliding serenely past on the moat but believe me I'm paddling just as frantically as their webbed underwater feet!

'I'll have a break once this is over. I'm working remember?'

'Excuse me, Robyn?' A small waitress hovers nervously at my shoulder. 'Mr. Scott has spilled his wine all over the table cloth. Have we any spares?'

'See?' I say to Matt. He raises his hands and gives me that crooked grin.

'I'll leave you to it, Ms. Wedding Planner Extraordinaire! Maybe catch you later for a dance? See if I've improved since Brad and Julia's?'

'Hmm, I'm not sure my toes can take that. They've only just recovered.' I laugh. 'Now get to that top table before your grass filled Yorkshires go cold.'

As Matt joins the bridal party I make my way from the Great Hall, smiling to myself as I recall the fun that we had at the Aussie wedding. Matt's possibly the worst dancer on the planet but he certainly knows how to make me laugh. Perhaps if I have a spare minute this evening I'll risk my toes again. It's not as though I'll be needing them for Swing Dancing any time soon. After the debacle at the competition I don't know if I'll be dancing with Jonathan again. Or even if I want to...

Grabbing the keys to the linen cupboard I leave the hall and venture into the warren of dark corridors. Two lefts, then a right I think? Or was it two rights then a left? I pause for a second as I try to get my bearings and suddenly the house seems very still and watchful. A portrait of a stern looking Tudor woman glowers down and me and for a second I feel quite unnerved. This house is just so old. The flagstones are worn smooth from centuries of passing feet and the dark corners brim with shadows. Even the stuffed corpses of long shot game regard me headily with glassy eyes. I rattle the heavy iron keys hastily, trying to remember which one opens the linen cupboard so I can dash in, snatch up a table cloth and scuttle back to the Great Hall where there's noise and laughter rather than this brooding quiet. Ah! That looks like the right key, it seems to be turning, let's see–

'Aargh!'

The keys clatter to the stone floor and my heart almost bursts through my chest when someone creeps up behind me and places a hand on my shoulder. I knew I should never have watched all those creepy *Most Haunted* shows with Gideon. Turning around I brace myself for a sinister hooded figure or at the very least a headless lady.

What I'm not expecting to see is a red faced Jonathan.

'Sorry, angel, I didn't mean to make you

jump,' he says, pulling me into his arms and raining kisses onto my face. 'I just couldn't bear to be apart from you for a second longer. Oh, God Robyn, I want you so much!'

Jonathan pushes me up against the linen cupboard door and his lips trail urgent kisses from the corner of my mouth across my throat and to the exposed flesh of my collar bones. He pushes his body hard against mine so that there's no escaping his arousal. Even his eyes are darkened with desire.

From horror to bodice ripper in less time than it takes to draw breath? This sudden switch of genres makes my head spin.

'Where can we go?' murmurs Jonathan, his breath hot against my skin.

Normally his slightest touch turns my limbs to runny honey and I've lost count of the times I've given in to his skilled touch when my head has been yelling at my heart to stop being such a sap. Even now his lips make delicious goose bumps ripple across my skin and for a second I want nothing more than to find somewhere quiet where we can be together.

But only for a second. Today my pragmatic head is well and truly screwed on. What *is* Jonathan thinking? I'm working, and on the biggest job of my career too! He knows that. I'm not just here for him to drag aside for a quickie. And in any case, his wife's only along the passage. It's totally inappropriate. And, actually, a little bit sordid.

'Jonathan! No!' I push him away. 'Not here, not like this! Anita's only down the corridor.'

'Forget Anita,' says Jonathan, shoving open the door to the linen cupboard and pulling me inside. 'It's over with her, it has been for years. I've been a fool not to have seen it sooner.' His lips are on mine again, hot hard and insistent and for a moment I find I'm kissing him back. His hands skim over my body and when we break apart our breathing is ragged.

'I'm leaving her, Robyn,' Jonathan says softly. 'It's over. I want to be with you.'

I goggle at him, totally speechless, which probably isn't the reaction he was expecting.

'Did you hear what I said?' In the half light Jonathan's sharp cheekboned face looms above mine. 'I said I'm leaving my wife so I can be with you. Say something, Robyn. This is what you want, isn't it?'

If he'd have told me this a month ago, maybe even two weeks ago on the eve of the swing dance contest then I'd have been jumping for joy. Sexy, handsome, clever Jonathan Broadhead leaving his unhappy marriage to be with me? I couldn't have contained myself. It would have been all my hopes and dreams come true, the most romantic moment of my life.

I just never thought it would take place in a linen cupboard and with my skirt around my ears like some floozy...

'Robyn?' His hands tighten on my shoulders. 'This is what you want?'

He sounds so unsure, so desperate that my heart constricts in sympathy. It *was* what I'd longed to hear him say but that was before he abandoned me at the competition and more importantly before I'd overheard the row between him and Anita. The pain etched onto her beautiful face told me more eloquently than any words that as far as she's concerned their marriage is very much alive.

Anyway, why were they fighting? Jonathan had seemed pretty insistent about something and if Anita had agreed it hadn't sounded as though he was about to end the marriage. How truthful is he being? As I look at his expectant and much loved face I know I can't make any decisions without knowing the full story. If at all...

'Please, Robyn! Say something!' Jonathan stares down at me. 'I know it's a shock but we're good together, aren't we? We love each other, I know we do! This could be the start of something really fantastic.'

I can't answer him now. I need some time.

'Jonathan, I–'

'Robyn! Robyn!' Through habit we both

spring guiltily apart as my name is shrilled from outside. 'Robyn! Did you find that table cloth?'

Mum!

'Right here!' I call brightly, extricating myself from his arms and scooping up a crisp sheet of white linen. 'Coming!'

Leaving the unanswered Jonathan in the gloom I join my mother outside. I don't think I've been so pleased to see her for years.

'Honestly,' she huffs, snatching the table cloth and stalking ahead of me along the corridor. 'You took your time, young lady. Whatever were you doing in there?'

Crossing my fingers behind my back and hoping that she doesn't turn round and see Jonathan uncurl his long body from the cramped space, I say brightly, 'Nothing!'

There are some things you just can't discuss with your mother, aren't there?

Back in the Great Hall the catering team is gathering up the plates from the starter. Before I can begin to collect my whirling thoughts I'm sucked right back into the action, sorting out a gluten free main course and taking a tiny bridesmaid to the toilet. When I next have a spare moment to look I see that Jonathan has slipped back into his place beside a skinny fashion editor. Anita, seated on his left, pointedly ignores her husband and remains deep in conversation with her neighbour while Jonathan turns his Armani clad back to her. Although he seems engaged by the blonde fashionista I can tell by the rigid set of his head and the muscle ticking in his cheek that he's simmering with rage. The same goes for his beautiful wife. Their row is clearly far from over.

I need to get to the bottom of this because like it or not I seem to he caught right in the middle of a major dispute between the Broadheads. And before I give Jonathan any answers I'm going to have to find out exactly what it is they're arguing about.

Chapter Twenty-Eight

It's that part of the reception where the food's been eaten, the speeches are over and there's a lull in the proceedings as everyone takes a breather before the evening celebrations. The guests have wandered outside where they flit through the fragrant gardens like designer butterflies or sit at tables sipping champagne. Inside the Great Hall all is still save the gentle chink of cutlery against bone china while the caterers clear the tables, rudely interrupted every now and then by the screech of feedback from the amps as *Blue Smoke* set up in the ballroom.

I've solved a minor crisis or two, held my breath all the way through Matt's speech (no rude jokes, thank goodness) and even helped Cerys unpin Saffron's heavy train so she can mingle more easily with her guests.

Could it be that I now have a minute all to myself? Surely not!

I run through my mental check list feeling pleased when I reach the end and confirm everything's completed. I glance out of the window to the rose garden where Matt's taking informal pictures of the bride and groom. Something he says makes Saffron throw back her head and laugh which makes me smile in turn because Matt's good humour is so infectious. Out of the corner of my eye I spot my mother and Davie Scott huddled together on a stone seat sharing a cigarette like a pair of naughty school kids. At least I hope that's a cigarette they're sharing...

Deep breath, Robyn, and repeat after me: you are not responsible for your mother!

Leaving Mum and Davie to it – ignorance is bliss after all – I decide to nip to the loo for a quick repair of my makeup and thorough inspection for rouge paint splatters.

Half way up the stairs I pass a very famous reformed boy band and nearly take a tumble because I'm so busy staring. God! I loved them when I was a teenager! Hmm, not sure about the matching white suits and spray tans though, what's that all about? Weaving my way past several soap stars, a stray Spice Girl and a gaggle of leather clad rockers I eventually make it to the top of the sweeping staircase, pausing for a second to appreciate the scene below. Wow! It's like being in a virtual reality version of *Scorching!* magazine. I can hardly believe I've been single handedly responsible, give or take a bit of meddling from mum, for such a major event in the celebrity world's social calendar.

Eat your heart out, Hester Dunnaway!

The ladies' rest room is actually Laney Scott's own bathroom and is attached to her gorgeous master suite, all Sleeping Beauty style four poster bed, drifting muslin drapes and a carpet so deep that I sink right up to my ankles. The en suite itself is enormous and would easily fit my flat twice over.

How the other half live, eh? I wonder what it would be like to be fabulously wealthy and spend my days in such luxury?

Hmm. Unless Prince William develops a sudden taste for petite twenty nine year old wedding planners I don't suppose I'll ever know!

Laney has thoughtfully placed a carafe of water just outside the entrance to en suite and two armchairs behind a beautiful Chinese screen so that weary guests can catch a few quiet moments before hurling themselves back into the wedding. I'm quite tempted to take some time out myself because my feet are throbbing inside my towering heels. How ever does Sarah Jessica Parker manage to traipse all round New York *and* pull gorgeous men with her feet in this kind of agony?

My thoughts filled with fantastic images of Manhattan and shoes I'm just about to open the en suite door when I hear a muffled sob from the far side of the screen followed by the low murmur of two people talking in hushed tones. Not wanting to disturb what's obviously a very earnest and private conversation I'm about to turn and leave when I overhear something that makes my hand freeze on the door handle.

'I just don't know what to do for the best,' a woman half sobs, while her companion soothes her. 'Jonathan won't listen to a word I say. He's so angry, Kathy. He really hates me right now.'

Jonathan? Hot with horror at eavesdropping, however unintentionally, I crane my neck and peer through the crack between the screen and the door. Sure enough the speaker is none other than Anita Broadhead, her face red and swollen as she dabs her eyes with a tissue.

'*He's* angry?' Anita's companion echoes. 'What's he got to be so angry about, for God's sake? You've always been honest with him.'

I'm in a horrible position. Do I turn on my

heel and leave them to have this conversation in privacy? Or do I stay and listen in, hoping that I may get some of the answers I've been looking for?

Robyn Hood, I admonish myself firmly, there's absolutely no choice here! Of course you're going to leave. And I am, I really am, except that what Anita says next really does stop me in my tracks. More than that. It paralyses me with total and utter shock.

'But I haven't been honest with him, have I? Jonathan went absolutely mental this morning when he found the pills in my wash bag. Of course he did! We'd agreed we'd start trying for a family once I'd finished the Biochem Project and he was back from Edinburgh. What's taking the contraceptive pill behind your husband's back if not lying?'

I'm suddenly aware of time slowing down around me. My heart seems to beat in slow motion and I'm holding my breath because if I don't I think I'll cry out. Jonathan's been trying for a baby with his wife? The same wife he claims neglects him and who he wants to leave so that we can be together?

Am I in a bizarre parallel universe or something?

'But you said you'd only talked about it?'

Anita takes a shuddering breath. 'That's what *I* thought but Jonathan totally flew off the handle. He says time's running out now I'm thirty-two, like I'm a giant ticking womb or something, and it's time I put him and our family first.'

Her friend snorts. 'Isn't that a bit rich coming from him, Nita? This is the same Jonathan we're talking about? The one who's always working or off on business trips?'

Anita blows her nose. 'That's his point. He's happy to work and support me, he always has been. He wants me to be at home looking after him and our children. Come on, Kath, you're his sister, you know what he's like. He wants my attention one hundred percent, he always has done, and he hates sharing me with my career.'

'He's hardly going to like sharing you with a baby then!' Kathy Broadhead points out. 'Besides, why should you be the one to give up your career? Why can't Jonathan stay at home and look after the sprog if he's so keen?'

They both laugh at this picture and I nearly do too. The immaculate Jonathan Broadhead with baby sick down his Turnbull and Asser shirt? I don't think so!

'I really don't think we're in the right place to have a child right now,' says Anita eventually as she shreds her tissue into tiny fragments. 'It's not just the career break, I can handle that, it's because things aren't good between us at the moment. Jonathan seems so distant and we're always arguing. I don't know what's gone wrong between us lately, I really don't.'

I'm crucified with guilt when Anita starts to weep again, burying her face in her hands. She may not know what's gone wrong between them but I certainly do. This is exactly what Faye was trying to warn me about.

'How can we possibly have a baby together unless things are right with us?' Anita sobs. 'Why can't Jonathan understand that and just listen to me? It's so bloody frustrating!'

'That's my brother for you. I blame mum, totally spoiling him for so long. I wouldn't panic though, hon, you know what he's like. It sounds to me like he's chucking his toys out of the pram because he hasn't got his own way for once.'

I think about how Jonathan pulled me against him in the linen cupboard and declared he was leaving Anita for me. Things are starting to make sense now. He'd never until that moment given me any indication that he might leave Anita, if his behaviour at the Swing Dancing Competition was anything to go by he's always seemed terrified of the idea. His sudden change of heart is down to wanting to lash out at his wife and nothing whatsoever to do with *really* loving me and wanting us to be together.

'Maybe,' Anita is agreeing, 'but I also know how much having a baby means to him. I love him so much, Kath, I really do. I just want to make him happy.'

'That's the story of Jonathan's life,' observes his sister, dryly. 'My advice is sit tight and don't do anything hasty. He'll calm down. He always does.'

'I hope so because I really do want us to be together and have a family all of our own.' Anita plucks another tissue from the box and wipes her eyes. 'I just want it to happen under the right circumstances.'

'I know,' soothes Kathy Broadhead. 'Come on, Nita. Deep breath. Don't let my git of a brother ruin today. I swear I saw Robbie Williams earlier, we can't have him seeing you looking all snotty! Blow your nose and fix your face while I get you some water. Oh sorry,' she adds surprised when she comes out from beside the screen to find me hovering between the loo and the bedroom, 'I didn't see you there! You're the wedding planner aren't you?'

'Yes!' I squeak. That sounds much better than your errant brother's girlfriend.

'Fantastic wedding,' Kathy congratulates me, her hauntingly familiar periwinkle eyes holding mine in a warm smile. 'I'm pretty sure my worse half is about to propose any day soon. At least he will if he knows what's good for him! You must give me your number.'

'Of course,' says my mouth while my brain screams *no way!* 'That would be lovely. Anyway, I was just on my way out. I'll leave you ladies in peace.'

I scuttle out into the passageway and eventually locate another loo where I lock myself in and lean my hot head against the mirror. Then I run the taps and scrub my hands over and over again with Molten Brown products, like some latter day Lady Macbeth. Oh God, I could scrub them all day and still not be able to get rid of this hideous creeping guilt. What can I do to put things right?

I raise my head and look in the mirror. My reflection stares back sadly. It's a bit of a no brainer really, isn't it? Now I know the truth behind the row, and more importantly the truth about his marriage, I'm going to tell Jonathan that I don't want him to leave Anita for me. Certainly not like this, in the heat of the moment and hitting out at the woman he really loves because he's hurt and angry. If I'm ever going to be with anyone I want it to be because they love me and can't live without me, not because they want to score points over someone else.

A single lonely tear rolls down by check and splashes into the basin. I wait for more to follow but to my surprise that seems to be it for now, which takes me aback because I do – did – really love Jonathan. I should be curled up on the floor howling in misery, or at the very least bawling my eyes out. Maybe I'm just in shock? After all it isn't every day a girl learns that her boyfriend's trying for a baby with another woman. Perhaps my emotions are too big to deal with right now? Probably tonight, wedding over and all alone in my big empty bed, I'll break my heart over Jonathan, howling until I look like a goblin and my neighbours hammer on the ceiling for me to shut up.

As I rearrange my hair and scrape off a few sneaky paint smudges I'm feeling a strange sense of calm because I know exactly what I'm going to do now. And actually I'm not surprised deep down because Jonathan's only been on loan to me really, he's never once said he's been unhappy enough to leave Anita, all the dreams I've savoured when we've been together are just that – dreams. Anita doesn't want their marriage to end and now I know that he doesn't really either.

I give my reflection a shaky smile. It's time to find Jonathan and put everything right.

I just hope I can find him before he speaks to Anita.

Chapter Twenty-Nine

'Excuse me young lady!' I've left the loo for all of ten seconds when a liver spotted claw grabs my elbow. 'There's no hand lotion in the ladies' cloakroom! It's an absolute disgrace. Whatever is Saffron Scott thinking? Every one knows I simply have to have hand lotion!'

'I'm so sorry!' I'm yanked out of the emotional quicksand and back into the wedding so fast that for a moment I feel giddy. Not that the aging soap star who's accosted me cares about this! She wants her hand lotion right now and there's no way she's letting me go until I can find some. Luckily Saffron warned me just how picky this particular guest can be and delving into my emergency wedding kit I pull out the bottle of Jo Malone Rose and Grapefruit lotion purchased especially for such a dire emergency. 'I hope this is OK.'

'Hmm,' she says through trout pout lips. 'Not bad. It'll do.'

I squirt a generous sized blob onto her Tango hued hands. Or at least that's what I intend to do. Unfortunately at the precise moment I'm decanting the gloopy lotion two tipsy models cannon into me and I fire a jet of hand lotion with pinpoint accuracy onto the passing front of a male news reader's trousers.

'Oh my God!' I gasp. 'I am so sorry!'

'My suit!' The news anchor wails, gazing down in shock. 'It's designer. Now look at it!'

'Stop making such a fuss,' snaps the soap star, tossing her dark extensions. 'It's not the first time I've seen you looking like that and I'm pretty sure it won't be the last!'

'Here, let me.' Rummaging in my trusty old bag I pull out a wet wipe, drop to my knees and start scrubbing at the stain. 'This should sort it.'

At least I bloody well hope it does.

'I'll leave you to it,' drawls the soap star to the news reader. 'You're clearly having the time of your life. We forty year olds simply can't compete.'

'Forty my arse,' he hisses. 'Don't think I haven't seen the black and white clips from your early days!'

'And don't think I haven't seen your toupee!' she retorts. 'Enjoy the youngsters while you can, darling. Don't mind me.'

My cheeks are flaming. On my knees and scrubbing a man's crotch is surely above and beyond the call of a wedding planner's duty?

'Good Lord! What sort of wedding planner are you?'

Great, just to add to my total humiliation here's Matt, grinning all over his face and clearly enjoying every minute of my embarrassment.

'Can I go next? I am the Best Man, so I must be qualified for extra special favours!'

'I'll give you a favour all right!' I mutter through clenched teeth. Suddenly I find I'm dangerously close to tears. 'It isn't what you think! I spilt some hand cream and-'

'Hey,' Matt places a hand on my bare shoulder and gives it a gentle squeeze. 'I know that! I was only teasing and,' he catches the eye of the poor news anchor, 'maybe a little jealous! After all, sir, I know you're pretty irresistible to the ladies.'

The news reader swells with pride. 'Well, it has been said a few times!'

'But firing hand cream at a guy to get his attention?' Matt puts his hands on his hips and gives me a stern look. 'That's a first!'

'And for me!' chortles the news reader, 'Although Angela Rippon once threw a stapler at my head. Bloody hurt too, she was a mean shot!'

'It's not coming off!' I wail.

'That stain's only getting worse, Robs. I'd give up before you wear a hole in the fabric.' Matt pulls my wrist aside and the three of us look down what can only be described as a hideous greasy stain.

Oh God. There go any profits I may have earned from today's wedding.

'That'll wash out,' says Matt breezily. 'Tell you what, sir, you and I are about the same size and build. How about I lend you a pair of trousers? I'm staying just along the corridor so it won't be any trouble.'

I open my mouth to point out that this has to be the most ridiculous idea since the Titanic's Captain decided to put his foot down. Matt is tall and rangy whereas the news reader is a dead ringer for Danny de Vito. Then I shut my mouth quickly because the poor victim of my killer hand cream is beaming from ear to ear.

'That's an excellent idea! Are you sure?'

'It's an honour. I'm a great fan of yours actually!'

Catching my eye Matt gives me a cheeky wink before sauntering off to his room with a flattered middle aged news reader in tow. Honestly! What a charmer! I must remember to take *everything* Matt says to me in the future with a lorry load of salt. Still, I certainly owe him one for defusing what was potentially an excruciatingly embarrassing situation, even the news reader has seen the funny side. I wonder how Jonathan would have handled things if he'd come wandering past? Somehow I don't think he'd have found anything amusing about seeing his girlfriend down on her knees attending to another man's crotch.

Not that I'm going to be his girlfriend for much longer.

Once I've reorganised my bag, and realised that the soap star has made off with the Jo Malone hand lotion, I've made up my mind that this is as good a time as any to track Jonathan down. I've got nothing to gain by putting things off.

I fight my way through the ballroom where the guests are going crazy to *Blue*

Smoke. I can't say I quite get the excitement myself, they sound like a pack of hyenas playing the dustbins to me, but everyone else seems to be ecstatic. Spotting Andy's Burberry cap bobbing up and down I wave at the van lads, both of whom give me Jack o'lantern grins and thumbs up in return. There's no sign of Jonathan though and I back out of the room, tripping over some cables and getting yelled at by the *Scorching* photographer on my way.

Upstairs I go again, trawling the dark passageways until I eventually track Jonathan down coming out of the gents.

'Robyn!' He lights up like a Christmas tree. 'There you are at last. I've been looking everywhere for you.'

'Can we talk?'

'Of course! It's all I've been able to think about ever since earlier on, well, that and how absolutely gorgeous you look.'

'Not here, somewhere private.' Grabbing his arm I drag him into the nearest unlocked room. Unfortunately I've chosen the improvised bridal suite and as we stand in the doorway I can hear the giggles of approaching people no doubt intent on strewing rose petals and Heaven only knows what else around the room.

'Quick! This way!' Shoving the surprised Jonathan into the bathroom (what is it with me and en suites today?) I kick the door shut and lock it behind us.

'Relax,' Jonathan says, trying to put his arms around me. 'I'm going to leave Anita for you so we don't need to hide anymore. I'm more than happy to tell everyone how I feel about you. I'll shout it out right now if you like.'

He opens his mouth wide and I clamp my hand over it.

'Don't be so stupid! This is your marriage on the line here, Jonathan. You can't chuck it away on a whim.'

'You are most definitely not a whim.' Pushing my hand aside Jonathan looks offended. 'Don't you know how I feel about you, Robyn?'

Quite frankly, no. I know that I'm in love with him and I know he fancies me, enjoys making love to me and dances like an angel but do I really know how he *feels* about me?

'So tell me,' I say, perching on a wash basin and lowering my voice to a whisper. 'How do you feel about me, Jonathan?'

'I adore you,' he smiles, leaning against the sink next to mine. 'I can hardly keep my hands off you, sweetheart. You know that.'

I *do* know that. The mind blowing limb tingling sex is going to be very hard to say goodbye to, but sex isn't love, is it? And a relationship based on sex, however amazing, is never going to go the distance. Whereas a relationship based on history and common ground and love at least stands a chance.

'I don't want you to leave Anita for me,' I blurt. 'She loves you, Jonathan, and I'm pretty sure you still love her.'

His dark brows meet in a scowl. 'Robyn, with all due respect you know absolutely nothing about my relationship with Anita. It's over with her and that's all that matters now.'

'Oh total crap, Jonathan! Just listen to yourself. Look, I'm just going to level with you – I know all about the big argument you guys had today. People who've given up on their marriages don't normally try for babies in my experience!'

'What!' Jonathan pales. 'Who told you about that?'

'I overheard Anita talking to your sister earlier and I have to agree with everything she said – you're being totally and utterly unreasonable. How could anyone with any sense think it's a good idea to have a baby when their marriage needs help first? It'd be like trying to stick Marie Antoinette's head back on with a Band Aid. If you actually *listened* to what Anita's been saying you'd know it makes perfect sense. She desperately wants to have a family with you but only when the time's right and you guys are on a more stable footing. And let's be honest, that's never going to happen while you're spending every spare minute with me, is it?

Or moping around the rest of the time sulking because your wife is inconsiderate enough to have a career?'

Jonathan's mouth is hanging open. So I plough on.

'I've loved every moment I've spent with you. You're handsome and funny and brilliant company. I've fallen head over heels in love with you Jonathan, but none of it is real. It's been beautiful, hearts and flowers and skinny lattes all the way but that isn't real life is it? Real life is what you have with Anita. It's all the domestic stuff and the rowing and the major life changing things, like who gives up work and when to have babies.'

'Why are you telling me all this if you love me? I thought you wanted to be with me?' Jonathan says so softly I can hardly hear him. 'I thought you'd be over the moon if I left Anita to be with you. I'm prepared to do it too, Robs. We're good together, aren't we?'

I try to swallow the football that's appeared in my throat. 'The best.'

'So why throw it away?' He cups my cheeks with his hands and turns my head towards him. His soft lips are only inches from mine and it takes every scrap of self control I have to resist one last bitter sweet kiss. But I have to resist because Jonathan's kisses always turn my bones to toffee and I can't weaken now, I really can't.

I cover his hands with my own. 'Because

what we have is *nothing* in comparison to a marriage! And your marriage is still very much alive, no matter how much you may try to tell yourself otherwise. It's real life, Jonathan, and real life is bloody difficult sometimes. What makes you think it would be any easier with me anyway? Once the dust had settled we'd soon be arguing about who puts the bins out and who goes to Waitrose.'

'We would not,' he says, with a weak smile. 'You'd do all that stuff, obviously!'

I poke him in the ribs. 'See! I knew it. But seriously, Jonathan, it couldn't work out. We both want such different things. You're ready to think about children, I'm years away from that. I've only just got my business up and running and I want to make a real success of it before I think about being ready for marriage and babies. We've got to face it; it's been beautiful and perfect and the sex has been amazing–'

Jonathan smiles at this and drops a kiss onto the top of my head.

'But it hasn't been real,' I finish. 'You need to sort things out with Anita and stop using me as distraction. There's no way I'm going to have anything to do with breaking up a marriage where there's still so much love left.'

Jonathan says sadly. 'No matter what you may think of me right now, Robyn, I do love you.'

I shake my head. 'You love an idea of me but you don't really know the real me, the one who wears tatty old pyjamas and eats toast in bed.'

'That's bollocks! I adore you. Your smile, your laugh, the way you're always happy-'

'Well, there's proof you don't really know me. I've cried over you far too many times!' I try to laugh but my throat is tight and my voice clots with tears.

'Oh Robyn!' Jonathan folds me into his arms and for a moment I cry into his chest, feeling really bleak because I know in my heart this is the last time I'll ever breathe in his special scent or be this close to him. He raises my chin and gently wipes my tears away with his thumb. 'This doesn't have to be the end of us.'

'Yes it does.' I swallow my tears. 'If your marriage is going to stand a chance then it has to be. I'm a wedding planner, not a marriage wrecker and I'm not going to give you an excuse to cop out of yours.' I place my palms against his chest and push him away gently. 'Go and find your wife, Jonathan and talk to her properly for once. Actually, don't just talk. Listen to her to and really hear what she's trying to say. I think you'll be surprised.'

The room is deathly quiet. The revellers have done their worst and moved on, probably to attach tin cans to Fergus's MG, and the coast is clear.

'You're an amazing person, Robyn.' Jonathan brushes his mouth against mine and I'm swamped with a longing so acute it hurts. 'I'm going to really miss you.

I close my eyes because I don't think I can bear to see him go. Then the door clicks shut and I'm all alone in the bathroom, only the scent of his aftershave and the lingering memory of his kiss evidence he was ever here at all.

'I'm going to miss you too,' I whisper to the empty room. 'So, so much.'

Blinking back tears I let myself out of the bathroom. Work's what I need to take my mind off everything. I look around the room and force myself into wedding planner mode, unhooking bras and pants from the headboard and removing the blow up sheep that some joker (Matt?) has left on the pillow. I rearrange the rose petals, dismantle a flower arrangement to add some more colour to the bedspread and exchange the bottle of champagne for the Bolly in the fridge. But all this work doesn't stop me from replaying my last conversation with Jonathan and as I finish up I'm feeling desperately sad.

Why is doing the right thing so hard?

Chapter Thirty

It's quarter to midnight and the evening reception's still going strong. The hot ballroom is heaving with dancing couples and outside in the twinkling lights of over one thousand white fairy lights guests sit and chat in the warm darkness. In a few minutes the caterers will serve the midnight supper and I can sneak off alone for a well deserved break. I can't face mingling with the guests – I've been carefully avoiding Matt for hours because I'm really not in the mood for dancing – and if I can lurk backstage for the rest of the night that will suit me just fine.

I know I've done the right thing telling Jonathan that he needs to make things work with Anita but it hurts like crazy. Everywhere I look I see couples; from Fergus and Saffron and Faye and Simon to, God help me, my mother and Davie Scott. Even Jonathan and Anita are together on the terrace, not holding hands or touching in any way but a million times closer than they were earlier in the church. Jonathan reaches out and brushes a lock of hair back from his wife's check. Anita smiles up at him, the lines of worry smoothed right away and the tear stains long since faded. They look like a couple again and although this is what I wanted I just wish it didn't hurt so much.

I turn away and pretend to check the food. If in doubt focussing on my work always helps. Look! The garnish is all wonky on the goats cheese crostini and some idiot has forgotten to fetch the Tuscan red pepper humus. And where's the ice sculpture? Just as well I'm on the job.

Putting my broken heart aside I hurry to the kitchen and chivvy on the caterers. Before long all the dishes are exactly where they're meant to be and the guests are soaking up the champagne with all the delicious nibbles. Once I'm satisfied everything's perfect I slip from the Great Hall, grabbing a couple of curried parsnip vol an vents on my way, and sit outside the kitchen door. The cool air soothes my flushed checks and as I collapse onto the door step my pulse starts to slow. It's time for me to relax; even if my personal life's a total car crash the wedding has gone beautifully. I ought to be turning cartwheels with joy, not feeling like throwing back my head and howling.

'Penny for 'em?'

Simon is leaning against the door way, tie loosened and holding a bottle of champagne.

'Believe me, they're not worth even that much.'

'I don't believe that for a second. Budge up,' Si sits down next to me, 'and have a swig of this to cheer you up.'

'It'll take more than champagne to cheer me up.'

'It's a good a place to start as any.' He passes the bottle to me. 'Besides, I don't think they've got any Malibu and pineapple.'

This reference to my revolting student tipple makes me laugh in spite of myself.

'Damn! I'll just have to slum it I suppose.' I take a gulp and pull a face when sharp biscuity bubbles explode across my tongue before fizzing into my empty stomach. I'd better take it easy; I don't want to turn into a drunken wreck just yet.

'I'm surprised you're still talking to me,' I say, passing the bottle back. 'I suppose Faye's told you?'

'A bit,' admits Simon. 'Sorry. Should I have pretended not to know? Are you angry with her for telling me?'

'Me, angry with Faye? You *are* joking? I think it's more the other way around actually. I thought you two hated me.'

'You silly moo,' Si puts his arm round me and hugs me. With a sigh I lean my head on his shoulder and go back twelve years quicker than you can say *time machine*. How many times has Simon comforted me over some useless man or another? I really need to move on.

'Of course we don't hate you. We've been worried sick about you. The other night Faye may have said some things she shouldn't but it's only because she cares, Robyn. She's been desperately afraid that you'll get hurt.'

'Well you can tell her she was right,' I admit sadly, going on to tell him my sorry tale. Si must be gagging to know every detail of his errant colleague's double life but good naturedly forgoes the gossip in favour of letting me off load. Every now and again he punctuates my narrative with exclamations of 'No way!' or 'Bastard!' but mostly he lets me talk.

'So it's well and truly over.' I finish. 'Jonathan wants to start a family with Anita and at the end of the day he still loves her. It was never really about me, Si, was it? I just caught up in something neither of us really understood and now it's finished. Jonathan's back with his wife, just as Faye predicted.'

Simon ruffles my hair. 'For what it's worth I'm glad it didn't work out with him, Robs. You deserve better than Jonathan Broadhead.'

Beyond the kitchen courtyard guests are starting to trail back to their vehicles. Engines roar into life and tail lights scatter ruby beams into the darkness.

'He's not all bad.' I say.

'I'm sure he isn't, but he's not the one for

you, Robs. You deserve someone who wants to be with you and only you, someone who really appreciates you for the fantastic person you are. And a married man was never going to be that person.'

'I think deep down I always knew that.'

'There's someone perfect waiting for you, babes, I know there is,' Simon promises. 'You're too special to be alone for long.'

While my dearest, oldest friend comes out with all the well meaning clichés that he can think of I munch on a vol au vent and watch the guests leave. Although the night is black as molasses there's no mistaking the tall silhouettes of Jonathan and Anita as they walk to their car, side by side and talking quietly, and a lonely tear rolls down my cheek and splashes into the pureed parsnip.

'It's just so hard to let him go. I'm going to miss him so much.'

'But Jonathan was always a married man,' Simon reminds me gently. 'He was never really yours to miss.'

I watch Jonathan's BMW pull away, the headlights sweeping along the drive. Simon's absolutely right. Jonathan was, and is, a very married man and that means he was never the one for me. Dwelling on something that was never going to be won't get me very far.

I jump to my feet. 'Right! That's my break over. I'd better go and supervise the cleaning up.'

'You need to clean yourself up,' Si observes, pointing to my skirt where sure enough a red wine stain has flowered across the delicate fabric.

'That's a mystery,' I say, 'seeing as I've not been drinking. Still, ruining my clothes is all part of being a wedding planner I suppose.' Along with throbbing feet, having my hand lotion stolen and, of course, scrubbing news readers' crotches!

Si gives me a kiss on the cheek. 'I'll catch you later. Call us, OK? I meant what I said. No one's mad at you. We were just worried.'

I'm not convinced Faye would quite share this point of view but it's a start I suppose. I've neglected my friends over the past months and I know I've got some serious humble pie to eat, so much so that it'll probably be my staple diet for weeks. As I return to the Great Hall and start removing dirty table cloths I comfort myself by thinking that although I may be dealing with the dregs of a wedding at least I'm not dealing with the dregs of a marriage. Look on the bright side, Robyn. This probably means you're single now.

Whatever single means.

I'm on all fours under a trestle table, picking up individual pieces of confetti, when I hear a familiar voice calling my name and a pair of Christian Louboutins stops inches away from my nose. Faye has finally tracked me down. What shall I do? Stay hidden under the table until she goes away or face her and the inevitable rollicking? Since today seems to have been a good day for getting everything out in the open I guess I'd better to go with the flow and just get it over with.

I poke my head out from beneath the table cloth. 'I'm here, Faye.'

'You're hiding from me under a table?'

I laugh in spite of myself. 'No! I'm clearing up. The table confetti's everywhere. But if it's OK with you can we leave the lecture for another time? I'm really not in the mood. You'll be glad to know you were right in any case. Jonathan's back with Anita and yup, I feel used and heartbroken, just as you predicted. Does that make you happy?'

Faye crouches down and peers in at me. 'Of course I'm not happy. How can you even think that? The last thing I wanted was to see you get hurt.'

Sharp bits of table confetti are digging into my knees but I'm not going to move until we've got to the bottom of this.

'There was more to it than that, Faye. You said some horrible things, especially all that stuff about trusting me with Si.'

'Can I join you?' Faye asks, pushing the table cloth aside. 'I'm feeling giddy bending over like this.'

If she wants to sit on a stone floor covered

with scraps of food and tired streamers than she can be my guest. She may find it harder to yell under the table.

'Sure. Feel free.'

Moments later Faye's squashed next to me, her long legs tucked beneath her and her neck cricked beneath the table. Maybe it's not such a bad thing to be short?

'I wasn't going to lecture you, Robs. I wanted to apologise for what I said at the Swing Dancing Club. Yes, I was angry and really hurt that you'd lied to me for so long but I know you never intentionally set out to hurt anyone.' She starts to shred a fallen streamer with her nails. 'I also think I re-acted as a wife rather than a friend, and I'm sorry about that, I truly am. I wasn't there for you and you needed me.'

I shrug. 'You're bound to see things from Anita's point of view, Faye. I've always appreciated that. That's one of the reasons I held back from telling you. I wasn't exactly proud of seeing a married man.'

'There's more to it than that though.' Faye turns to look at me and her eyes shimmer with tears. 'Simon's been working so late recently and it's crossed my mind a few times that maybe he could have found some-one else too. I know it's totally ludicrous–'

'Bloody right it is! Simon adores you! He'd never look at anyone else!'

'It doesn't always feel like that, Robs, when

you're the nagging old bat at home. I couldn't help identifying with Anita Broadhead in that respect. In any case what I'm trying to say is that my own fears probably made me hypersensitive to any talk of affairs. When I saw you with Jonathan, who claims to work every bit as hard as Si, I just went off at the deep end.' She takes a deep breath. 'I'm so sorry for not listening to you and I'm more ashamed than I can say about all the horrible accusations. Can you ever forgive me for being a crap friend?'

'Only if you can forgive *me* for being a crap friend and not telling you the truth,' I choke. Then we're hugging and crying and laughing all at once and suddenly splitting up with Jonathan doesn't seem half as painful. Maybe my heart isn't quite as irretrievably broken as I'd thought?

'God, I can't cry now!' I laugh through my tears. 'I'm far too busy! There's still a thousand bits of confetti to pick up.'

'Right then.' Faye bunches her Ronit Zilkha skirt into her fists and gets down onto her hands and knees. 'We'd better make a start, hadn't we?'

We grin at each other and even though I feel like my emotions have been churned round in a giant food mixer I'm no longer so desperately sad. My most important friendships have survived intact. What could really be more important than that?

An hour later I'm rummaging beneath the top table and wondering how on earth a leopard print thong has managed to get hooked to a table leg when my phone rings so loudly that I jump and crack my skull on the table.

'Ow!' I wail into the receiver.

'There's no need to cry just because you haven't seen me for a few hours,' says Matt Knowles.

I sit back on my heels. 'I've just banged my head on a table, thanks to you!'

'Head banging at this time of night? Is that a good idea? Even Davie Scott's given up and gone to bed.'

This hasn't escaped my notice. And neither has the fact that my mother has also vanished...

'I'm clearing up,' I explain. 'I'm under the top table picking up all the mess that you guys dropped. I don't suppose you've lost a leopard skin thong by any chance?'

'No, mine are all zebra print,' Matt doesn't miss a beat. 'I waited for you in the ball room, Cinderella. What happened? I was looking forward to taking out your other foot.'

'Crisis with the midnight supper,' I say, which sounds better than saying that my love life was in total meltdown. 'I think the jazz band's still going though if you want to try and do a bit more damage?'

'That would have been great but I'm actually on my way to Heathrow. That's why I'm ringing – I couldn't find you to say goodbye, probably because I wasn't crawling under tables, and I didn't want to leave without telling you what a brilliant job you've done today.'

'Thanks Matt.' I feel a warm glow of pride. 'I'm really glad you had a good time.'

'It was a great wedding, the best ever. The memory of you and that poor news reader will keep me laughing all the way to Amsterdam!'

In the darkness of my under-table lair my lace colours. 'Amsterdam?' I say quickly, to cover my embarrassment. 'That sounds glamorous.' Images flit through my mind's eye; red light districts and girls with glossy mouths posing in windows. Something deep inside me twists.

'Yeah, dead glam,' laughs Matt, 'if pictures of computer components are your thing! Still, it pays the mortgage and no doubt some computer geeks get off on it! Anyway, I didn't call to talk about that.'

'Oh?' I say. 'What did you call for then?'

I can't see Matt but I can imagine him rolling his eyes and raking a hand through his curls. 'God! You're going to make me work hard here, aren't you? I was just thinking it was a shame I didn't get to see much of you today. Would you like to catch up sometime when I get back? Go for dinner or something? I know a great greasy spoon.'

I don't know what to say, so I say nothing.

'Only if you want to, of course,' Matt adds quickly. 'You're probably flat out with weddings.'

Is he asking me out? My first instinct is to agree and say I'm totally busy but then I think about how much fun I've had with Matt and all the crazy situations we've shared lately, from wandering through London to the sensitive way he rescued me from total mortification earlier on. Maybe it's time I stopped being suspicious of any man who isn't married?

'I'm wedding free for a bit,' I reply slowly. 'Actually, there's a dance at my local swing club next week. If you're up for it I could teach you some moves?'

'Could we try something less painful? Maybe you could pull my teeth out with pliers instead?' Matt suggests. 'Or how about I bring my camera over and show you the finer rudiments of photography?'

I laugh. 'Matt, I know all about *your* photography remember? No more insect pictures, thanks! Maybe we should forget swing dancing and taking photos?'

'I absolutely agree,' Matt says. There's a pause and in the stillness across the network something shifts and changes between us. 'Maybe we can find something else to do?'

I say nothing but my imagination is starting to warm up. How strong was that champagne?

'Such as?' I whisper.

'Who knows?' Matt replies slowly. 'Maybe we'll discover a shared passion for something else entirely?'

My mind is whirling which I'm sure isn't just down to concussion. 'And what exactly do you have in mind, Mr. Knowles?'

'Well,' Matt says thoughtfully, 'I know you may take a bit of persuading, and you're probably not that kind of girl, but you never did give those insects a fair go! Maybe we could go on a nature walk sometime and peer under a few rocks?'

'How can I resist an offer like that?' I laugh.

'With difficulty I hope!' In the background I hear a chime and the crackle of a tannoy. 'I've got to go,' Matt says. 'They're calling my flight. I'll call you, OK? Don't go looking at worms without me!'

As he rings off I find I'm laughing out loud, my heart suddenly lighter than the meringue crumbs I've been scooping up.

I shake my head. Well, whoever said common interests were everything? Maybe it's time I discovered if opposites really do attract?

Finding out suddenly feels as though it could be a whole new lot of fun...

The publishers hope that this book has given you enjoyable reading. Large Print Books are especially designed to be as easy to see and hold as possible. If you wish a complete list of our books please ask at your local library or write directly to:

Dales Large Print Books
Magna House, Long Preston,
Skipton, North Yorkshire.
BD23 4ND